I0762501

ARCHITECT

The Goodpasture Chronicles
Book 3

Eald Talu House

R.J. Halbert

To Kelton & Kennedy, may the truth of our foundation reveal revelation and hope to your future generations.

Architect
The Goodpasture Chronicles

Architect Hardcover : 978-1-963366-19-8

Published by:
Eald Talu House
(A Division of Novus Press Works)
Nashville, TN 37215

We cannot control what life throws at us, and we cannot control what breaks us. What we can control is how we respond and how we tell our stories. The Goodpasture Chronicles is how I've chosen to tell my story. My hope is these words resonate and leave an impact of power that leads to healing and restoration. May you, the reader, have eyes to see and ears to hear the whisper.

To my one true love and partner for life, Jason. I could not have done my part without you. Thank you for choosing to walk the hard road with me. You taught me how to dream big, take risks and create more than I thought was possible. Outside of our two children, I could not be more proud of something we created together as our heritage. I'm so proud of you, my love.

And to our future grandchildren, I can't wait for the day that you read The Goodpasture Chronicles. That is the day you will see what full redemption and restoration looks like. May it blow wind in the sails of hope for your future, and establish an unbreakable anchor of truth to steady your feet as you head off into your own adventures. And may you always find home in these pages. - Rhonda Halbert

As excited as I am seeing this trilogy come to life, I could never have foreseen the depth of healing and joy that would come from the process. Rhonda, I'm so proud of what we created during the darkest days of our lives. We have built many things together - our family, our homes, our careers - but this is the one that will endure long beyond us.

As I said previously, I come from a long line of storytellers. But the greatest Storyteller of all continues to write our story - with twists, turns and mystery. He spoke in parables, inviting us to see ourselves in the lives of others, revealing unseen truths. It is my prayer that these stories do the same for future generations, and all who encounter our tales.

Many times I have heard, "Never let the truth get in the way of a good story." I would say, "Never let a good story be told without revealing the truth."

I think we're finally home. - Jason Halbert

CONTENTS

PROLOGUE

HE ARRIVED JUST before dusk, too late to search the ruins. And yet, the wind whispered for him to try. Or maybe it wasn't the wind at all.

The man sighed and shook his head, then ran gnarled fingers through his cloud-white hair. Today he felt old. Today he *was* old. If only he had waited a few months longer. What was time to ruins, anyway?

What was time to him?

He shook his head, straightened his back, then turned in a slow circle, looking for anyone who might deign to question what he was doing on this island. Anyone who might jeopardize his mission. But only the tumble of stones stared back at him.

He sniffed at the air, smelling the salt of the sea and the memory of ashes. The lighthouse had fallen victim to multiple earthquakes over the centuries and was little more than a pile of stones now. Or perhaps its demise was delayed justice from his long-silent God.

He glanced back toward the mainland and saw the flickering lights of a transformed city. Most of the royal quarter was underwater, but the city itself remained a vibrant, if more compact, trading hub. He paused to reflect on his all-too-brief visit to the once-magnificent library that had been built, like the lighthouse, to honor the conqueror who founded the city. He relished the days he had spent studying, researching, learning from the greatest collection of scrolls ever collected in one place. Surely there would never be another library like it. But this was no time to reminisce. The sun was setting and soon the island would be covered in darkness.

The man turned back toward the ruins, imagining the lighthouse as it once was, towering above, higher than the falcon flew. As the fading daylight washed across the rubble, the stones began to glow like jewels. He wandered among them, searching the ground for evidence of the lantern chamber, perhaps a shard of glass or a sliver of the grand mirror. But as the shadows grew longer, his hope dimmed.

Just then he saw a glimmer, a reflection from something half-buried in the sand and silt. He hurried over to it as fast as his aching bones would allow, careful not to trip on the jagged rocks, then bent down and pushed aside the surrounding debris. He grasped a piece of metal by its edge and pulled it free. To a casual observer, it might look like trash; a piece of a broken shield or perhaps something washed ashore from a shipwreck. But he knew exactly what this was. It was the reason he had risked such a dangerous journey to this very place.

He brushed his hand against the metal and some of the dirt and ash fell away, revealing a faint, if unreadable symbol etched into its surface. This wasn't just any scrap of metal; it was once part of a silver box. A box that he knew all too well.

The man continued to dig around in the dirt and found two more remnants of the silver box. As he stood there, holding the fragile silver fragments, night fell across the landscape. And yet, a subtle blue glow remained. He felt the ancient power imbued into the remnants subtly pulsating in his hands. He carefully hid them in his satchel, dousing the glow.

He had found what he was looking for, but the hunt was far from over.

In truth, it was only beginning.

CHAPTER ONE

AKOLO SAT ON a flat rock and attempted to kick the dirt and sand from his sandals. He was only moderately successful at this now-familiar evening routine. His feet hurt, his back hurt and his head hurt from walking under the relentless, blazing sun. But for a moment, anyway, he chose to overlook the pain of traveling. Behind him, the sun was setting, painting a golden glow on the hilt of his sword. Well, it was more of a dagger, but it was his, a gift from the king himself, or so the high priest had told him.

"For being a good and helpful servant," the high priest had said. They had even given him a belt and a leather sheath to hold what he now considered his second-most-prized possession. The bracelet his friend had given him still held highest honors. Trailing both of these beloved items, but not far behind, was the fire opal that he kept hidden in the pocket of his tunic. He slipped his hand from the hilt of his dagger into that very pocket and caressed the stone. It was both cool and warm to the touch, something that continually bewildered him but also felt right somehow.

The caravan he'd been traveling with was far smaller than the one that had escorted him to the king's palace so many months ago. He counted seventy-three travelers, including himself. He seemed to count a lot of things lately. His friend with the bracelet taught him. It helped to pass the time during the long walks—people, steps, pomegranate seeds, days and nights. Some of the seventy-three travelers he had met before, including the high priest, of course, and his family, but most were strangers. Soldiers made up the rest of the group. Unlike during the previous trip, when they didn't understand the power within the holy items they carried, the soldiers took great care to distance themselves from the mystical items that were being returned to the temple in his hometown.

But was it his hometown anymore? He had learned long ago that his family was gone. His sisters, mother and father—dead. The king had said so. Unless…

No. They were gone. He was well and truly alone.

Sadness and anger swirled within him. Like…what was that word his friend had used? *Tornado*. They swirled like a tornado.

Akolo knew they had been traveling exactly twenty-one days so far because of the marks on his belt. He made one with a sharp stone each morning when the sun rose, much as his friend had done to tally the days they lived in the palace.

That seemed so long ago.

Akolo missed his friend. The guards were mystified by the boy's sudden disappearance, even delaying their departure from the palace by a day in order to search for him. Akolo didn't know where his friend had gone either, which was exactly what he told the king when summoned to him the morning they were supposed to depart. If Akolo closed his eyes, he could still see the king's piercing stare, the furrowed brow; he could still feel the sweat dripping down his neck as he awaited the king's response to his assertion. Akolo *was* telling the truth. He didn't know where the boy…where…Zach had gone.

Zach.

Already the name felt foreign to him. As if the months spent with his friend were a dream. Akolo looked down at the bracelet on his wrist.

"No," he said aloud. "Not a dream. It was real."

"What was real?"

The voice came from behind, startling him. He didn't need to turn to know to whom it belonged, though. They might have only been traveling for twenty-one days, but Akolo easily recognized the high priest's daughter's honey-sweet voice. He turned halfway around and looked up at her. She stood mostly in shadow, a silhouette against the setting sun, but firelight from the altar in front of him danced in her eyes.

Akolo didn't have a word for the way Esme made him feel. But if he did, it would have been a big word, something with lots of colors and facets, like the myriad stones on the king's crown. He stared at her eyes, her emerald-green eyes, the color unlike any he had ever seen, and he'd seen a lot of colors. Especially in the Royal Gardens, with its many flowers. Her long hair was dark, like midnight, and tucked like a shadow behind her rust-colored hood. Akolo had always believed his mother was the most beautiful woman in the world.

Now he wasn't so sure.

Akolo felt guilty, and maybe a little embarrassed, at this thought and turned back to face the raging fire. Maybe in the firelight, she wouldn't notice his flushing cheeks.

Esme walked up beside him and paused, also staring into the flames. He stole another glance at her, studying her distinct profile in the flickering light, admiring the slope of her nose, the gentle curve of her chin. He longed for her to turn toward him, but somehow also feared her gaze. Not because she was scary. Quite the opposite. She was hope and peace and joy and wonder.

All the things he once enjoyed with his family.

Akolo turned back toward the fire and sighed.

"What was that for?" Esme asked.

He didn't dare look at her. His feelings were too close to the surface. Memories of his family could so easily bring tears.

He cleared his throat. "I just…" He paused, then thought of a way to change the subject. "I just was wondering what the fires were for."

Esme tapped his shoulder, urged him to slide over. The touch of her hand against his bare arm felt like a spark, but he didn't hesitate. He scooted over so he was just barely balancing on the rock, giving her more than half of the surface for herself.

"They remind us of our god. Do you not light fires for your god?" she asked.

Akolo thought back to his time at the palace. He had seen the fires before but hadn't asked about them. He'd been too busy playing the role the king said he was born for: to be an intermediary between the king and the God of Akolo's people. That word had confused him at first, but Zach explained it later. He was a go-between. Like a messenger. He had another role, too: to imbue artifacts with his God's power. *Imbue.* Zach had to explain that word to him, too.

Akolo let his mind wander further back in time, to his observations of the temple practices at home: the incense burning, the animal sacrifices. Both of those used fire. But this fire before him was something different. An improvised square stone structure with sides as long as the tallest man among them, and walls as tall as Akolo's waist had been filled with branches and sticks gathered from bushes and trees and even some of the dried fruit they had brought with them, then lit with one of the torches the soldiers carried. The flames had started out small, then quickly grew to the height of three men. The fire continued to rage as soldiers added more fuel to the pyre. Its shape reminded him of the tower where he and his friend had stayed for months.

"Not like this," he said, finally answering Esme's question.

"I don't fully understand it myself," said Esme. He felt the shrug of her shoulders against his. "I'd ask my father, but he probably would just say I needn't worry about such things." Her voice brightened when she spoke up again. "Good thoughts, good words, good deeds."

Akolo scrunched his face into a question and turned toward her. "Huh?" he said.

"It's what our God asks of us," she said. Then she corrected herself. "I mean my God. I don't know yours."

Akolo thought about that as the sun finally set behind them. "I guess my God asks that, too." But was that right? The only things he really knew about his God were that he was powerful and that he dwelled in the temple and sometimes whispered to the special people who were allowed into his presence.

People like him.

As the sun disappeared behind them, the camp took on an eerie glow. A number of men, including Esme's father, the high priest, stood near the fire. Too close for Akolo's comfort, but the men didn't seem bothered by the heat.

The two of them sat in silence for a few minutes, listening to the men's whispered prayers accompanied by the spit and spat of sparks. The sound was mesmerizing, like a song you couldn't quite hear.

Akolo's eyes felt heavy. He would sleep well tonight; he was sure of it. Even on the rocky ground.

"I'm sorry about your family." Esme's words drifted like ash into Akolo's thoughts and lingered there. It was the first time she'd acknowledged his tragic story. But what do you say to that?

He decided on the simplest of responses, to avoid tripping over words or stumbling into a deeper sadness. "Thanks."

"My father really likes you," she added a moment later.

That brought a small smile to Akolo's face.

"I do, too," she added.

Warmth poured over Akolo like sweet honey dripping from the comb. This time, it wasn't from the nearby fire. He turned toward Esme, but something off in the distance drew his attention. Flickering lights. But they were nowhere near any town or village.

The prayers abated. Soldiers rushed to douse the tower of flames, scooping sand onto their long tunics and pouring it onto the makeshift altar.

New whispers reached Akolo's ears, but these weren't prayers. These were words of warning.

"We must leave at once!" The words cut through the eerie silence like a sharpened sword through a ripe pomegranate. Akolo wasn't even sure who spoke them. He was too focused on the soft hand that had grabbed his.

CHAPTER TWO

ZACH COULDN'T RECALL the last time he felt so rested. He looked up from his nearly empty plate to check the kitchen clock not for the first time since returning home.

Time.

He couldn't make sense of it. But who could, really? He'd been away for a long time. The calendar said it was a matter of weeks. But his gut said it was far more. Was his gut lying to him? If his gut was lying to him, his hair certainly was not. It had grown at least six inches since his family had last seen him, and his curls were unruly.

"Well?"

Zach turned toward the sound of Ariel's voice. She sat to his right. His mother was across from him, his father to his left. He was home. Eating breakfast. With his family.

"Well, what?" he said.

"Are you going to tell us about your little adventure or not?" she continued. Ariel's tone was a blend of curiosity and snark. Yeah. He was definitely home.

"I'm not sure what to say." This was becoming truer by the minute. After sleeping in his own bed for eleven hours straight, he was still only waking up. His mind was always a little fuzzy first thing in the morning, but this was a different kind of fuzzy. When he tried to recount recent memories, they skittered away, hiding just in the periphery. He could only see glimpses: an ancient land; a man with a patch over one eye; a palace; a magnificent, terraced garden. Lots of stone and sand.

And a boy. This memory was both the most insistent and the blurriest. He struggled to pull it into focus.

"It all seems like a dream, you know?" he said finally. That was the truest thing he could say.

"It's okay if you don't want to talk about it," said his dad.

Zach turned to look at him. His father's gaze had always been a little intense, usually in a good way, but there was something different about his eyes today. They were softer. More like his mother's eyes.

"So much for story time at the Keanes." Ariel's half-whispered words sounded a lot like a cartoon "harrumph" to Zach. The thought made him laugh.

"What's so funny?" asked Ariel.

"Nothing," said Zach.

"Fine. If you aren't going to talk about your adventure, can we talk about what happened last night?" Ariel asked.

"What do you mean?" his mother asked. Zach had seen his mother wipe away tears more than a few times since returning home. She was doing it yet again.

"The house? Did no one else feel the house shake last night?"

Zach didn't recall the house shaking, and by the blank looks on his parents' faces, neither had they. Then again, they all had been a little distracted by his return.

"Do you mean from the storm?" his dad asked.

Ariel huffed again, then abruptly scooted away from the table, the chair nearly tipping over when she stood.

"No, Dad! I know what a storm sounds like. In case you forgot, like everyone else, I've already been through a few so far! I don't get it!" she said, fire in her voice. "It's like you're all hypnotized or something. Can't you see it? This place, this house is trying to destroy us! Why can't anyone else see that?" She stood there for a nanosecond, then spun on her heels and left, heading for the stairs at first, then doing a 180 and walking toward the front door.

“Ariel…wait…” Lyana started to get up.

“I’ll go,” Ian said. He placed his hand on Lyana’s, keeping her from following Ariel, then stood. “We’re all a bit out of sorts, and for good reason. It’s entirely possible we missed something yesterday with all that was going on. I’ll make sure she has space to speak her mind.” He took a sip of his coffee, then followed after Ariel.

Zach didn’t think it was as simple as everyone being “out of sorts.” Something strange had happened, but he couldn’t wrap his mind around it. Usually, Zach would be the first to offer theories, but now he found himself just as silent as his parents. The house definitely had been up to something. But was that something nefarious or helpful? The answer to that question was just as blurry as his recent memories.

“I don’t know why my memory is so messy,” he said once the front door had closed behind his dad. “Maybe writing things down will help me remember.” Zach excused himself from the table, started toward the stairs as his sister had done, then paused. He stepped toward his mother and gave her an awkward hug. All his hugs felt at least a little bit awkward, but this one seemed important. She held him tight for a moment, then released him.

“I think that’s a good idea,” she said. She wiped yet another tear from her eyes. Maybe the hug was a bad idea after all.

“I can help clean up from breakfast first…” he offered.

“I’ve got this. You go do what you need to do,” his mother said. She turned to look out the kitchen window.

Zach studied her profile for a moment, then headed upstairs to his room.

• • •

“Ariel, hold up.”

Ariel didn't want to "hold up." She wanted to keep walking. She had started down the long driveway, but without any destination in mind. She just wanted to be as far away from this house as possible. Why couldn't her parents see the truth? It wasn't safe here. Still, she slowed her pace, allowing her father to catch up. She didn't turn to look at him.

"Honey, I'm sorry if we've not been listening to you. We've been distracted and..."

"Ya think?" She immediately regretted her tone. "Sorry. I'm just..." She stopped walking but didn't dare turn toward her father. It wasn't that she was afraid he'd be angry; she simply didn't trust her own emotions in that moment. "Last night," she began, then took a deep breath to steady herself, "I felt the house shake. Could it have been from the storm? Maybe. But by then the storm had mostly subsided. It felt more like an earthquake. Or at least what I think an earthquake would feel like. I don't know. Something just felt really off..."

"Maybe it..."

She didn't let him finish. "Something has felt really off about this house since pretty much the day we moved in. You know I'm right. Please tell me you know this." She definitely couldn't turn toward him now. What if he didn't acknowledge the truth? What if she was the only one who remembered everything that had happened to them?

"I do know this."

She took a deep breath.

"There is something about this place," he continued, then stopped. "But your mother is convinced that we need to be here. I'm not sure how to explain it. It's like...something bigger is at play. I didn't know what to believe before. But now? I think she's right."

Ariel was incredulous. "What changed your mind?" she snarked. "Was it the murdered chickens? Zach's disappearance? Or the way he suddenly reappeared in a flooded storm shelter? I don't get it,

Dad. I honestly just don't get it. Nothing good has happened since we moved here..."

"Wait, that's not entirely true, Ariel..."

"It's not? Okay." She turned toward him, steeling herself from the twisting emotions that threatened to spill out of her. "Tell me three good things that have happened to us since we moved."

When her father didn't immediately respond, she huffed, "I thought so," then started walking down the driveway again.

"Wait, I..."

"Just leave me alone!" She felt a little bad about that and added, "Just for a little while, okay? I promise I won't get lost in the woods. I'll be back later. Maybe by then you'll have come up with a list." She didn't need to say that last part, but it slipped out anyway. Her father didn't reply. And he didn't follow. In a matter of minutes, she was alone, surrounded on both sides by rows of tall trees and thick privet. Daylight flickered through the leaves, painting dappled shadows on the path before her.

She walked in silence until she reached the road at the end of the driveway, then found a fallen log to sit on. She bent forward, her head in her hands, and willed herself to cry. To feel something. But all she felt was anger. And sadness. They had almost lost Zach, but she was feeling a different kind of loss. The loss of her entire family.

• • •

Zach stared at the blank page in front of him. He had considered typing his thoughts on his computer but then thought better of it. Technology had always been a fascination of his, but right now he wasn't sure he could trust tech. Pencil and paper surely wouldn't betray him.

He laughed at his cartoon-like paranoia, then put pencil to paper and began to write.

I don't know where to begin, but here's what I remember.

I was heading to my room…weeks ago? Months? The calendar says weeks, but my brain says it was longer. Anyway, I think I walked through a time portal or something like that. Suddenly, it was a long time ago, in a galaxy far, far away. Kidding. It was this galaxy. But the "long time ago" thing was true.

Time travel isn't anything like what you see in movies. I didn't see any swirly colors or anything like that. One minute I was home, the next I was there. I guess there might have been some fog or mist or something between places.

The thing that's clearest to me is the trip home. I remember running down a long hallway and opening a door, then climbing a bunch of stairs only to end up in the tornado shelter outside my home. But all the other memories are difficult to describe. It's like when you wake up from a dream and you know it was really specific and clear while you slept, but the words to describe that dream don't exist or something. I do know there was a king and a palace and a high priest with one eye and a boy about my age. Maybe a little younger. And there was a temple. I remember a dream my sister and I both had a while ago—yeah, we had the same dream, or it appeared like we did anyway—and it was a lot like that.

But was this just a dream, too? And if it was, where have I been for the last few weeks?

Gotta say, writing this down isn't helping much. But it does feel good to hear the scratch of graphite on paper again. I mean, it's annoying, too, but it's familiar. Most of those hazy memories are the opposite of familiar.

That's all I have right now.

Oh, one more thing. For some reason I wanted pomegranate seeds for breakfast. We didn't have any, but Mom said she'd get them next time she went shopping. Here's what confuses me, though—I don't think I've ever had pomegranate seeds. So, what is that all about?

Zach set his pencil down and took a moment to review his work. His handwriting had always been a source of pride—he was meticulous with every stroke, often to a fault. But it had been a while since he held a pencil, and the lack of practice showed in slightly uneven lines and a few crossed-out words. He considered starting over, then shrugged and decided "good enough" was enough this time.

"Huh," he said aloud. "Good enough" was a new feeling.

• • •

Lyana had just finished loading the dishwasher when Ian walked in the front door. She didn't need to ask if he'd had any success talking with Ariel. She didn't even need to see the look on his face. Ariel had been holding things together by a thread for quite a while. And yet somehow Ariel had remained calm and collected when Lyana went on a manic painting spree, driven by images in her head she couldn't shake. Images that led Ariel to figure out where Zach would be found. Lyana glanced over at the stack of paintings that sat on the kitchen counter. It had all been too much. No wonder Ariel was falling apart.

"She doesn't want to talk," said Ian. He stood by the door, looking defeated.

Lyana walked over and wrapped her arms around him. He hugged her in return, and they stood there in silence for a moment.

"She doesn't want to stay here," Ian said, still holding tight to Lyana.

Lyana gently pulled away from the hug and looked her husband in the eyes. "It's understandable," she said. Then she laughed. "Moving to Littleton has been the most…confounding experience for all of us. Maybe most of all for Ariel. I mean, she's a teenager, and that's difficult enough as it is." She sighed. "But…"

"You still believe we need to stay. That this is meant to be."

She nodded.

"I wish I could explain it to Ariel, but I barely understand it myself," said Lyana. "I wasn't so sure before. But now? I'm convinced that this is exactly where we're supposed to be."

She had felt that way for a long time. Zach's disappearance should have made her question the journey they were on. Instead, it only reaffirmed that they were doing the right thing by staying in Littleton. In this house.

"You know," began Ian, "we're kind of like the characters in those horror movies who stay in the scary house even though they know there's a killer loose. Everyone watching the movie is shouting, 'Get out of there!'" He paused, then shook his head. "But, no, this is different because there's no killer here."

Lyana suddenly felt cold. What if she was wrong? What if the house *was* trying to hurt them?

"Ariel is shouting at us to get out," said Lyana. Was Ariel the only sane one in the family?

Neither of them spoke for a moment.

"Do you remember the day she tried to run away from home?" asked Ian.

"How could I forget?"

"She was almost twelve. And so upset that we wouldn't let her have a pet snake."

"She didn't get very far…"

"No. But she had her little suitcase all packed and ready to go."

Lyana shook her head, recalling the way Ariel had huffed and marched right out the front door. Ian had followed a short distance behind to make sure Ariel was safe, but the very idea of her daughter running away from home was seared into Lyana's brain. She was confident Ariel would be back soon—she'd only packed a few crackers and a bottle of juice, after all—but that didn't do much to mitigate the heartache she felt as she watched her only daughter walking away.

Lyana gasped as that same feeling bubbled to the surface again.

"Are you okay?" Ian asked.

"I just hope we're doing the right thing, you know?"

All those years ago, they had given Ariel space to express her disappointment. And that was all she needed. Just twenty minutes later, she was back home, hugging her mom, apologizing for running away. She still wanted a snake, of course. But she would wait until she was an adult and living on her own to get one. She hadn't said another word about a snake since.

They could laugh about the experience now. But today's concern was anything but a laughing matter.

Wind whistled through the kitchen window. Strangely, Lyana didn't remember opening it.

"Ariel will be okay. I'm sure of it. She just needs more time to process everything. I mean, all of us do," said Ian. "Maybe Zach most of all."

"I have so many questions to ask him. But he seems hesitant to talk."

"Give him time," said Ian.

"I wonder what he must be thinking."

They had so little information about what had happened to their son, it was impossible to guess what he was going through. Lyana hoped they could have a long talk with him soon. Once the fog cleared.

"How are we going to explain Zach's sudden reappearance?" said Lyana. Everyone had presumed he was dead. That thought dropped a sinking feeling in her stomach.

"I've been thinking about that a lot," said Ian. "What if we say he got lost in the woods. Maybe he hit his head and lost his memory and was taken in by someone who is off the grid and didn't know about the missing person report."

Lyana shook her head. "That's like a terrible movie plot. No one is going to believe that."

"Okay, what about this: He hit his head and got lost in the woods and then found shelter in a cave that happened to be a wolf's den, and the wolves helped keep him safe until he regained his memory."

"That's even worse. Be serious, Ian. This is going to come up."

"Should we just tell them he time-traveled somewhere for a few weeks and then suddenly reappeared in our storm shelter?"

Lyana laughed. "That might be more believable than your other suggestions."

"Maybe we should just ask Zach. He'll probably have a good idea or two," said Ian.

Lyana paled. "Lloyd was there. What if he says something? We'll be branded as the crazy family."

Ian placed his hand on Lyana's shoulder. "Lloyd is a good man. I don't think he'll say anything. At least not anything that makes us seem crazier than we already are. For all anyone knows, he borrowed that truck to pump water out of our house. No one needs to know any more about that."

"I hope you're right."

"And I'm sure Ariel will be fine in time," said Ian. "She just needs some space."

Lyana wished it was that simple. Something even deeper than the mysteries surrounding their house was bothering her daughter.

• • •

An unfamiliar car slowed to a stop along the road by their driveway, and Ariel stiffened. Thoughts of kidnapping came, unbidden. Or maybe they were bidden. She had, after all, lost her brother for weeks and there still was no explanation for his absence.

She relaxed when Lloyd climbed out of the passenger seat, then sent the driver on her way.

"Hey, Ariel." He walked up to her and stopped. "Out for a little fresh air?"

"Something like that." Maybe Lloyd would have some wisdom about their situation. "What...what happened out there yesterday?" She gestured in the general direction of their house.

Lloyd shrugged. "Something that's impossible to explain, I think."

"Ya think?"

Lloyd laughed. "What do you think happened?"

"I think this house, this land, is haunted and we're just being toyed with before something truly terrible happens," said Ariel. She hadn't put it into such succinct words before.

Lloyd nodded. "Could be," he said. "Or it could be an avalanche of strange coincidences."

"Could it?"

Lloyd shook his head. "Probably the haunted thing," he said. "We may never know. I suspect that will be difficult to accept—not knowing. But sometimes not knowing is the best we can hope for."

"I just don't know what's true anymore," she said.

"'Doubt is the key to knowledge.'"

"What does that mean?"

"It's an old Persian proverb. I have a feeling it may apply here. Or not." He shrugged again.

Ariel liked the way he shrugged. He seemed so comfortable in his own skin. But how could anyone be comfortable in their own skin after experiencing so much heartache? She couldn't imagine what it was like for Lloyd to lose his wife and daughter so suddenly in a car accident. Well, maybe now she could imagine it a little. But she didn't want to.

"I just came by to collect the truck," he added. "I'm assuming your parents…and Zach…are home?"

"Yeah. Unless they've all been swallowed up by a random vortex."

"I'll be careful to avoid any random vortexes." Lloyd started down the driveway, then paused. He turned to Ariel. "Let me know when you want to schedule that burping contest now that Zach is back." He winked at her.

Ariel laughed, despite herself. Lloyd didn't wait for a response. He wasn't expecting one anyway.

Zach is back, she thought.

But where had he been?

CHAPTER THREE

THE JOURNEY HAD been long, too long, and with too many sleepless nights, thanks to the risk of rogue armies that had little love for the king and his conquests. But Akolo was finally home. Such as it was. The first thing he noticed was the smell. The Jordan River valley had a distinct odor—something like earth and water and fish and flowers. After getting permission from the high priest, he had asked Esme to accompany him on a walk to revisit the house where he had been raised. He wasn't eager for her to see his certain tears, but he didn't want to go alone either.

"It's this way," he said as they wove through the narrow stone-paved streets. Some of the sandstone houses were just as he remembered. Others appeared to be abandoned or badly damaged by fire. People milled through the streets as if it was just a normal day, but it was the opposite of normal. Akolo worried that he might recognize an old neighbor or someone he would sometimes see at the temple—but he was just as worried that he wouldn't.

He paused when he turned the corner onto the street where he'd grown up, stopping so suddenly Esme bumped into him from behind.

"What is it?" she asked.

Akolo swallowed hard. The house where he'd spent the entirety of his life, until being stolen away into captivity by the king's conquering army, was gone. There was nothing left of the building he'd called home. An entire row of houses was missing.

"It's gone," he said.

"What's gone?"

"My house." Akolo didn't even try to fight the tears. They flowed freely as he walked slowly along the dusty street, stopping only when he reached a fence. The entire block where he once lived had been leveled and replaced by a stable. Horses stomped and stirred up dust in what used to be his living room. Just beyond the stable, through a wide gate in the city wall, the river gurgled along as if nothing had happened. But something had. Something awful.

Akolo leaned against a fencepost and dropped to the ground. He pressed his hands to his eyes, feeling the dirt mingle with his tears. Esme sat beside him. The wind shifted and the smell of animal sweat and manure replaced the smell of the river. These scents weren't anything Akolo hadn't experienced before, especially during their long journey back to the Jordan River Valley, but now they made him want to throw up.

Esme didn't say anything. She just sat there next to him. He was thankful for that.

Akolo closed his dirt and salt-crusted eyes and dropped his hands to his lap. He had been struggling mightily with remembering things lately, but he couldn't allow his memories of home to fade. He reached for the most vivid ones he could recall and replayed them in his mind. Laughing with his sisters as their father made funny faces at them behind their mother's back. The look his mother gave when she realized what he was doing. Helping his mother grind the grain to make bread. Staying up late so he could take in the sounds of life going on around him. He loved to eavesdrop on his parents and their neighbors from the bedroom he shared with his sisters. The sound of familiar voices engaged in conversation, occasionally littered with laughter, had always given Akolo a true sense of peace. Of safety. He would often fall asleep to those sounds.

But now the only sounds he could hear were the animals' snorts and his own snuffling.

Esme placed her hand on his, bringing Akolo back to the now. He looked down at her small hand on his, then risked a glance at her face. Those dark eyebrows, the tease of hair that had slipped out of her hood. The weight of his loss was heavy, indeed. But the lightness Esme brought him would not go unnoticed.

A loud snort behind him startled Akolo, and he jumped to his feet. He turned to see a horse staring at him, her long nose inches from his own. The horse snorted again. Esme stood up and laughed, then Akolo couldn't help himself. He laughed too.

"I think she's saying thank you," said Esme.

Akolo reached up to stroke the horse's long snout. "What is she thanking me for?" asked Akolo.

"For sharing your home, of course," said Esme.

Words caught in Akolo's throat, but then he smiled. "You're welcome," he said to the horse.

"We should probably get back," said Esme.

Akolo nodded, took one more long look at the ghost of his childhood home, and the river beyond, then started back along the narrow path through the city, Esme at his side. Just when he thought he might reach over to take her hand, she took his.

"Is this the way to the temple?" she asked, squeezing his hand gently.

Akolo felt that lightness again. "Yes," he said. He knew the way all too well.

They zigged and zagged through narrow alleyways until they reached the wall that protected the temple. A few sections of the wall were partially damaged, perhaps due to a battle, or maybe just from time itself, but mostly it looked as it had when he visited with his sisters. Just inside the north gate, he glanced at the offering table where he'd hidden a year earlier. It was here where he'd discovered a precious stone, the one he'd given away to…to someone. Had he given it away? He reached into the pocket of his tunic and touched the cool stone that never left his side. Too many of Akolo's memories were missing or indistinct.

"This is your god's home?" Esme's sweet voice brought Akolo out of his reverie. She was looking up at the massive tower and the intimidating stairs that led up to it.

"Yes," said Akolo. But was it really? He had felt his God's presence while at the king's palace, too. Maybe it wasn't about the building at all. Surely, then, it was about the holy artifacts—the golden coffer they had carried out of the city and now had returned to its original home.

"It's wonderful," said Esme. "Your god must be something special."

It was impressive, thought Akolo. But what was it his father had said? He could almost hear his father's voice telling him about the magnificence of the first temple. Why was that memory so vivid, and the ones from his time at the king's palace so blurry?

"Can we go inside?" asked Esme.

Akolo shook his head. "No. We can climb the steps to the door, but only the high priest can enter."

"You mean my father?"

Akolo furrowed his brow. Could the high priest of another god enter his God's temple? The high priest hadn't dared to enter the makeshift temple at the king's palace. Only Akolo was allowed inside.

"I don't know," said Akolo. He walked up the first set of stairs and sat down. Esme followed cautiously behind, then sat next to him. From this perch, they could look across the city to the river. He could almost make out the stables where his home once was.

"But *you* can go inside," said Esme.

It was then that he realized the truth. Yes. This was why he had been spared. This was his destiny.

His purpose.

"Yes," he said, answering Esme. "I can."

Akolo wondered, *Am I a high priest now?*

CHAPTER FOUR

ZACH WANTED TO disappear. He had told his parents not to let the school make a big deal about his reappearance, but either they hadn't talked to the right people, or the "right people" had ignored his request.

"Zach," the principal repeated from the podium at the front of the auditorium. "Would you stand please?"

The eyes of everyone in the assembly were surely on him, but Zach kept his gaze at the floor. He had hoped sitting in the back row might keep him from any unwanted attention. No such luck.

Zach's teacher walked up behind him and whispered, "It's okay, Zach. They just want to celebrate you." She placed a hand on his shoulder and waited.

Slowly, he got to his feet, still unwilling to look at the people around him. There was silence at first. An awkward, awful silence. And then the applause began. First, from the teachers and adults in the room, and then the entire auditorium erupted in applause and hoots and hollers. Awkward, awful hoots and hollers, he thought. Zach nodded, then sat down, pulling his arms around himself as a shield. The noise faded and the principal thankfully moved on to the next subject for the assembly.

His first days back had felt strange. He had missed a lot of schoolwork, but none of his teachers required him to do all that work. Instead, they offered to bring him up to date during lunchtime sessions, which he didn't have any say in, apparently. He'd endured the first couple of sessions rather well, but soon realized he wasn't as far behind as the calendar might suggest. Or maybe he was just smarter than most kids his age.

This thought made him smile. He *was* smart.

Even with all the special attention, though, Zach was glad to be back in the regular routine of school. As the images from his adventure faded, the immediacy of school was a kind of relief. He liked studying. He liked learning. He was even beginning to like hanging out with some of his peers in the cafeteria or the school library. But one thing hadn't changed since his adventure: He was always happiest when he was home. Despite the inexplicable experiences he'd had there, the house—especially his room—had become a sanctuary. Even the woods on the property felt like a safe place. Saying that out loud would have brought more curious, judgmental stares, of course. Shouldn't he be afraid of the woods? they'd argue. No. He loved the woods. He loved exploring. He wasn't about to stop doing that.

Besides, he was on a mission now. Every chance he could get, he would go online to research ancient cultures, particularly ancient Mesopotamia, which was where he was certain he'd gone during his time away. Even if it was all just a crazy dream, he needed to know more about the place, the people. And then there were the many books in Marshall's cabin. Like Zach's father, Marshall was a student of ancient cultures. Zach couldn't wait to soak up as much knowledge as possible from Marshall's vast collection.

Zach was munching away on pomegranate seeds at lunchtime when a group of classmates came over and sat down at his table. He knew the kids' names, but before his disappearance, not one of them would have known his.

"Hey," said Matt, clearly the alpha of the small group, based on how he took the lead.

"Hey," said Zach.

"Is it really true that you were in a coma all that time?"

Zach had heard a bunch of wild explanations for his absence, but this one was new.

"A coma? Nope. Pretty sure I'd remember if I was." Zach realized the silliness of his answer the second the words poured out. But no one laughed.

"What *do* you remember?" Matt asked. The other kids stared at him, clearly anticipating some crazy response.

"Not much, really." He'd already told a bunch of people this, including a policeman, two doctors, and a woman he thought might be a psychiatrist. Or maybe psychologist. He wasn't exactly sure of the difference. He made a mental note to research that so he *could* be sure. He cued up the explanation he and his parents had concocted: that he had some kind of brain "hiccup" that left him without a memory of who he was—a sort of amnesia; that he'd wandered in the woods for a day or more before finding an abandoned cabin; that he'd stayed there, feeding himself from canned goods in a well-stocked pantry, until one day when his memory just returned without warning. Then there was the detailed explanation for how he found his way home, following a creek behind the cabin that eventually led him to his house. This is where people would usually gasp and say, "Wow, how crazy that you could have just followed that home on the first day." Yeah, if his brain had worked properly, he'd reply.

But the kids at the table didn't ask follow-up questions. They just nodded, said, "Glad you're back" and walked away.

It was probably the most benign interaction he'd had since his return just about a week ago. He smiled. Maybe things would be back to "normal" sooner rather than later.

• • •

Lyana stood and admired her cleanup work. The chicken coop hadn't housed chickens for quite a while, but now it was finally cleaned up. Ian had suggested they take down the coop and replace it with beehives. Lyana wasn't convinced Zach would be okay with that. Besides, she liked the little coop, even if they didn't have chickens.

Then again, she thought, it would be nice to have fresh honey less than a minute's walk from the kitchen.

A cool breeze rattled the tiny door of the miniature bungalow. The decision to raise chickens was a wild, spur-of-the-moment idea, but once they'd discovered the cute Tudor-style chicken coop online, there was no turning back. They fenced the tiny building that resembled their house, if only slightly, with an area far larger than the few chickens they were raising needed, optimistic that they might someday add a second coop and more chickens. But that optimism had been shattered the day Lyana found the fence broken and every one of their chickens dead.

Lyana shook the image from her head, recalling that her next thought in that moment was that Zach had succumbed to the very same fate. But no. Zach was fine. Zach *is* fine.

Zach should be home from school any minute.

She looked back toward the house and the long driveway, then checked her watch. No, not quite yet.

Lyana took a deep breath, held it in, then released it. As she did, a faint voice blew in with a breeze. The words were indistinct. Were they words at all, or moans from the trees bending in the wind? She turned her head this way and that, hoping to better hear the sound.

She'd heard enough voices since their move to Littleton to keep a therapist busy for years, but she had been so very hopeful that Zach's return might mean the end of them.

The words flitted past her again, this time with more intensity, causing the sibilance of the s's to buzz at her like a bee.

This isn't over.

"What? What isn't over?" Lyana spun around, looking for the source of the voice. But, as expected, she found nothing. The last time she'd heard a voice, she was sure it was from the daughter they'd lost to a miscarriage. Avril. But this voice sounded different.

Lyana took another deep breath and resigned herself to a familiar if unwelcomed truth: Her family's unpredictable, ever-evolving story *wasn't* over. She knew there was more to the strange occurrences. There had to be a purpose for it all.

But what did the voice mean?

What was yet to come?

Her thoughts were interrupted as she stumbled over the uneven ground. Ruts had been cut into the lawn by the truck Lloyd had driven the night Zach returned. She recalled their conversation just a few days before when he'd come to collect the truck.

"Lloyd, I don't know how we can thank you," Ian had begun. Lloyd, in typical Lloyd fashion, shrugged off the thank-you.

"I think of you as family," he'd said in reply. "I mean, if you're comfortable with that."

They were. Of course they were. Then there was a long, awkward silence. Lyana was cuing up the right words to say about what Lloyd had witnessed when he broke the silence.

"Strange night last night, don't you think?" he'd said.

"Yeah, about that..." began Ian.

"I'm so glad Zach found his way home," Lloyd interrupted, waving Ian off. "I look forward to hearing all about his adventure. Until then, I know nothing. I just happened to show up when he returned."

"How will you explain the truck?" Ian asked.

"Well, you did have a bit of a flood, didn't you?"

Lloyd had winked at them then. That little action immediately eased the growing tension in her stomach.

Lloyd was indeed a good man.

• • •

Ian glanced over at his son, who was busying himself with homework at the small table in Marshall's cabin. Zach had practically pleaded with his dad to let him come along on his visit.

"I can do my homework later," he'd argued.

Ian instead agreed on a compromise, allowing Zach to join him as long as he brought his homework and worked on it while he and Marshall talked.

"Maybe Marshall can help me with my history homework," Zach had replied.

"Why, because he's old?"

"No. Well maybe that. But also because he's smart." Zach quickly added, "Not that you aren't…smart, I mean. But he's a different kind of smart."

Ian didn't press the issue. Besides, having Zach around when they talked about the house might be wise. Zach was good at solving puzzles.

Marshall had been unusually quiet these past few days. Ian had a ton of questions for him but was so occupied sorting out the issues prompted by Zach's sudden reappearance, he hadn't yet confronted him. But the questions couldn't wait any longer.

"I can't believe I'm about to ask…but is this property cursed? Did you know Zach would be found in the tornado shelter? What secrets have you been keeping from us?" he began.

Marshall nodded at Zach, who was scratching away with a pencil on a sheet of paper.

"Zach needs to know this too," said Ian. He walked over to the table and looked at the paper Zach was working on. Something about Greek mythology. The topic brought a slight shake of the head and a half smile from Ian.

"Ian, honestly I'm not really sure what I should or shouldn't say," Marshall replied. He handed a steaming cup of tea to Ian.

"So, you *do* know more than you've shared?"

"I know…shadows of things," he replied.

"What does that mean?" Ian wasn't angry at Marshall, but he was getting annoyed by his cryptic answers.

"It means I'm nearly as mystified as you about what's been happening here," Marshall answered.

Ian was usually pretty good at reading people. But Marshall was a true enigma. Still, that word, *nearly*, stood out.

"You said 'nearly' as mystified. So, you do know more than you've let on."

Marshall pointed to the unoccupied chair across from Zach, and Ian sat. Marshall then dragged a stool over from his desk that was littered with carvings of animals in various stages of completion, along with a generous dusting of wood shavings. That explained the subtle sweetness in the air. Well, that, and the tea. Marshall sat on the stool, facing Ian and Zach.

"Black cherry," said Marshall, reading Ian's mind, not for the first time. "I prefer cherry wood when carving."

"How long have you been carving stuff?" Zach was tapping his pencil eraser on the table to whatever rhythm he heard in his head. Or maybe he was counting to himself.

"Oh, a very long time. My uncle…" Marshall paused.

"Mr. Goodpasture," Zach interjected.

"Hey, aren't you supposed to be doing your homework?" Ian asked. He pointed to the paper.

"Almost done," said Zach. "I'm just trying to remember the Greek equivalent of the Roman god Mercury." He started shuffling through his textbook.

"Hermes," said Marshall. "Messenger of the gods."

Zach looked up at his dad and raised his eyebrows. "See?"

"I knew that," said Ian. He reached across the table and ruffled his son's hair. Zach didn't seem to mind.

"I have lived a very long and...complicated life," Marshall began. Ian sensed a shift in the caretaker's tone. He sounded almost apologetic. "But there are some memories, some knowledge that eludes me. Things that seem just out of reach..."

"Me too!" said Zach. "That's what I've been trying to say!"

Marshall nodded at Zach. "I can tell you this for certain: There is something bigger than us at play here."

"Isn't that kind of obvious?" said Zach. He was stuffing his homework and textbook into his backpack.

They'd already experienced more than a few supernatural events. The house wiring that nearly destroyed Lyana. The voices she was hearing. The bees in Zach's room. Zach's disappearance, and a most unlikely reappearance. Had Zach really traveled through time as he'd suggested during the one detailed conversation they'd had since his return? All the clues Ian and Marshall had collected pointed to that hard-to-believe reality, too. Did any of it make sense? Only if "something bigger" was at play in all this.

Marshall smiled. "I guess it is a little obvious," he admitted. "But what I'm suggesting is that this is all connected. These aren't random events."

Ian had suspected as much but couldn't put his finger on what that connection was. Until now.

"It's you," said Ian. "This isn't just about us; it's about you." He worded it as a statement rather than a question, but it was a shot in the dark.

Marshall seemed to shrink, his shoulders slumping.

"I think it's about all of us," he said.

"It's not random," said Zach.

Marshall shook his head. "I wish I could say more. I wish I knew what exactly I could say. But…there are still a lot of unanswerable questions."

Ian's stomach dropped. What did he mean by that? He was almost afraid to ask.

"Are we in danger?" asked Zach. He was bouncing his pencil on the table again. There was a pattern to it, but Ian couldn't quite figure it out.

"Everything has worked out so far," Marshall answered. Then he paused. The silence in the room grew until it was almost overwhelming. Finally, he added, "I think that will continue to be the case."

Ian wasn't reassured, but it was clear from his tone Marshall wouldn't be providing more answers today. "From now on, just don't keep anything from us, okay?" he said. Marshall nodded and Ian decided to change the subject. "Have you gotten any further with the translation?" Ian remembered speaking in a foreign tongue just before they cracked open the rusted door in the dirt to discover the flooded tornado shelter, but could only recall a few of the words. Marshall had no recollection of the strange outburst.

"You were on the right track. It's an extinct language. Akkadian."

"Of course!" said Ian. "*The Epic of Gilgamesh.*"

"What's that?" asked Zach.

"It's one of the oldest examples of written literature, an epic poem—like the *Iliad* or the *Odyssey*," said Ian. He pointed to Zach's backpack. "It's Sumerian. That's even older than Greek or Roman mythology. It was written in Sumerian, then translated into Akkadian, if I recall." He looked over at Marshall. Marshall was nodding.

"What is it about?" Zach asked, wide-eyed.

"Take a wild guess," said Ian. He was enjoying this moment.

"Gods?"

"Yes, and..."

"Monsters?"

"Yup," said Ian.

"And a king who wanted to cheat death," added Marshall.

"Now that's cool," said Zach. "But...what does that have to do with us?"

Ian looked over at Marshall. "Were you able to successfully translate the words?"

Marshall's expression was unreadable. "Some of what you remembered was apparently gibberish, because it was untranslatable."

Ian's heart sank.

"However...I was able to translate a few words. And, frankly, this is still somewhat of a guess, since we have no context."

"I wish I could have remembered more," said Ian. "But It all happened so fast."

"Yes."

"What did you find out? What words did you translate?" asked Zach.

"There are three," began Marshall. "The first is *plan*. The second is *future*." He hesitated. "It may actually be something more specific like *tomorrow*, but again, without context..."

Ian tensed. "What was the third word?"

Marshall looked Ian directly in the eye. "*Harm*."

Zach's expression went from curiosity to fear and then to confidence in a nanosecond. "Maybe that was about me? I mean, I could have been harmed, right? But I wasn't. I'm fine! I'm right here and everything's fine." He looked to Marshall, then back to Ian. "Everything's fine, right, Dad?"

Ian nodded. "Everything is fine, Zach," he said. He didn't dare look at Marshall.

What if the message was a warning?

CHAPTER FIVE

ESME WAS AKOLO'S best friend. There was no disputing that now. She instinctively knew when he was feeling overwhelmed or sad or disappointed and knew exactly the right words to help him sort through those feelings. He had experienced plenty of those feelings in the years since returning home.

Home.

Home was once a place—a house filled with family that he knew would always be there for him. But with his house and family long gone, home meant something different to him now. Esme helped him to understand that "home" was really about people. She ought to know, he thought. She was far from the place of her birth, the place where she had grown up.

An image of the king's palace slipped into Akolo's thoughts. He saw the king's fancy throne room. A courtyard with a fountain. Did it have water in it? He saw a tall tower and felt a breeze blowing through its windows. And there was a makeshift temple. Was he remembering it right? The images were fuzzy at the edges, like a fraying rug. A boy about his own age flitted among the scenes like a shadow, then disappeared altogether. So many of his memories were uncertain. But there was one that remained clear as day.

He is outside the temple and a young girl about his age is standing next to the high priest, looking over at him. Her eyes are so green.

Esme was right. Home isn't just about a place. The high priest who continued to mentor him was the closest thing he had to a father now. That thought always brought both a smile and a tear. Akolo felt safe in the high priest's presence, but the man was more than a little intimidating. Sometimes, though, Akolo saw a sparkle in his singular eye.

With wise counsel from the high priest, and frequent encouragement from Esme, Akolo had settled into his role as intermediary. And though he felt more kinship with Esme's people than his own, he served the people of his hometown well.

In this moment, he was not sure what that meant. One thing was certain: He did not expect to see a sparkle in the high priest's eye.

Akolo was doing his best to remain calm. He was not looking forward to this conversation. He sat on the bench outside of the high priest's meeting room, a golden chalice set beside him, and he shifted his position not for the first time. As he waited, he recalled the moment when his heart nearly stopped beating.

It was the night before. He was in the temple room. A room he'd been in dozens if not hundreds of times by now. Before his brief exile, he'd spent many hours outside the temple, helping his sisters and his mother with the preparation for the temple offerings. But the first time he had entered the small space upon his return, it felt foreign to him. It didn't feel right that he, once a servant to servants of his own high priest, now had sole access to this place where the holiest artifacts were kept, the place where his people's God resided and communicated with them.

Akolo had just set the chalice given him by an ambassador of the king onto the holy chest and was standing there, waiting for… something to happen. Sometimes nothing happened at all, even during a blood moon. That had been a difficult message to give to the high priest.

"Nothing happened," he'd said. The high priest had studied him closely then, looking for a lie, perhaps. But it wasn't a lie. The item he'd been tasked with imbuing—a crown, of all things—just rested there on the chest. There was no blurring of the air, no glowing lights, no whispers from God indicating the crown had been blessed. That was the first indication that imbuing objects with this deity's power was not as simple as bringing them into the small room.

"We will try again next blood moon," the high priest had finally said before dismissing Akolo.

But during the next blood moon, the high priest had sent a shield, not a crown. Sure enough, the moment Akolo had placed it on the chest, the air turned cold, the gems on the shield began to glow, and faint whispers filled the room, or at least Akolo's head. He was pretty sure no one else could hear what he heard. And even if they could, they wouldn't know what was being said. He barely did himself. The message was typically brief and often cryptic. Like a poem he could feel in his gut but didn't quite know how to express in words.

But last night was different. The usually faint whispers grew in volume and in depth. What typically sounded like a waft of wind or a whisper seemed to be coming from underneath the floors, through the walls, and inside his body—inside and outside all at the same time. This time he heard a voice that sounded like a waterfall, and the message was strong and clear.

Mene, Mene, Tekel.

He had heard these words from his father once during story night before the temple was taken, but he couldn't remember their significance. The sound continued to swell with intensity, and he felt the rumble in his chest as he heard it again.

Mene, Mene, Tekel.

He covered his ears and slumped to the ground as light and sound collided and threatened to overwhelm him. Then in an instant, the sound climaxed, followed by a deafening silence. A still, small whisper filled the room.

In Hedyeh rā bā to sharik mishavam.

Akolo was pulled out of his memory by the sound of a spear smacking the ground in front of him.

"The high priest will see you now," the guard snapped. He didn't look pleased, but when did guards ever look pleased? Akolo wondered.

Akolo stood and walked into the high priest's room. It had once been where the high priest who had served Akolo's people lived. Akolo had only ever visited it once, when his mother sent him there with a basket of fruit not meant for an offering but as a gift to the high priest himself.

But that high priest was long dead.

Akolo swallowed familiar waves of anger and heartache as he stood in front of the massive table. It wasn't this high priest's fault that his family was dead. It was the king's. But the high priest was there to do the king's bidding. That remained true.

"Akolo," began the high priest. He pointed to a bowl of fruit and nodded.

Akolo wasn't the least bit hungry, but he reached for a pear and slipped it into his tunic pocket.

The high priest raised an eyebrow. "Saving it for later?" he said.

Akolo nodded.

The high priest looked Akolo up and down. "We really need to do something about…that." He gestured at Akolo.

"About what?"

"I think it's time you started wearing a robe."

Akolo didn't think a robe would make his role better—he liked the simplicity of his garb. But he nodded again anyway.

"Tell me, young Akolo, what did your god say to you last night?"

The high priest waved at someone behind Akolo. The guard walked in, carrying the chalice he'd left on the bench like it might break at any moment. Or turn him to ash. He set it on the table, then quickly backed out of the room.

Akolo swallowed hard.

"Please share," the high priest added. Akolo had a hard time reading the old man's expression, half hidden as it was behind one black eye patch.

"I heard Him speak," said Akolo.

The high priest gestured at the chalice.

"No," said Akolo. "It wasn't about the chalice. I…it wasn't imbued. I'm certain of it."

"What did He say?"

Akolo took a deep breath, then spoke as clearly as his nerves would allow. "He just said 'Mene, Mene, Tekel.'"

The high priest sat back in his chair, lifted his hand to stroke his long beard. It was an action Akolo had seen many times.

"And what do you think it means?" the high priest asked after a moment's silence.

Akolo was afraid of this very question. He had rehearsed a response, but the words failed him. "I…I don't know for sure," he began. "But…" Another deep breath. "My father once told me a story about our God speaking to another king. Then he said 'Mene, Mene, Tekel, Upharsin,' which means 'You have been weighed, found wanting, and will be divided.' But he definitely did not say Upharsin this time. Then he said something I did not understand—it sounded like your language."

The high priest leaned forward, intrigued, and stared intensely at Akolo, waiting for his next words.

"He said, '*In hedyeh rā bā to sharik mishavam,*' or something like that. I don't know what that means, but I have a strong feeling we need to choose wisely what we ask Him to bless."

But what did "choose wisely" mean? Akolo had no clue. The high priest stroked his beard again, sitting in silence for what felt like an eternity, then nodded.

"Good," he finally said. "This is good to know. I will send a courier to the king with this news. Perhaps then he will..." He stopped. "Thank you, Akolo. This is helpful."

Akolo had expected a rebuke. Instead, the high priest seemed pleased.

"But what does it mean?" asked Akolo.

"You may go," the high priest began. Then he held up his hand to stop Akolo. "But first, stop by the tailor's hut so he can measure you for a robe." He waved his hand. As Akolo walked out the door, he heard the high priest call after him, "And please be discreet if you plan on visiting my daughter today."

Akolo thought he heard the guard laugh as he passed by, but he chose to ignore it and kept on walking down the hall, out the grand doorway, and down the many steps into the temple courtyard. He almost walked right by the tailor's hut. After pausing to catch his breath, he walked inside and was immediately greeted by the tailor, a short man with a kind smile and sleepy eyes.

"I was expecting you," said the tailor.

Akolo shouldn't have been surprised by this. The high priest's reach was undeniable. He had eyes and ears all over the town. Just what did he know about Akolo's meetings with Esme?

• • •

"I thought I'd find you here."

Esme's honey-dripped voice eased Akolo out of his pensiveness. He'd been at the stables for more than an hour, sitting on what had become his favorite rock, listening to the sounds of the animals going about their lazy day and the rushing of the river just beyond the gate. She sat down beside him. He awkwardly shifted to his left, putting more distance between them than he would have liked.

"What's that all about?" she asked, indicating the gap between them.

"Your father issued a stern warning about us spending time together." Well, that wasn't exactly what he'd said, but Akolo didn't want to press his luck.

"My father? A stern warning?" Esme laughed.

"Well, it felt like a stern warning," said Akolo.

"He's just looking out for his youngest daughter," said Esme. "His favorite daughter," she added with another laugh.

Akolo laughed, too. His tension eased.

"He said something interesting, today," Akolo began. "Or rather, started to say something, then stopped."

Akolo shared the conversation he'd had with Esme's father. "What do you think he was going to say about the king?"

Esme didn't reply right away. She stood and walked over to the fence to pet a horse that had wandered close to them. The horse snorted its approval. "I have heard rumblings," she began.

Akolo joined Esme at the fence, making sure to keep the appropriate amount of space between them. Lately, that had taken more and more intentional effort. All he wanted was to be close to Esme. "What kind of rumblings?" he asked.

"I don't think I should say," she said.

"Okay."

Esme gently nudged Akolo with her elbow. "What? You're not going to pester me about it?"

"I've learned that when you want to tell me something, you will. And if you don't? There's no amount of pestering that will change your mind."

She smiled. "You've learned well," she said.

"So..." Akolo began, "I was fitted for a robe."

"I know."

Akolo sighed. "Is there anything you don't know?"

"Probably. But I'll find out soon enough."

Esme reached over and took Akolo's hand, then turned to him. "Here's what I can tell you," she said, looking him straight in the eyes. "My father thinks the king is making too many mistakes." She squeezed his hand. "But you didn't hear that from me. In fact, you didn't hear it at all."

"No, of course I didn't hear it." He had to turn away from her gaze. It was too much, too intense. "What else didn't I hear?" he added as he turned back to look at the horses.

She let go of his hand and softly slapped him on the shoulder. "You are something, Akolo. That's certain." She returned to petting the horse. "The king has many enemies," she said, ostensibly to the horse. "Their power is growing, while his own power is weakening. There will be a reckoning. Maybe not soon, but eventually. And my father..."

Akolo waited for her to continue. No words followed.

"Let's just enjoy the sunset," she said. The words seemed to catch in her throat.

"Yes," said Akolo. He wanted desperately to take her hand in his, but before he could convince himself that would be okay, something startled the horses. The one Esme had been petting darted away to join the rest.

Seconds later, thunder broke the silence. Akolo turned and looked across the city to the temple tower. An ominous band of black clouds blocked the sky behind it. Lightning flashed and lit up the tower in silhouette, followed by another roll of thunder.

"We should go," said Esme. She started off at a brisk pace toward the city center, Akolo following close behind.

After a few steps, she stopped and abruptly turned toward him. A gust of wind whipped her hood away. Long black hair blew wildly across her face. Those green eyes bored into Akolo's soul and his heartbeat raced. Before he could react, she stood on tiptoes, gently wrapped her hands around his head and pulled him down into a kiss. She then turned and ran, disappearing down the narrow alleyway before the first drops of rain landed.

Akolo was frozen in place, stunned by the taste of Esme's lips. He was still standing there when the deluge began. The downpour of cool water brought him back to the moment. It was only then that he noticed a hooded stranger peeking around the corner of what he had thought was an empty building. As soon as Akolo noticed him, the figure disappeared into the blur of rain.

Fear replaced the wonder that had settled in Akolo's gut.

The high priest had eyes and ears all over town.

CHAPTER SIX

ARIEL PRESSED "SEND" on her phone and immediately regretted it. "Is there a way to unsend?" she wondered aloud, frantically searching the internet for an answer. But it was too late. She'd already received a reply.

Of course. See you there.

She breathed a sigh of relief. She didn't quite know how to read Garrett. He seemed like a genuinely nice guy, but he was fickle. Unpredictable. He didn't fit in any particular group in school and relished the idea of avoiding labels. It was one of the things Ariel liked about him, despite how it also made her feel slightly uncomfortable around him. Or maybe *because* it made her feel uncomfortable.

"I need a ride into town," she said as she walked into the kitchen. Her father was cleaning up the dishes from a late breakfast she'd chosen not to participate in. "Unless you want me to walk..."

"No, I'll take you," Ian said. He went back to working on the dishes. A moment later, he paused and turned back toward her. "Do you mean now?" he asked.

Ariel almost replied with "duh," but instead chose the higher ground. "If that's okay."

"It's fine. I need to take Zach into town later for an appointment. I could pick you up then. Would that work?"

"Like, when?" she asked.

"Around two, two thirty?"

"Yeah, that works."

"What are you planning on doing downtown?" he asked.

She knew he would ask that. "Maybe shop a little? Maybe just walk around for the heck of it."

"Okay. Give me a minute."

That was surprisingly easy, thought Ariel. She had expected more grilling about her intent at the very least. It wasn't like she asked for a ride to town often. In fact, this was probably the first time in months. She made a mental note to window shop for a minute before heading to the park. That would make her answer at least partly truthful. And despite her frustration with her parents, she still didn't relish the idea of lying to them.

Her dad dropped her off in front of the diner just before eleven.

"See you around two, then?" she said.

"Might be as late as two thirty." He reached over to brush something off her shoulder. "You had a leaf stuck there." She undid her seatbelt and opened the door. "Is everything okay?" he asked before she closed it.

"Well, I still think we should move, but otherwise...everything is fine," she said with a smirk. It wasn't, of course. And her dad, of all people, should have known that. He might be stubborn, but he wasn't stupid.

"Okay. Please know your mom and I are open to talking. We don't want you to keep all that stuff locked inside. It's not healthy."

"Got it." She closed the door. Her dad didn't pull away from the curb right away. He was probably trying to come up with something profound to say. Or something funny. Something to make her laugh.

It might have worked, too. Not because her disappointment in her parents was fading, but because she was anxious about spending time with Garrett. Anxiety often accompanied complex emotions. She thought back to the moment she'd figured out the puzzle of her mother's frantic paintings. She should have been terrified by the implications that her brother was locked inside the tornado shelter, and of course she was, but she'd also felt exhilaration at her discovery. Her mother would likely explain her complex cocktail of emotions as one of the many unexpected joys of adolescence. She would be partially right, of course, but Ariel knew it was something more. Something she'd buried deep inside years earlier. Something that was threatening to bubble to the surface in light of all that had happened to her family. But not yet. Not today.

Ariel waited outside the diner for a few minutes, then started heading toward the city park. A cool breeze tempted her to zip up her hoodie, but she didn't like the way she looked with it zipped up, so she endured the chill as she crossed the street and walked over to the swing set. The playground here felt like a second thought of city planners; the ball fields took priority. It wasn't as modern as the neighborhood park near her school, but there was a kind of old-school charm about the rainbow-painted merry-go-round, the all-metal monkey bars, and the towering A-frame swing set featuring a half dozen wooden swings. She considered testing her strength on the monkey bars but opted instead to sit on the swing farthest from the sidewalk. She found it odd that the playground was practically empty on a weekend day around noon, but she didn't mind the quiet.

"Hey, sorry I'm so late."

Ariel startled at the voice coming from behind her. She turned her head to see Garrett walking up to the swing set.

He sat in the swing next to her. "I guess swings are kind of our thing now," he said.

Ariel laughed. "I guess so."

"This isn't some kind of regression therapy, is it?" asked Garrett.

"No. I just like…wait. You think I need therapy?" Ariel hoped Garrett would catch the lightness in her voice.

"Don't we all?" He caught it.

"Maybe I am regressing a little bit," she offered.

"Missing the good ol' days?"

"Something like that." She started swinging in earnest, feeling the wind in her face, the tickle in her stomach.

"Things going okay with your family?" he asked.

"Wow, are *you* my therapist now?"

He laughed and started swinging and soon was matching her pace.

"Things are...okay," she said. "Just dealing with the usual stuff. Annoying parents. An annoying brother..."

"I wouldn't know."

Of course not. Garrett was an only child and had been living with his grandparents for at least a few years now. That much she'd gotten out of him the last time they hung out at a park.

"Sorry," she said. "I didn't mean to be insensitive..."

"No offense taken," said Garrett. "I was just stating a fact. I mean, my Papa and Nana can be a bit much at times, but I just figured that was because they're old."

Ariel smiled. "You call them Papa and Nana?"

"Old habits die hard, Air."

Air. There it was again. His nickname for her. She couldn't love it more.

They didn't talk for a while and that was just fine with Ariel. She really didn't have an agenda. She just wanted to be around someone she liked. Someone who didn't expect anything from her except just to "be."

• • •

"Good afternoon, I'm Dr. Lee. "Please sit wherever you're most comfortable."

Zach was busy studying the diplomas hanging on the wall near the doorway. Finally, he found what he was looking for. Dr. Lee had a PsyD in psychology from Baylor University. So, she was a psychologist, not a psychiatrist. He wasn't sure why that mattered, or if it did. But at least now he knew.

Zach looked at his dad. Two cushioned chairs and a couch had been arranged in the large office in front of a simple but clearly very expensive wooden desk. Ian nodded toward the couch with a question mark in his eyes.

Zach took a seat on the right side of the couch, leaning against the armrest. It was a leather couch, but soft, supple, one that had gotten plenty of use. Zach generally didn't like things made of leather—they reminded him of cows, and even though cows were among the gentlest of creatures, according to Wikipedia, Zach was uncomfortable around them. *Probably stems from childhood trauma*, he thought, imagining the psychiatrist addressing this unusual phobia. Was it a phobia? No. He just didn't like cows.

Ian sat next to him. Zach noted the way his father caressed the cushion after he sat. The contented look on his face suggested approval. His dad probably didn't think of cows when he sat on leather couches. What were his dad's phobias? Well, other than snakes. *That would certainly count as a phobia*, he thought.

"I thought we could begin by simply sharing a little bit about ourselves," said Dr. Lee as she settled into one of the cushioned chairs. "If you don't mind, I'll go first."

She proceeded to share about her educational journey and her clinical experience as a psychologist, then finished with a brief mention of a husband and two grown children, both of whom lived out of state. Zach thought that last part was probably unnecessary, but figured she was just trying to be personable.

"Now, tell me a little about yourselves."

Zach waited for his dad to start talking. Instead, he looked at Zach. "You want to go first?"

No. He didn't. He really wasn't sure why they were here in the first place. Actually, he did know why. The detective they had talked with after Zach reappeared had "strongly suggested" they speak with a professional about his disappearance, and in particular, about his missing memories. After a family meeting, they all agreed that Zach and his dad would meet with Dr. Lee "to satisfy the curious and silence the judgmental" as his mother described it. To better hide their lie, really. Because no one would believe Zach had traveled thousands of years back in time. Most of the time he didn't believe it himself. But what other explanation was there for his somewhat random collection of strangely specific memories?

"I'm Zach," he began. "Zach Keane. I'm a good student and I like studying things like history and bugs and numbers, and we used to have chickens, but a wild animal killed them all. Oh, and tornadoes. I like tracking which way they might go, and I like movies, and I like pancakes, especially with chocolate chips." He couldn't tell by their faces if this was too much or just what she wanted to hear. Reading body language was a big challenge for him. "Oh, and I have a sister. She's not terrible, but…"

His dad gave him that look—the one he used in public when Zach over shared. Dr. Lee didn't press him for more. That was a plus in Zach's book. His dad took over, sharing a little about himself and their family and the reason they had set up this appointment. Zach zoned out, trying to read the titles of the many books in the shelf behind Dr. Lee's desk.

"Zach?" his father said.

"Sorry, I was a little distracted. I get distracted sometimes. What was the question?"

"Dr. Lee wanted to hear what you think happened."

"You mean in general?"

"Just share whatever you feel comfortable sharing," said the doc. Zach hated that word *share*. It sounded so juvenile.

"Okay." Zach took a moment to put his thoughts in order, then told his version of the story. It was like a play in four acts: He went out for a walk in the woods; something happened inside his head, and his memory got jumbled; he found an abandoned cabin (he thinks) and lived off canned foods for weeks; then his memory returned, and he found his way home. There was no way to make it sound more believable. The family had all agreed on that, too. But it was the best they could come up with. Getting a clean bill of health from the hospital made Zach feel better, but it didn't add credence to the "brain hiccup" part of their story. He didn't love the MRI, though. Too claustrophobic.

When he'd finished talking, Dr. Lee didn't say anything. She hadn't even nodded along when he was speaking. Her gaze was intense, but not unkind. She finally nodded, to herself, it seemed, then made a few notes on her notepad. Zach wondered if a notepad was standard equipment for all psychologists.

"Do you want to talk about any of the dreams you remember?"

Wait. Did his dad say something about his ancient memories? Zach tried to rewind the conversation in the office, but there was a gap missing. Probably when he was reading all the book titles.

"You mean like about ancient things?"

"Whatever you can recall," said the doc.

"Mostly the dreams are kind of blurry," he offered. It was true enough. "But I do remember one with a tent and a high priest or someone like that." The dream he and his sister had shared before his time travel. Seemed safe enough to talk about that one. He offered as much detail as he could.

"Your father is a professor of history, is that right?" She looked at his dad.

"I teach about ancient cultures," Ian clarified.

"That's probably where I got it," said Zach. "The dream, I mean. I read some of my dad's books sometimes."

That seemed to satisfy Dr. Lee. Their session went on for another half hour or so, but nothing more was said about Zach's disappearance.

Mostly they talked about things Zach liked to do. He had plenty of specifics to share, especially about bees. He'd become an expert on bees. He avoided them in the real world, but figured the more he knew about them, the safer he'd be. Dr. Lee had laughed at that little play on words. Zach liked her. She didn't say much but didn't seem to judge him either. But wasn't that her job? To judge people? Maybe she was just good at doing it quietly.

When time was about up, Dr. Lee asked if Zach had anything else he wanted to share.

There was that word again. But he did have something. He'd just remembered one of his dad's phobias.

"My dad hates pork belly," Zach stated, smiling. "I mean, he loves bacon, but if you call it pork belly, he gets all squeamish and stuff. Anyway, is that a normal phobia?"

Dr. Lee laughed again. "That's a new one for me," she said. "But words do matter, don't they, Zach?"

He didn't need to think about that for long. "Yeah, they do."

"My secret's out," said Ian with a slight giggle.

"I wonder if they serve pork belly at the diner?" said Zach. Ian ruffled Zach's hair. Zach used to recoil at that kind of touch, but lately he'd been enjoying it. Welcoming it, even.

"Speaking of which, we need to go collect your sister."

They said their goodbyes and left.

"Well?" his dad asked as they left the building.

"She's nice."

"But?"

"Do we need to do that again?"

"Only if you want to," answered Ian.

"Okay. I'll think about it."

And he would, too.

• • •

Ariel stole a glance at Garrett. He was facing straight ahead, swinging with purpose.

"What are you thinking about?" she ventured.

"Chocolate chip cookies," he said, without hesitation.

Ariel laughed. "Why chocolate chip cookies?"

"Why not chocolate chip cookies?" He looked over at her and smiled.

This was it. The one thing that made her second-guess her desire to move back to Boston. To move anywhere but here, really.

Garrett.

He jumped off the swing, landing perfectly, then sending his arms into the air like an Olympic gymnast.

"The Russian judge gives you a nine point seven," said Ariel, in an awful approximation of a Russian accent.

"Only a nine point seven?" Garrett pouted. "Let's see you do better."

Ariel swung her feet to gain height, readied herself, then on the next swing forward, jumped. She landed unevenly on the pea gravel and slid toward Garrett. Instead of him catching her like in one of those predictably schlocky Hallmark movies, she knocked him to the ground, landing beside him.

"Oof. The Irish judge gives you a four point four," said Garrett in a perfect Irish accent.

"Fair," she replied. Ariel was still brushing the gravel from her palms when Garrett stood and reached for her hand to help her up.

"Thanks." She was disappointed when he took his hand away. Maybe she wanted to be in one of those predictably schlocky Hallmark movies after all.

It was nearly two o'clock. Why did time move so quickly when you wanted it to go slow, and so slowly when you wanted it to go fast?

"I should get going. My dad could be here any time now," she said.

Garrett nodded. "Your dad seems pretty cool."

"How would you know anything about my dad?"

"I might have searched him on the interwebs," he said.

Ariel punched Garret in the arm. A little harder than she intended. "Stalker! Tell me you didn't!"

"Maybe I did?" he said with a shrug.

"Well, the 'interwebs' only tell part of the story. You know that, right?"

"Of course. I just think it might be cool to have a dad who knows so much about ancient stuff."

Ariel nodded. "It's mostly not terrible," she said. And that was true. Her dad wasn't an evil tyrant. Her mom wasn't the wicked witch of the west, either. And her brother, for all his faults, was just a typical younger brother. Well, maybe not typical, but he wasn't so bad.

"You are lucky to have both parents," said Garrett. "And an annoying brother," he added.

"Yeah, I guess." She desperately wanted to tell him about the strange things that had happened in her world. The house that was trying to kill her family. The enigmatic caretaker. And the still-unsolved mystery of what happened to her brother. But it wasn't the right time. This had been the best of days, and she didn't want to ruin it.

Garrett's expression went from pensive to goofy in a nanosecond. "Race you to the street?"

"What are we, five?"

"Sure. We're five." He took off. Ariel chased after him, laughing the whole way.

It felt good to be five.

When they got to the street, Garrett paused. He turned to Ariel and smiled. "I won."

"Pretty sure it was a tie," said Ariel. Garrett had totally won.

"That was fun. Speaking of, I was wondering, like, if maybe you were wondering, I don't mean, well, what if...would you, I don't know, want to, maybe, if you want to, go out..." he began.

"You mean on a date?" she interrupted.

Garrett blushed. It was the cutest thing Ariel had ever seen.

"Is that what the kids are calling it these days?"

She laughed. "Yup."

"Then yes. On a date."

Butterflies. She actually felt butterflies in her stomach. "Yeah, sure. Why not?"

"Cool." He smiled again. She couldn't get enough of his smile. "Do you like bowling?"

She harrumphed. "No. I hate it."

"Me too," he said.

"Then bowling sounds perfect," said Ariel.

"We can hate it together!"

Together. What a perfect word.

CHAPTER SEVEN

AKOLO HAD NEVER been more nervous. Even standing in the presence of an all-powerful, invisible entity paled in comparison to what he felt while waiting outside the high priest's meeting room. This time his fear didn't have anything to do with what he learned in the temple. He was thankful there was no guard standing nearby to silently judge him. Most of the guards had been recalled to the king's army. The word on the street was that the king's influence was fading fast. They needed all the soldiers they could find to fight battles on multiple fronts. Akolo had even wondered if he'd be conscripted into service. The high priest quickly rejected that idea, restating what Akolo already knew: He was needed at the temple, perhaps now more than ever. With limited opportunities to imbue objects with his God's power, every chance they got could be the difference in the king's attempt at world dominance.

"Come in, Akolo."

He walked in and was surprised to see the high priest wearing a simple tunic instead of his colorful robe. The black eye patch remained, but in simpler garb, the high priest looked less imposing. Still, Akolo's insides were in turmoil.

"What can I do for you today?" the high priest asked. He looked more tired than usual.

Akolo had often wondered what it must be like to have the role of high priest so far from his home, from his people. Of course, he did still make offerings at an altar they'd erected near the southern wall—far enough from the temple so as not to offend the local God. But it must have paled in comparison to the high priest's role back at the palace.

"I know there are proper ways to do this," began Akolo, "but since I am the only one left from my family, I don't know any other way except simply to ask."

The high priest offered a sly smile. "And what do you wish to ask?"

Akolo cleared his throat. "I wish to ask for the hand of your daughter in marriage," he said, choking out the last word.

"Which daughter?" the high priest said, his smile never wavering. "I have three."

"Esme. I wish to marry Esme," Akolo said.

The high priest laughed. It was a rare sound from this man who'd been as much a father to Akolo as a mentor.

"And what does Esme think of this idea?" he asked, raising his one visible eye.

"She…I…I haven't asked her yet? That's why I'm here. I know my family is supposed to ask, but…well, I already said that."

"You haven't talked about it at all?"

"Not in so many words," said Akolo. But they had dreamed out loud more than once about what it would be like to share a life together. They had simply never used the word *marriage* in their conversations.

"Do you think she'll have you?" asked the high priest.

Akolo furrowed his brow. "Isn't that up to you?" he asked. He had learned about the traditions shared by Esme's people, mostly from discussions with a friendly guard, and knew that most marriages were arranged by the parents and were typically based on social standing or family honor. That wasn't so different from his own traditions, or what he could recall of them anyway. What did he really have to offer? Yes, he played an important role in the temple. But he had no wealth, no social standing to speak of. What if the high priest denied his request?

The high priest stood and walked over to Akolo. He stood in front of him and placed his hands on Akolo's shoulders. "I don't think she would ever talk to me again if I said no." He squeezed Akolo's shoulders, then pulled him into a hug. It was the first time the high priest had hugged him. "Of course I give my permission. It will be a joy to bring you into our family." He stepped back and folded his arms, smiling at Akolo.

Akolo's heart raced. This couldn't have gone any better.

"Thank you, sir. I promise I'll be the best husband..."

"Whoa, hold on there, young man. Save the promises for the wedding. That's when they matter most."

Akolo nodded. "Yes, of course."

The high priest gestured toward the door. "Well, what are you waiting for? Go tell your bride-to-be the good news!"

"Thank you again! I...I just...thank you!"

Akolo walked briskly out the door, then ran down the hall and down the steps outside the temple building, taking two at a time and nearly falling at least twice. Esme was standing near the gate where Akolo had found his precious stone so many years ago. She smiled when she recognized the same expression on his face.

"Esme, will you marry me?" He was certain her answer would be yes, but he felt nervous, nonetheless.

"What took you so long?" she said.

"I...I was just talking with your father..."

"I don't mean about coming to see me just now." She offered a sly smile.

Akolo furrowed his brow, then it dawned on him what she was saying. He took his time with important decisions. Too much time, it seemed.

He took her in his arms, breathing in the intoxicating scent of her hair. "I won't make the same mistake twice," he said.

There could be no better moment than this, thought Akolo.

• • •

A few months had passed since Esme said yes, and now the blood moon was rising. The light emanating from the sword he'd placed on the chest was as bright as any he'd seen before. This was a special blessing to be sure. The high priest would be pleased. And the king doubly so. But was it too late? The rumblings about his fading power had grown louder.

Akolo reached into his robe and pulled out his fire opal. He'd kept this stone for so many years now. He held it in his hand and watched as it, too, began to glow.

"I know you have blessed me in many ways," he said in a quiet voice. "But I would ask one more blessing from you." Akolo waited for a whispered reply.

None came, but that wasn't unusual. This God was a capricious God who spoke only when He willed to speak.

"I am to be married soon," continued Akolo, "to the most wonderful woman, Esme." He laughed. "But of course you must know this already." The stone glowed brightly in response. Akolo felt its warmth in his hand. "And you surely know what I am about to ask, but I will ask it anyway: Will you bless my marriage to Esme? I can think of no better thing than to spend my life with her. I promise…I promise to be a strong protector, to serve her, and to love her for all time."

The stone glowed even brighter.

Architect.

A sudden wind picked up in the room, swirled around him, and then settled. Akolo heard the soft voice but didn't understand. What did he mean by "architect"? The king had sent the royal architect with them to lead the rebuilding of the temple. But little had been done in the years since Akolo's return to the Jordan River Valley. Or was the message for him? Maybe God was asking him to build a house for Esme. He could certainly do that. He added the word to a growing collection of cryptic messages. Some found meaning over time, like the warning about not abusing this mystical power through reckless imbuing of objects and artifacts. But others continued to puzzle Akolo. As always, he would tell the high priest about this latest word. Perhaps he would know its meaning.

The glowing sword faded into darkness, soon followed by his stone. He pocketed the stone and offered thanks for allowing an audience yet again. He never wanted to take these moments for granted. Carefully, he lifted the sword, then backed out of the small room.

The light pouring in through the windows of the surrounding temple building briefly blinded him, as it always did. He allowed a moment for his eyes to adjust, then marched into the high priest's room, unannounced. The room was uncharacteristically empty. He placed the sword on the table, turned, and left.

Esme would be waiting for him at the tailor's hut.

He saw her there, talking with the tailor's wife, a seamstress herself, out front. When they noticed him, they abruptly stopped talking. The tailor's wife excused herself and disappeared into the hut.

"Making secret plans?" asked Akolo as he walked up to Esme.

"Secret plans?" She took his hands in hers. "No secrets between us, Akolo. We were discussing my wedding dress. It's going to be… well, I suppose the details can be a secret. You'll see it soon enough."

"Five days," said Akolo. He'd been marking the time. The thought triggered a vague memory from his past. Someone he once knew marked the days, too. Not counting down to a wedding though. Who was that? he wondered. And just what was he counting?

He shrugged the incomplete memory away and focused on Esme. Her smile had faded.

"What is it? Is something wrong?" Akolo asked.

"My father..."

"Wait, he didn't change his mind, did he?" The thought sent chills down Akolo's spine.

"What? No. Of course not. He's very happy that you will join our family." She squeezed his hands. "It's just that..."

"Don't keep me waiting. What is it, Esme?"

"A courier arrived yesterday with a message from the king. My father is being recalled to the palace. He is needed there."

"When?"

"He was supposed to leave immediately, but...he has decided to stay for our wedding. He will leave soon after."

"But...what is to become of me?" Akolo regretted the selfish tone the minute the words fell out of his mouth.

"You? Do you mean us?"

"Yes, yes, of course I meant us. I'm sorry. It's all so sudden."

Esme dropped Akolo's hands and turned away. "He asked if we would come with him."

Akolo's throat suddenly felt dry. "What did you tell him?"

"I told him my husband would be the one to make that decision."

Husband. He was about to be a husband. The thought brought a small smile to Akolo's face. It quickly faded. "But what would happen to the temple? Who would speak to God on behalf of the king? On behalf of the people?" *On behalf of my people*, he added silently.

Esme turned back toward him, showing a tear-stained face. "When I am your wife, my loyalty is to you. I will do whatever you choose."

"Then it's a choice?"

"Please, just talk with my father. I…" Esme took Akolo's hand and kissed it. "I have more preparations to make for our wedding. I must go now." She offered a forced smile, then turned and walked away.

Akolo's heart sank.

He had come to love his life here. The Jordan River Valley was home once again. He couldn't imagine ever leaving.

• • •

"Good thoughts, good words, good deeds," repeated Akolo. The high priest had agreed to blend some of Akolo's traditions into the wedding ceremony but insisted on including these words from his own tradition, stating that his god would be offended if they were ignored.

"But I thought your god was a kind, loving god?" Akolo had said to Esme when they were finalizing the plans for the ceremony.

"Can't a kind, loving god be offended?"

He had no response to that question. What did he know about Esme's god? For that matter, what did he know about his own God? Maybe all gods were mysterious.

Akolo's hands were sweating. Still, Esme did not let go. She was resplendent in a long, silky green dress decorated at the sleeves and the hem with blue and yellow jewels. A spiraling pattern of golden threads snaked around the dress's neckline. Esme's eyes sparkled even brighter with the green-and-gold silk wrap over her black hair. Akolo was certain she was the most beautiful woman ever to grace this world.

When he looked into her eyes, he saw infinite beauty. He saw unfailing love. He saw hope and grace and wonder and possibility.

She was everything.

They would make a life together in the Jordan River Valley.

"And now, we shall all enjoy the sweetness and abundance of a feast made for a king."

Did the high priest wink at Akolo then? It was impossible to tell with one eye covered by a patch. Akolo noted that gold threads with a snakelike pattern matching that on his daughter's dress had been sewn into the black patch. It was a nice touch, if a little distracting.

The high priest gestured at the tables of fruits and nuts and honey and other foods that had been spread out behind them. "And may God bless you with many children," he added.

Children. The thought equally thrilled and frightened Akolo.

The musicians began to play. This was his cue that the ceremony was over. Akolo bent forward to kiss Esme. There were tears in her eyes again, but these, surely, were tears of joy.

The feasting that typically lasted for days had been shortened due to the imminent departure of the high priest and his entourage, but there was no shortage of celebration among the locals who had become like extended family to Akolo. Only once since his return had someone approached him with questions about the fate of his parents and sisters. He had answered honestly, prompting tears and a much-needed hug from this stranger who used to dine with his mother and father long before Akolo was born. But then? Nothing. It was as if the entire community had forgotten the siege from years earlier. Many had died in the battle, of course. Still others had left the Jordan River Valley entirely, in search of a safer place to live and raise their children. So maybe it wasn't so strange that they had forgotten.

Akolo took his wife's hand and led her to the feast tables.

Children.

What will our children be like? he wondered.

Esme read his thoughts.

"We will have the most wonderful children," she said. She pinched a pomegranate seed between her fingers and lifted it to his lips.

CHAPTER EIGHT

ZACH'S ARMS WERE tired. He'd been scrubbing away at the mud-caked walls of the storm shelter for almost an hour, and he was ready to be done. The only thing that had helped pass the time was the old AM radio he had brought with him to help quiet his thoughts while he did his chores. He found himself scrubbing the mud in the same rhythmic pattern as the church bell in the song that was currently playing on the radio.

I used to rule the world
Seas would rise when I gave the word
Now in the morning, I sleep alone
Sweep the streets I used to own

"You never know when a tornado might appear," Ian said to himself, making Zach roll his eyes. He'd done his research. Zach knew there had only been one tornado of any significance in the area in the past seventy-five years, and while that was a one on the Enhanced Fujita Scale, it resulted in minimal damage and exactly zero deaths.

This only added to Zach's confusion about why Mr. Goodpasture had built the shelter in the first place. They weren't in any kind of tornado alley. Zach shrugged and went back to scrubbing the wall while singing along.

It was a wicked and wild wind
Blew down the doors to let me in
Shattered windows and the sound of drums

People couldn't believe what I'd become
Revolutionaries wait
For my head on a silver plate
Just a puppet on a lonely string
Aw, who would ever wanna be king?

"Let's take a break," his dad said.

"Finally," said Zach with a big sigh.

His dad laughed. "I think Marshall and I can finish this up." He looked over at the caretaker, who nodded in reply. His bearded face was caked in mud. Zach almost laughed at the image, but something in the old man's expression made him pause. Why did he seem so familiar to Zach, anyway? Of course, they'd spent lots of time around him after moving into the house he'd sold them. It was a silly question. Zach shook it off, turning his attention to the project he was eager to begin.

"Why don't you clean up and call it a day," his dad added.

"Cool, thanks," Zach replied. He tossed the muddy rag onto the stairs, wiped his hands against his pants, and climbed out of the shelter into the dappled sunlight.

"I'm going to work on my project," he called back to his dad.

"Do you need any more supplies? I can run to the store later..."

"Don't know yet. I'll let you know if I do."

Zach had determined that journaling wasn't his thing. That was Ariel's thing. He'd decided to go a different route in an attempt to remember the details of his time-traveling adventure. He couldn't call it that in casual conversation, of course. But he liked thinking of it that way inside his own head. Time travel, for all its confusing rules and twists and paradoxes, was still cool. He didn't want to lose sight of that.

He also didn't want to lose sight of the images that lingered at the periphery of his thoughts. He'd decided to create a 3-D model of the palace that played such a key role in his memories. It wouldn't be an exact replica—there were too many holes in his memory. But it might tease more of the hidden stuff out into the open. Was that a good thing? He wasn't so sure. One thing he was sure about was that he loved constructing things. Armed with a boxful of cardboard, paper, tape, glue and the best scissors he could scrounge from the kitchen junk drawer, he was eager to get started.

He'd brought a card table up from the storage closet and set it up in the only corner of his room that wasn't already occupied by furniture or other half-finished projects.

"How to begin," he said to himself. He set a piece of paper in front of him and began to sketch what he could recall about the palace. First, he drew the long hallway and the rooms that lined it on either side, one of which he remembered living in for a time. Then he added the steps to a courtyard. And then…what else?

Zach saw the blurry outline of a fountain in his memories. But was that in the courtyard or somewhere else? Was it a working fountain? Too many questions. He decided to put it on the far side of the courtyard, near an exit that led to…to what? The temple?

Frustrated, Zach set his pencil down and went to lie down on his bed. He reached for the book he'd borrowed from his father's study, then just as quickly abandoned it to the bedside table. The title had caught his interest, but the writing was extremely dry and boring—the kind of book only professors like his dad could love. He picked up *How to Build a Time Machine* by Brian Clegg instead. His dad had ordered it without hesitation. That was unusual. Typically, his dad would ask for three good reasons to purchase something that wasn't already in the budget. That wasn't a problem: Zach could always come up with three good reasons. Except maybe when it came to videogames. But this time his dad didn't even ask for one. Zach wondered how long this season of unusual grace would last. He didn't really want to take advantage of it—he was just glad to be home after all—but if it meant a new book or two, an extra slice of pie, or a half hour later bedtime, he wasn't about to complain.

The book was exactly the sort of thing he loved—hard science but delivered in a way that only made your head spin a little. He might never fully understand particle physics or quantum theory, but that wouldn't stop him from trying. It wasn't actually a how-to book, but Zach was smart enough to know such a thing couldn't possibly exist. So far, though, it was a fun read.

After a few pages, his eyelids became heavy, despite the compelling subject. He drifted off into a shadowy dream.

Startled by a loud buzzing, he awoke. He sat up suddenly, swatting his hands around his head, sure that the bees were back. But as he became conscious of his surroundings, he realized there was no buzzing sound at all. His book remained opened on the bed beside him. He looked at the TARDIS clock on the wall. He'd only been asleep for minutes.

Fuzzy images from his dream began to congeal. Shelves in a terrace wall filled with clay pots and urns. Beehives. *Ancient* beehives. He jumped off his bed and went back to his table to draw what he had seen. Another picture brightened into his mind's eye. A tower. An ancient tower with a staircase that led to a room. A room with a window. No, two windows.

He knew this place.

More images appeared in his head, appearing and disappearing rapidly like the pages of a picture book being flipped. He sketched like a madman, hoping to get everything down before the images faded from view.

• • •

I hear Jerusalem bells a-ringin'
Roman Cavalry choirs are singin'

Be my mirror, my sword and shield
My missionaries in a foreign field
For some reason, I can't explain
Once you'd gone, there was never, never an honest word
And that was when I ruled the world

Marshall shook his head. "I don't recognize that," he said.

"That's 'Viva la Vida' by Coldplay, the British band?" Ian replied.

"Believe it or not, I know *that*, Ian. I was referring to the object in your hands," Marshall said as he reached over to turn off the radio Zach had left behind in his rush to leave the shelter.

Ian turned the clay shard over in his hands. "It looks ancient," he said.

"Might be from an oil lamp," said Marshall.

"Yes, that's what I was thinking." He rubbed his fingers along the broken edge, careful not to cut himself. "But how did this get in there?" He pointed at the tornado shelter.

"Hmm…" Marshall reached his hand out. Ian handed him the shard. Anyone unfamiliar with ancient cultures would likely have overlooked the triangle-shaped piece of dried clay. Ian's experience on archeological digs had prepared him well for moments like this.

"Did your uncle collect pottery or other ancient artifacts?"

Marshall lifted the shard to his nose and sniffed. "He was a student of ancient history. It was his interest that sparked my own." He held the shard out to Ian. "Do you smell that?"

Ian sniffed. "Olive oil?"

"That's my guess."

"That's a potent smell. There's no way that scent would have endured across centuries." Ian took a deep breath. "This just adds more credence to the time-travel thing." He shook his head. "It makes zero sense. Why would Zach travel back in time? What was the purpose of that?"

Marshall pocketed the shard. "I wish I knew," he said. "I sincerely wish I did. But at least he's home now."

Yeah. He's home. For now. But what was the next surprise awaiting his family?

"Maybe we should close the door now?" Marshall raised his eyebrows.

Ian helped him to lift the heavy door, then drop it into place. Marshall started to walk away. Ian hesitated.

"I need to check something," he said. He bent down and lifted the door a few inches, then let it drop again. "Did that sound strange to you?" he asked.

"Strange like how?" the caretaker asked.

"I don't know. Like…like it's a much bigger space below?" They'd spent hours cleaning mud out from the shelter. At the bottom of the stairs, the boxy room was barely big enough to fit five, maybe six people. It was not a large space.

Marshall shrugged. "Bigger on the inside?" he said.

"Is that a *Dr. Who* reference, Marshall?"

"Dr. what?"

"*Dr. Who*."

"I'm not familiar. Is that a television program? I don't watch much TV."

"We'll have to remedy that," said Ian.

Marshall began walking away again. Ian followed close behind. The old man had promised not to keep any more secrets from Ian.

Was he keeping that promise?

• • •

Lyana turned toward the source of the noise. It was rhythmic and predictable. Like the slow drip of a water faucet. She got up from the living room couch and walked into the kitchen, then pressed down on the faucet handle to make sure it was off. There were no splashes of water in the sink. She paused to listen. The sound continued but seemed to be coming from the pantry.

Most people would think it odd to hope that the dripping was a leaky pipe, but that's exactly what Lyana was hoping. A leaky pipe would be something they understood. Something they could fix. The other alternative was more than Lyana wanted to deal with.

She stepped into the pantry and paused again, listening.

The dripping continued, but Lyana couldn't pinpoint its location. The sound came from all around her.

Drip. Drip. Drip.

"What is this?" she said aloud.

First the water. Then the wind.

Lyana froze.

"Who are you?" she said aloud, her voice cracking. This was not the voice of Avril, the daughter they had lost to miscarriage. This was someone or something altogether different. Something darker. Something sinister? "What do you want?" she asked. A puff of water vapor escaped with her words. The room had turned ice cold.

First the water. Then the wind.

Lyana clenched her fists and screamed in frustration. "Arrgh. What. Do. You. Want?"

Drip.

She wrapped her arms around herself and watched condensation puff into the room with every exhale.

A moment later, silence. The drips had stopped dripping. The room had warmed. Lyana stood there until her frayed nerves began to settle, afraid of the voice returning, and somehow also wishing it would.

She needed answers.

• • •

Zach scooted his chair back. The floor was littered with paper and cardboard scraps and balled-up clumps of tape. Drops and stripes of glue painted the cluttered table. He picked at some that had dried on his fingers. There was something satisfying about peeling glue from your skin.

"Whoa." Ariel's voice. He didn't turn around.

"What do you think?" he asked, gesturing at the three-dimensional paper-and-cardboard model in front of him.

"I think you should be institutionalized," she snipped.

Zach spun around to face her. "Hey, that's not…"

She held her hands in front of her. "Sorry, sorry. I didn't mean that. I just meant…" She gestured at the mess. "It looks like the aftermath of a hurricane in here."

"Yeah, yeah. I know. I'll clean it up. I meant, what do you think of the model?"

"It's…" She stepped closer, studying the complex structures.

The actual placement of the various buildings was only a guess. And the scale was certainly off. But the more he looked at his construction, the more Zach was certain he'd nailed most of the basics, if not the details.

"What is it?" she said finally.

"It's where I went," said Zach. "I mean, I think it's where I went. Or what I dreamed. Or something."

She pointed to the area outside the courtyard that featured a tent-like structure.

"That's…is that from my dream?"

"You mean 'our' dream? It's a makeshift temple or something."

She nodded, her eyes still focused on the model.

"I think I was there," he said. He bent forward and straightened the tiny tent.

"You need to show this to Dad and Mom," she said, backing away from the table. "But do not, I mean do not, tell *anyone* else about it. You can't. They'll put you away for sure."

"Ariel, stop..."

"I'm serious, Zach. I don't care how cool you think this is, you can't tell anyone else about it. Okay?"

Zach's excitement faded. "I could tell 'em it was for a school project?"

"Just don't."

"Fine." Zach sighed heavily.

Ariel paused at the door. Zach tried to gauge her expression, but she was unreadable. She'd been hard to read for a while now. "It's really good, though," she said. "I mean, it's actually kind of impressive."

"Thanks."

He turned back to the table after Ariel left.

It *was* kind of impressive.

CHAPTER NINE

AKOLO FOUND HIS wife sitting on a flat rock that overlooked the rushing waters of the Jordan River. Instead of calling out, he paused, stood stock-still and watched her. She had freed her long black hair from its confines behind the hood of her robe. Unlike many of the local women, she didn't often wear a veil, so it wasn't unusual to see her like this. However, there was something in her posture that concerned Akolo. She was bent slightly forward. Not quite in the position of someone crying, but nearly so. She reached up and ran her fingers through her hair, then pinched a strand and held it in front of her face. She turned then and noticed him looking at her. Her smile was genuine, but the lines on her face told Akolo she was troubled.

He knew this conversation was coming, but he dreaded it.

Akolo walked over to his wife and sat next to her, wrapping his arm around her small frame. She wouldn't look into his eyes.

"Esme…" he began.

"Look at this," she said, interrupting him. She picked at her hair until she'd found just what she was looking for and held the strand forward for him to see.

"You have the most beautiful hair…" he began.

"Don't you see it?" she asked.

"See what?" Yes, he did see it.

"It's turning grey," she said.

"It's just a few grey hairs…"

She froze him with a stare he'd seen more than once. The "please stop talking and consider what I just said" stare. He nodded slowly.

"We're running out of time, Akolo," she added. The depth of sadness in her voice made Akolo swallow hard. He knew she was fighting back tears. He felt his own queuing up as well. He leaned over and gently kissed the top of her head.

He wanted to say something to reassure her. Offer words that erased the sadness and heartbreak caused by years of childlessness. He desperately wanted to tell her that they would be parents, if not soon, then someday.

But they had already seen so many "somedays" pass them by. He pulled her closer but felt some resistance to his hug. "I'm running out of time," she clarified, gently pushing him away. She turned toward him. Her emerald-green eyes were indeed pooling with tears.

And there it was. The hard truth. She was getting older. Not quite past childbearing years yet but closing in on that heartbreaking reality.

And yet Akolo wasn't aging at all. Though he'd lived the same number of years as his wife, he looked no older than his twenty-something self, aside from a few more laugh lines and a dotting of age spots on his hands.

"Have you heard nothing from..." Esme couldn't finish the question. But Akolo knew what she was asking.

Akolo shook his head. He had not heard a single word about their situation from the deity he'd shared an audience with over these past years. How many had it been since they returned to his home village? Fifteen? Twenty? Time was a tricky thing to hold on to, especially for Akolo, who somehow seemed to exist out of time as much as in it.

"I will ask again," he said, reaching his hand up to wipe away her tears. "Maybe this time..."

But would it be any different? Akolo had grown weary of asking the God who resided in the temple for something so personal. He recalled the joy of their wedding day, the words of hope and encouragement from the high priest, Esme's father. *May God bless you with many children.*

But which God? The god of Esme's people? Or the capricious God who lived in the temple, the God Akolo served in ways both obvious and vague? He had oft wondered if the two gods were one and the same, simply going by different names. He had meant to talk with the high priest about that, but before he could find the courage to ask, the high priest had been summoned back to the king's palace. In the intervening years, reports from that part of the world had become less and less frequent and were rarely full of good news. The king who had conquered so much of the world had begun losing more battles than he won. What did that mean for Akolo, who had been conscripted into this role as mediator with his own people's God on behalf of the king?

While they sat there listening to the rushing river, a young boy ran up to them, then stood there breathless. He looked to be about the same age Akolo was when the king had raided his town and taken him far away to live in the palace.

"Sir," he began, then paused again to take a breath. "A visitor…"

"What is…" began Akolo.

"Please, take a moment to catch your breath," said Esme, interrupting her husband. She was always the patient one. The compassionate one. He loved her for that.

"Someone has come from far away. He…he wants to meet with you both."

"Who is it?" asked Akolo.

"He…" The boy paused, scrunched his face into a puzzle. "I don't know his name. But…he's very old."

Esme's eyes brightened. "Could it be…?"

They stood and followed the boy to the temple grounds. A white-bearded man in a dusty purple robe stood there. His arms went wide.

"Esme!"

"Father!"

The high priest had aged so much since the last time Akolo had seen him. He looked frail as he steadied himself with a carved wooden cane. Even his eye patch looked ancient. Esme stepped up to her father and waited for his welcome. He pulled her into a hug, and a tear rolled down his weathered face.

"It has been too long, my daughter," he said. "But you look as lovely as ever." The high priest looked over at Akolo. "You haven't aged at all." The implications were clear. He gently released Esme from the hug, then had to steady himself with the cane. His gaze remained on Akolo. "We must talk," he said.

"Father, you must be tired from your journey. Perhaps some rest would…"

The high priest reached over and gently laid a hand on Esme's shoulder. "There is little time to rest," he said. He turned again to Akolo. "Shall we meet in my old room?" A small smile appeared on the old man's face. "I mean, your room." He nodded toward the temple building.

"Of course," said Akolo.

"I'll go fetch some food and drink for you," said Esme, and she was off. She was always so good at reading the room. She knew her father needed a private conversation with Akolo.

"Come, let us talk," said the high priest. He moved surprisingly fast for an ancient man wielding a cane.

When they walked into the spacious anteroom, Akolo headed for the table he'd spent so many years seated behind, counseling the lost, offering hope to the hopeless, and pondering his role in the grand scheme of things, then paused, gesturing for the man who used to sit there to take the preferred seat. The high priest simply shook his head and sat on the other side of the table instead. A loud sigh escaped his lips, and Akolo sensed it was from much more than a long trip.

"Young Akolo," he began, then laughed. "I suppose you're not so young anymore." He raised an eyebrow.

"It is good to see you again," said Akolo. "What brings you back to…the Jordan River Valley?" He stumbled over his words, eager for the high priest to get to the point. Something in his gut told him the news from the king wasn't good.

The high priest took in a deep breath. "I have missed this," he said. "The scent of water and fertile soil. This is the smell of life." He closed his eye, apparently lost in a memory. When he opened it again, he was staring directly at Akolo. "The king has asked me to bring the chest and its artifacts back to the palace."

Akolo tried not to show his surprise, but the words felt like a gut punch. He and Esme had made a life for themselves here in the city of his childhood. There was no place he'd rather be.

The high priest continued, "Perhaps you have heard, he has lost some battles."

"I have heard rumors," said Akolo.

"Do you remember when you took the king's goblet into the holy place? The look on the king's face when he sipped the blessed water?"

Akolo nodded. That image was seared into his brain. He could still feel the way his body shook from nervousness, awaiting the king's response to his first "official" act as a representative of his people's God.

"He wants that again," said the high priest.

"But that would mean…"

The high priest held up his hand to stop Akolo's reply. "I told him no."

Akolo was stunned. Despite his reputation as a kind and fair ruler, no one challenged the king. His power was unmatched in the known world. At least it had been.

"Are you happy here?" asked the high priest.

Akolo nodded, then added, "Yes, of course. Esme and I are very happy. Except…"

The high priest raised his eyebrow. "Except?"

"We have failed to bring children into this world." He shook his head at his awkward wording.

The high priest's brow furrowed. "You haven't failed," he began. "You just haven't been successful…yet."

Akolo opened his mouth to respond, but his old mentor lifted his hand again to stop him.

"You have asked your god to bless you with children," he stated. Of course he had.

"In hedyeh rā bā to sharik mishavam."

Akolo looked confused.

"It means 'I share this gift with you.'"

"I'm sorry, but what does…?"

"Do you remember your god saying this to you?"

Akolo did. He nodded.

"Do you think asking to be blessed with children is a gift?"

"I…I do…but surely He meant the gift was for the king, not me."

"Are you not the one he chose to create the gifts for the king? It seems like an honorable request to have just one gift for yourself." He paused, tilted his head just a little. "I know that look in your eyes, Akolo. You believe that Esme is too old to bear children. That it's too late for you. Is your god so small that…" The sound of footsteps stopped him.

Akolo turned to see Esme standing in the doorway, a tray of food and drink held delicately in her hands. She offered a smile, but it didn't quite reach her eyes.

"Come, my daughter," said the high priest. She walked into the room, set the tray down on the table, then turned to leave. "Please, stay," her father said.

"I should leave you to your…"

"Please," said the high priest. He gestured to the chair beside him. She sat.

The high priest started to speak, but a cough interrupted his words. He lifted the cup in front of him and sipped until the cough had subsided. "I am old, much older than when I was last here," he began. "But I am no less wise." He looked from Esme to Akolo. "I have seen evidence of your god's great power. Perhaps you are asking the wrong question? Maybe it's not 'Will you bless us with children?' Perhaps the better question is simply 'How?'"

Akolo didn't know what to say. The high priest had indeed been a wise teacher and mentor for many years, but this didn't sound like wisdom at all. It sounded like the ramblings of a man who'd lost touch with reality. There was no question about 'how' they might have children. The process was as old as humanity itself. He felt his cheeks burning with embarrassment and looked at his wife, expecting to see a flush in her cheeks as well. Instead, he saw a smile.

The high priest looked between the two of them, then burst out laughing. He laughed until he was coughing again. A few sips of water ended the coughing fit, but a smile remained plastered on his face.

"There are many facets to every question," he said. His smile faded. "Have you forgotten how to listen?" he asked, staring at Akolo. It wasn't an accusation, though. Merely a question. And a good one. Akolo had not been good at listening lately. It had been weeks since his last audience with his God. Perhaps his growing frustration about their childlessness had plugged his ears to God's words.

"I will listen," he said.

"Good," said the high priest. "And now I must go. I don't know what awaits me back at the palace, but I suspect this will be my last visit with you." He reached over and took his daughter's hands. "You will be blessed with children," he said. "I am sure of it."

Akolo wanted to scold the old man for offering such baseless hope. But he held his tongue. Perhaps there was wisdom in the high priest's words after all.

How, he thought.

• • •

After a tearful goodbye, the high priest and his small cohort left to return to an uncertain future at the palace. Akolo wanted to reassure Esme that her father would be okay but thought better of offering up hollow words. Had he not just secretly chastised the high priest for that very thing? Would the old man even survive the long journey home?

After the high priest was gone, Esme sat for a long time in the temple courtyard next to a small pool that usually sat empty. Today, however, it was full of rainwater. She reached over and troubled the water, then touched her wet fingers to her lips.

Everything she did was magic to Akolo. The way she would tilt her head when considering a reply. The twitch of her nose when she was about to call him out on something he'd said or done that she deemed inappropriate. The brush of her fingers on the back of his hand whenever she passed him in the hall.

Oh, to have children with this woman, he thought. There could be nothing better.

Akolo looked up into the night sky. The moon was red.

He walked over to his wife, kissed her on the top of her head, then donned his robe to enter the holy place. She could never enter that room. But what if she could? Would she be blessed with a long life as he had? Was it the room that changed him?

No, not the room.

The deity who resided there.

Akolo reached into the robe pocket and found his fire opal. The one he'd been given by…by someone long ago. Why couldn't he remember that when he could so clearly remember when he'd found a similar stone in that courtyard below where his wife now sat in apparent mourning? He was just a boy then. And the stone…the stone…

Was that it? Was the stone the secret to his youthfulness? But no, he'd given his away. This one was from…what was it from? A crown?

No, a sword. Akolo shook the muddled thoughts from his head and placed his stone on the altar.

He took a deep breath, inhaling what had become a familiar taste—like the charged air before a storm.

"How?" he asked aloud. Just the one word. Any god worth his salt would know what he was asking. But just what was he asking, really?

The stone began to glow. And then something else happened. Something he'd never seen before. A cloud formed around the stone and began to swirl. A whirlwind of light and color. Akolo leaned closer. The swirls were random at first, then they began to congeal into a specific form.

The snake eating its own tail. The ouroboros.

The high priest had a tattoo of this image on his arm. Akolo had asked about it once.

"It is the symbol of life, death and rebirth," had been the response.

Life, death, and...rebirth.

The swirling cloud grew brighter, until it was almost too bright to look at. Then, suddenly, it went dark.

Akolo knew what he must do. He couldn't be certain it was his own idea, or one given him by the deity he'd so honorably served all these years. But either way, his new mission was clear.

A smile came to his face.

"This is how."

• • •

Akolo lifted the necklace, turning it this way and that. He nodded. "This is perfect," he said. He emptied a bag of coins on the counter. The jeweler picked up two coins and offered his thanks.

Akolo pushed the rest of the coins toward the man.

"They are all for you," said Akolo.

"I can't accept that. It's too much," he replied.

Akolo insisted. "This necklace is worth ten times that amount."

The incredulous jeweler bowed and thanked Akolo for his generosity, promising to give some of the coins to the needy who begged just outside of the city walls.

Akolo thanked the man again and walked out of the small building into the blinding sun of a blisteringly hot day.

He knew where to find Esme. She was sitting by the horse corral. A foal had sauntered up to the fence and was reveling in Esme's gentle attention. She was so good with animals.

And she would be even better as a mother.

"Esme," he began. She turned her head toward him, the sunlight filtering through her flowing black hair. "I have a gift for you."

He held the necklace out to her, the fire opal glinting in the sun. When she took it in her hands, her eyes glowed greener than ever before.

Yes, this was how.

CHAPTER TEN

"FIRST THE WATER. Then the wind." Lyana felt a chill as she repeated the words she'd heard.

Ian furrowed his brow and tilted his head up and slightly to the right. It was a look Lyana had seen hundreds of times—his "thinking deeply" look. It was such a predictable habit that sometimes he exaggerated it when asked a simple question, just to get a smile out of Lyana. But not this time. Ian was doing some serious mental calculations.

"What do you think it means?" she asked, after giving him a moment to process.

"The water—that surely was the flood. Right? And it was windy then, too. A blustery day."

Lyana smiled. "Are you seriously referencing Winnie the Pooh right now, Ian?"

"What? Oh…no, I didn't even think of that. *Winnie the Pooh and the Blustery Day.* Now there's an ancient memory."

"The kids never really got into Winnie the Pooh," said Lyana.

"I tried. But no, those films were already old when I saw them as a child. Still, they're kind of unforgettable." He tilted his head again, but this time it was accompanied by a slight smile.

Lyana wondered if Ian was going to start singing something from one of the films in Pooh's voice. He used to do voices a lot, especially when the kids were small. He'd even tried some out on her when they were dating, which prompted more than a few eyerolls from Lyana. Still, there was something endearing about the childlike side of her husband. She missed that.

Instead of singing, though, Ian's eyes went wide. "What if the wind hasn't happened yet?"

"What do you mean?"

"First the water. That has to be the flooded creek and the storm shelter. Then the wind. What if there's another storm coming?"

"Do you mean that literally or metaphorically?"

"Both."

Lyana tensed. Ian had told her about the words Marshall had translated. The third word that haunted her. *Harm.*

"We have weathered so many storms, Ian," she said. "I don't know if we can handle another."

Ian pulled Lyana into a hug. "We will weather whatever comes our way."

Lyana nodded into his shoulder. This was the side of her husband she loved the most. His confidence, his assurance. His protection. That, too, had gone missing far too much in the past few months, but she didn't question him in this moment. He was right. They *could* handle anything as long as they were together.

Then why did she still feel so unsure?

• • •

"I'm sorry to bother you about this again."

Sheriff Blackstone stood outside their front door, wearing an obviously apologetic expression. A woman Ian didn't recognize stood beside him.

"It's fine," said Ian.

The sheriff turned and gestured to the woman. "This is Angela Miller. She's with…" He hesitated, but Ian already knew what was coming next. "She's with CPS."

"And why exactly is CPS here?" Ian felt a potent mix of anxiety and frustration bubbling up, but he hid both behind a polite smile. They'd already answered so many questions about Zach's disappearance.

"Angela is new to the agency," said the sheriff, as if that answered his question. In a way, it did. "She just wants to talk with Zach for a bit. I already told her everything we know…"

Angela stepped forward, reaching her hand out to Ian. He took it and they shook hands briefly. "I, too, would like to apologize. I've been briefed by my staff and Sheriff Blackstone about your son's disappearance and…reappearance. It's just such a fascinating case, you know? Since I'm new to CPS, I just wanted to get a chance to talk with Zach firsthand."

"You don't trust the reports?" said Ian.

Her eyes went wide. "Oh, I'm sure the reports are entirely accurate. It's just…" She paused, then leaned forward as if sharing a secret with Ian. "I'm curious, you know? I want to meet the young man who endured…what was it, weeks lost in the woods?"

"If you've read the reports, then you know…"

"Yes, yes. I really am eager to believe those reports. I am, Mr. Keane. I think talking with Zach would go a long way toward helping with that."

Ian invited them into the house. "I'll go see if he's interested in talking," said Ian. What choice did he have? If he told them to go away, that would just make him look guilty. But of what? Sheriff Blackstone had called the case "closed," but Angela Miller looked like someone with an agenda.

He walked over to the stairs and climbed them, silently counting each one as Zach did. He continued down the hall and knocked on Zach's door.

"Come in," came Zach's voice.

Ian opened the door and leaned in. "There's a woman here who wants to talk with you. About your...adventure." That's what they called it now: his adventure. It was shorthand for something that was far more complex and nearly impossible to describe anyway.

"Is it a reporter?"

"No."

"Is it the therapist? I liked talking to her."

"No, it's someone new. She's..."

Angela Miller startled Ian by sidling up next to him in Zach's doorway. "My name is Angela Miller. I'm with CPS. Do you know what that is?"

"Child Protective Services," said Zach matter-of-factly.

"Yes." Her eyes went to the expansive paper model that filled the table in his room.

"Wow, that's impressive. What can you tell me about that?" she asked.

"It's just something I made," said Zach. "I have a...vivid imagination."

Ian smiled. "He's really into ancient architecture," he said.

"Like father, like son, right?" she said. So, she'd done at least a little research. "May I?" she asked, pointing to the model.

"Sure," said Zach. "Just don't touch anything, okay? It's kind of fragile."

Ian knew better. The model was anything but fragile. Zach was meticulous with just about everything he did, but this was his masterpiece. It was as good as any reproduction Ian had seen in the many museums he'd visited over the years while pursuing his love of ancient cultures.

The sheriff had followed Angela up the stairs and was standing in the hallway, subtly shaking his head.

"I'm sorry," he mouthed.

Ian nodded, then turned his attention back to Zach. He had slipped out of his desk chair and was standing behind his model, hands indicating the construction like a student presenting at a science fair.

"It's something I saw in a dream," said Zach. "Well, maybe I saw it in one of my dad's books, too," he added.

"It's really quite spectacular," said Angela. She turned to Ian. "Would it be okay if I spoke with Zach for a moment…alone?" She turned to Zach. "And would that be okay with you, too?"

Ian watched Zach's expression. It didn't change. "It's fine," he said.

"I'll wait downstairs," said Ian.

"I'll join you," said Sheriff Blackstone.

"Okay," said Zach. He didn't seem fazed at all.

Ian followed the sheriff down the stairs and into the kitchen.

"Can I get you a cup of coffee?" Ian asked. He wished Lyana would hurry up and return from the grocery store. She was always good at reading awkward situations. She'd have some thoughts about Angela Miller, that's for certain.

"No thank you," answered Sheriff Blackstone. "I almost told her no," he continued, referencing the stranger who was upstairs grilling his son. "You've been through a lot. I sure didn't want to add to that, but she was rather insistent. I don't think she has ill intent, though. She's just really puzzled by this story. We all are."

Ian was surprised. He squinted at the sheriff. "Do you think we're hiding something?"

Sheriff Blackstone raised his hands and shook his head. "Me? No, not at all. It's a mystery, to be sure. But sometimes that's what we end up with—a mystery."

Ian liked the sheriff. He was a good man with a good heart.

"Maybe I'll have a cup of coffee after all. If it's already made, that is."

Ian nodded and went to the old coffee maker sitting on the kitchen counter. The espresso machine they'd bought a few weeks earlier still sat unused. Ian made a mental note to study the instructions soon. They really did need to up their coffee game at home.

Ian delivered a cup of coffee to the sheriff and poured one for himself, and they sat at the kitchen table, sipping in silence. It was only five minutes later when Ian heard Zach's door open. Zach exited first, followed by the CPS worker. He led her down the stairs and paused at the kitchen, looking at Ian.

"Can I show Ms. Angela your books?" he asked.

Ian raised an eyebrow. "Which books?"

"The ones with your name in them," he answered.

Ian laughed. "I suppose." He scooted his chair back and led them to his office, where he pulled a few books off the shelf and set them on his desk.

"You wrote these?" asked Angela.

"Well, these two." He indicated two of the books. "I was just a consultant on the others."

"That's amazing," she said. She really did seem a little starstruck. Only bookish people were impressed by authors. Maybe Angela Miller wasn't so bad after all.

"Thank you for showing me," she said. "And thank you, Zach, for talking with me." She turned to Ian. "You have a wonderful son here. I'm so glad he found his way back home."

"We all are," added the sheriff. He stood and patted Ian on the back. "We'll get out of your hair now. I think we can finally call this case closed. Right, Ms. Miller?"

She paused before nodding, seemingly lost in thought. "Yes, of course. Thanks again for your time." She started toward the door, then paused and turned. "You really should write about this," she said, then fumbled with her hands to gesture indiscriminately. "I mean about Zach's 'adventure.' It would make a fantastic novel."

Ian ushered her and the sheriff outside. “I might just do that,” he said.

Just five minutes after the sheriff’s car had left the property, Lyana pulled up. Ian met her in the garage and helped to carry the groceries in.

“I thought we were done with all that,” he said as he placed a jug of milk in the fridge.

Lyana’s sigh drew his attention.

“What?” he asked.

“Maybe I’m just overthinking things, but…you wouldn’t believe the looks I got at the grocery store. I mean, it was just from a couple people, but they were practically boring a hole in my head with their stares. I don’t think this thing will be going away for a while.”

“We need some kind of natural disaster to take people’s minds off our family saga,” said Ian.

Lyana gently slapped his shoulder. “Don’t even say that!”

Ian shook his head. “Sorry.”

Lyana took a deep breath. “Well, maybe just a tiny earthquake.”

Ian laughed. “I love you, you know that?”

“I do.”

Zach had stayed behind in Ian’s office, poring over a book that he’d unearthed. He walked in just as Ian leaned in to kiss Lyana.

“Ew, get a room,” he said.

“You’re next, buddy,” said Ian. He turned toward Zach, and Zach took off toward the stairs. Ian chased him to his room, then stopped, leaned against the doorjamb. “How was the chat with Ms. Angela?”

“Fine.”

“Do you want to talk about it?”

“Nothing to say, really. She just asked how I was doing. If I felt safe, stuff like that.”

“And?”

“I told her the truth.”

Ian paused. When more didn't come, he prompted Zach, "And that is?"

"I'm doing fine. And I feel safe."

Ian walked over to his son and ruffled his hair. Unexpectedly, Zach wrapped his arms around his dad for a hug. It was nearly enough to make Ian cry. His son wasn't known for physical affection, but something had changed in him since his adventure.

"I'm so glad," said Ian.

So very glad.

• • •

"Whoa, that was epic, Air!"

Ariel had never heard so much enthusiasm from the usually subdued Garrett. But he was absolutely correct. Getting a strike from a bowling ball she had rolled backward between her legs was an incredible bit of luck, but no less amazing for that. They were well into their second game but had given up trying to get a decent score and instead were resorting to all kinds of improvised trick shots. This was the first that had succeeded in knocking down pins.

"Thanks." Ariel offered an exaggerated bow, then returned to her seat to sip her Dr. Pepper. The fountain drink was flat, which would usually bother her. She was particular about her Dr. Pepper. But she didn't care; she was having the best night she'd had in a long time.

Garrett picked up his bowling ball and walked up to the edge of the lane, turned around, then rolled the ball backward between his legs in an attempt to duplicate Ariel's feat. The ball rolled slowly down the lane for a few feet before dropping into the gutter with a gentle thud.

"Well, that was equally epic," said Ariel, her voice dripping with what she hoped sounded like lighthearted sarcasm. Garrett responded with a defeated look. Ariel felt a twinge of guilt, but then Garrett flipped his disappointment into a goofy grin.

"Thank you, m'lady," he said, offering a bow that mimicked her own.

They were both chomping on cold, cardboardy pizza when a group of four teenagers commandeered the lane next to theirs. Ariel recognized a couple of the kids as classmates but didn't remember their names.

Garrett turned to glance at the new crew, offered a polite nod, then turned back to Ariel and rolled his eyes. It was all she could do to keep from laughing. Apparently, she didn't hide her response well enough.

"What are you laughing at, freak?" This from the shortest girl in the foursome.

Garrett started to turn back to the newcomers, but Ariel gently grabbed his elbow and stopped him.

"Ignore them," she said. She was saying this to herself as much as to Garrett.

"Beat up any other students lately?" The taller, dark-haired girl had her hands on her hips, looking like a cliché from some lame TV show.

"Not yet," said Ariel. "But I'm making a list. Can I have your names, please?" This time it was Garrett who couldn't hold back his laugh. The boys who were accompanying the girls also snickered, garnering glares from their dates.

"You need serious help," said the short-haired girl. She turned toward her friend and pointed toward the counter. "We're going to ask for a different lane. This one is infested." She grabbed her friend by the arm and led her away. The two boys who had remained silent just shrugged and followed them, bowling balls in hand.

When they were out of earshot, Garrett looked at Ariel and said, "Maybe we're done bowling for the night?" His voice was gentle and kind. He wasn't stating a certainty; he was inviting her thoughts on the matter. It might have seemed a little thing, but his tone and words mattered to Ariel. She'd felt ignored at home for far too long.

"Hmm..." she said. She glanced over at the foursome, who were now walking toward a lane on the opposite end of the alley. "Does that mean they won?" she asked.

"If we quit now, you mean?"

"Yeah."

"Nah. It just means we reached peak epicness. How can we top the last frame, anyway?"

"Yeah. Yours especially," added Ariel.

Garrett's smile was the best thing she'd seen in forever. She wanted to freeze that moment. But just as she thought that, a torrent of darker thoughts rained on her daydream. *What if he's not for real? What if Garrett turns out to be a fraud? What if this...whatever it is...crashes and burns? What if...*

"You in the mood for some real food?" Garrett held his half-eaten pizza slice by the crust and pointed it toward the door like an arrow.

Ariel took a deep breath and shoved the doomscrolling thoughts aside. Maybe Garrett was exactly who he appeared to be.

"I am," she said.

"Cool."

"The diner's not far," said Ariel. She felt safe in the diner. She wanted to share that safe place with her best friend.

Friend. Or more?

"Brilliant idea," said Garrett.

As they walked by the counter at the front of the alley, Garrett let the woman standing there know they were ending their bowling early. "In case you need to reset the lane or something," he said.

Kind. *And* considerate.

What is this dream I'm in and please don't let me wake up.

• • •

They sat across from each other in Ariel's favorite booth on the far side of the diner. For a moment she thought Garrett might sit next to her, but then she shrugged off the idea as silly. *Only weird couples do that*, she concluded.

After they ordered their drinks and a plate of nachos, Garrett reached over and took Ariel's hand. She thought for a moment he was about to offer a prayer, but instead he gently lifted her hand and pointed to her ring.

"Tell me about that," he said.

Ariel had forgotten she'd put the ring on. It was something her mother had given her when they lived in Boston. A single amethyst set in silver. Or white gold. She didn't remember which.

"Just something my mom gave me," she offered.

"Wow, compelling story," said Garrett. He set her hand down but let his fingers remain atop hers. Butterflies were congregating in her stomach, threatening to wreak havoc on her carefully controlled exterior.

"I'm quite the storyteller," she said. He just smiled and sat there, waiting for more. "Okay, fine. I'll elaborate. But only because you have cheese sauce on your face."

"I do?" He lifted his hand from hers and picked up a napkin, then proceeded to dab at his face randomly, asking, "Did I get it?" each time. Finally, he just licked his lip to erase the cheese he obviously knew all along was right there.

"You're insane," said Ariel. She spun the ring Garrett had noticed.

"I am," he said. He nodded at her. "Now, about that ring?"

Ariel sipped her perfectly carbonated Dr. Pepper, then leaned back against the padded vinyl of the booth. "It was a kind of promise ring," she began. Garrett raised his eyebrows. "Not *that* kind of promise ring," she quickly clarified, then began to blush. "I mean, I don't know what kind of promise ring you were thinking about, but this is different. I was going through some…stuff…and she gave me this along with a promise to always be there for me, to always be truthful." The memory stirred two distinct feelings in Ariel. First, thankfulness. The promise meant something to her then. But then disgust.

"Then why are you scowling?" asked Garrett.

"Me? I'm not scowling," she argued. Was she?

"There's more to the story." Garrett scooped up a glob of cheese and salsa with a chip and balanced it between his fingers before stuffing it into his mouth. Then he lifted the napkin again to delicately dab at the corners of his mouth, which turned up into a smile.

"Look, can we change the subject, please?" She really didn't want to talk about this.

"Okay." He shrugged and sipped his lemonade.

That was too easy, thought Ariel. Way too easy. He didn't say anything more. He just kept eating the nachos and looking at her.

"Fine, fine!" She hadn't meant to say it so angrily. "Sorry. It's just that…my parents haven't been keeping up their part of the bargain."

"I thought it was just your mom who promised…"

"They're both lying!" The words just flew out of her mouth. She wished she could take them back, but it was too late.

Garrett set the chip he'd picked up back on the plate and reached across the table to take Ariel's hands. Instead, she pulled them back and folded them across her chest, then immediately dropped them to her side when she realized she was becoming a cliché herself.

"You can talk about it if you want, but it's fine if you…"

"I don't," she said.

"Okay," he offered, then reached for a chip.

She gently slapped his hand away. "How can you do that?" she asked.

"Um, because I'm hungry?"

"No, not that. I mean, how can you just let things go so easily?"

He shrugged again. "I'm just trying to be sensitive to you…"

"Everyone has issues with their parents, okay?" she interrupted. "I'm sure you have…" She stopped, realizing her error. "I'm sorry," she said. "I wasn't thinking. I'm truly sorry." Ariel felt like a fool.

Garrett nodded. "Didn't we already have this conversation at the park?"

"Yeah. We did. Or something like it."

"This thing with your parents is really troubling you, isn't it?"

"It is."

"Maybe you'll want to tell me more about it sometime. Or maybe not. I'll leave that in your court. Meanwhile…" He reached across the table with napkin in hand. Ariel recoiled at first, then leaned forward. "You have some cheese on your face."

Ariel didn't resist as he wiped her upper lip.

"Thanks," she said. "And not just for…this." She pointed to her mouth.

"Of course."

• • •

Dear diary,

I know I said I wasn't going to say "dear diary" anymore, but I've changed my mind. I'm fickle. So, sue me.

Anyway, this is going to be the shortest entry yet. I've got nothin'. Seriously, how can words describe this night?

She closed her diary and stared up at the ceiling. Music was drifting into her room from downstairs. She couldn't remember the last time her parents had stayed up so late together just listening to music. Maybe they were feeling nostalgic.

Ariel wasn't sure what she was feeling.

Like a river to the sea
I will always be with you
And if you sail away
I will follow you

That's when she recognized the song.

Give me one more night
Give me just one more night
Oh, one more night
'Cause I can't wait forever

CHAPTER ELEVEN

AKOLO LIFTED HIS young son onto his lap, and they looked out across the city from a bench just outside the temple building. The boy was not quite three. With his green eyes and olive skin, he was looking more like his mother every day.

In his younger years, Akolo had never fully grasped the scope of his hometown. It was a small, densely populated city built on a hill and surrounded by two concentric walls, some of which had been destroyed in past battles and had yet to be repaired. The Jordan River flowed nearby, bringing with it the stuff of life. But it was the freshwater spring in the center of the city that made it such a desirable place to live. He'd explored much of the city's maze-like alleyways as a child, to be sure, but the view from this vantage point had been reserved for the elite members of the otherwise close-knit community.

He was one of the elite now. Perhaps the only one. The community had reshaped itself upon his return from the king's palace with the high priest and others of his tribe, and over the years, he had taken on more and more responsibility with his people. After Esme's father left to return to the king, everyone looked to Akolo for leadership. He was not a natural leader, but he had learned enough in his years under the high priest's tutelage to know the value of delegating. And in the years since, the city had continued to grow and thrive, rebuilding itself into something that nearly matched its earlier status before the destruction by the invading army. This city had been through so much, and yet it still stood strong. Akolo marveled at its resilience, and the resilience of the people who lived here. They, like the freshwater spring, continued to bubble with life.

"Papa, look." His son was pointing to the east. Far beyond the city's majestic walls, smoke spiraled into the sky. Perhaps it was nomads making an offering to their god. Or warming themselves from the cool of the coming night. Or was it something to be concerned about? Akolo made a note to ask the commander of their small local army.

He inhaled deeply, then exhaled. His son mimicked the exaggerated breath. Akolo smiled and ruffled the boy's hair.

Esme had gone to milk the goats they'd inherited from a neighbor who had recently died.

"You must have them," the man had said. With his dying words, he had offered a gift to the high priest "who remains unchanged." No one called him that to his face, but whispers had found their way to him. Some whispers even compared him to Melchizedek, though Akolo believed he was just a myth. Secretly, he bristled at being called the high priest. He felt uncomfortable comparing himself in any way to Esme's father—the man who had mentored him after the king had taken him into captivity so many years ago. The high priest had become like a second father to him, not only training him to be a man of God but also teaching him how to lead others in the ways of tradition and faith. And though they came from different religious traditions, the lessons were incredibly valuable to the young Akolo.

Akolo wasn't so young anymore. He had stopped counting the years, but while his outward appearance changed slowly, he felt every single year in his soul. Every joyous moment and every heartbreak stood in shadows of thoughts, stepping into the light periodically to remind him of all that had gone before.

One of those joyous moments had come just a week earlier, with the news that Esme was pregnant. "Another son," she had declared, despite any way to be sure. Akolo never questioned his wife. She was as wise as she was beautiful, and her beauty knew no bounds.

Akolo sensed movement behind him and turned to see the changing of the temple guards. It still hurt his heart that he had to post guards in front of the building where the ancient, mystical chest and its artifacts lay. But after three misguided citizens' attempts to go into the inner room, he had no choice. His advisors had suggested they didn't need guards since any who entered that space were killed immediately. Akolo didn't agree. No one could know why they'd tried to enter into God's presence. Perhaps their intentions were nefarious. Maybe they wanted to steal the artifacts—they clearly held great power and significance. But what if they simply wanted an audience with God? An answer to prayers?

"Then they should come to you," his closest advisor had argued.

Perhaps they already had. Akolo had petitioned his God for so many things on behalf of his people—health, peace, abundance, safety, grace. Sometimes the answers were clear, but often they were as murky as the Jordan after a storm. Akolo's God was very mysterious and often misunderstood by the people, but Akolo knew he was always welcomed.

But no, Akolo couldn't abide the idea of leaving the temple building unguarded. He would protect the people from themselves.

"Mama!" His son wriggled and turned to greet his mother, his arms outstretched. Akolo set the boy down and stood, then walked up to collect the milk-laden jar so she could pick up her wide-eyed son. Soon, she wouldn't be able to pick him up so easily, but he knew she would still try. Little fingers reached for the pendant around her neck and gently turned the stone over so he could study its swirling colors.

Akolo often marveled at his good fortune. Though the weight of his responsibilities sometimes felt more like a burden than a gift, there was never a day when he didn't thank his God for the love of his wife, the bounty of one healthy son and another on the way, and the great beauty of the world around him.

There could be no better life than this.

• • •

The news was devastating. The high priest who taught him so much, Esme's father, was dead. The courier who had brought them the news had also brought something else. A cough that quickly morphed into something much worse. Less than a week after his arrival, more than three dozen residents were now immobilized by a persistent, ugly cough and dangerously high fever. Akolo had little time to grieve the loss of his father-in-law; he was much too busy trying to help coordinate efforts to care for the sick and prevent others from catching whatever this was. Esme desperately wanted to help as well, but he couldn't let her risk her own health, or the health of their two young boys. Against her wishes, he sent them to a house on the outskirts of the city and begged her not to interact with others until the outbreak was over.

But would it end? Or was this just the beginning of an unavoidable catastrophe?

Akolo bowed as he entered the temple's holy place and kneeled before the chest. Without his fire opal, the room remained dark as night. After a season of little more than regular offerings and quiet supplications, he had resorted to outright pleading with the God who resided in that space.

"Please," he would begin, "bring healing to our people."

Sometimes he would add that because he had asked for so little of late, this request surely could be granted, as if that mattered to a God with unlimited power.

Today he added one more request: "Protect Esme and my boys from this disease. I could not live without them." Was it a selfish request? Perhaps. But what else could he do but plead? For years, his God had been silent. Was he even listening anymore?

There is always a price.

A light flashed in the small room, briefly blinding Akolo. Had he heard that right?

"I will pay whatever it costs," he said aloud.

He swore he heard a sigh. But no, just silence. For a moment he wondered if he'd imagined the voice. But then the truth settled into his heart. Instinctively, he knew what he was to do. He quickly left the chamber, then returned a few minutes later with a wine-filled goblet. He gently set the humble cup on the chest, then backed away and bowed before it.

"Bless this wine with your healing power," he said. The words came to him as if from somewhere else. He glanced up to see if the goblet was glowing, but nothing happened.

He remained in the silence, awaiting more. He tried again, this time scrunching his eyes and raising his voice, "Bless this wine with your healing power!" More silence. In a flash of anger, he slammed the goblet onto the chest, breaking it into pieces. "Why do you keep your voice from me when I need it most?! My people—your people—are dying. Do you even care? What do you want from me?!"

He raised his hands to the heavens with a shout, and as he did, he noticed a gash on his wrist carved from a shard of the goblet. A drop of blood fell into the wine. Suddenly, the chamber filled with the sound of rushing waters echoing off the cold, stone walls, and the glowing goblet lit up the whole room. Time expanded, then contracted, then seemed to stop altogether. Once again, the room grew dark and silent. There were no more instructions. No more words from the powerful God who had helped a king conquer many lands. The same God who had given him a family. And now, the God who would heal the people.

Akolo collected the goblet and backed out of the chamber, driven by an uncertain hope. The sky was black. He couldn't begin to guess how long he'd been inside the holy space.

He paused at the top of the temple stairs, wrestling with himself about where to go first. He pictured his wife and children, who had so far been protected from this plague. But for how long? Perhaps the imbued fire opal would protect Esme. But what of his children?

The sound of coughing interrupted his thoughts. He turned to see one of the guards on his knees. The other guard had scooted farther away from him.

Akolo walked up to the stricken guard and held the goblet out in front of him.

"Sip from this cup," he said. After an extended coughing fit, the guard nodded, then took in the smallest sip of wine. Immediately his cough subsided. A moment later, he was able to stand.

"How do you feel?" asked Akolo.

"I feel…better," he answered. "Alive," he added.

Akolo offered a sip to the second guard, despite his protest that he "felt fine."

As Akolo marched down the temple steps, he knew a long night was ahead of him. He headed first to the home of the jeweler, one of the first who had come down with a fever. He was met there by the man's wife. She was wearing a scarf around her face, but that did not disguise the tears in her eyes.

"You should not be here," she began.

Akolo gently placed his hand on her shoulder, then walked up to the bed where the jeweler lay, sweating and shivering under a thin blanket.

"Drink." Akolo offered the goblet to the man, but he couldn't lift his head. The man's wife handed Akolo a wet rag.

"It's the only way I can get water into him," she said, her voice barely a whisper.

Akolo dipped the rag into the wine, then held it up to the man's lips. If even a drop could make its way into the man's throat…

The jeweler's eyes grew wide. His shivering stopped. Color returned to his face.

"It is a miracle!" said his wife. Fresh tears dripped from her eyes. But these were happy tears, thankful tears. Akolo offered a sip of the wine to her as well, and she obliged.

"I must visit all the sick and those caring for them," Akolo said. "Can you help me find them?"

She nodded, went over to kiss her husband on the forehead, then gathered a shawl to wear into the cool of the night.

They traveled from house to house, offering the wine that never seemed to diminish to everyone they found. Sadly, it was too late for the courier who had brought the news and disease to his city. He had died just minutes before they made it to his tent. Akolo had paused then, wondering just how powerful his God was. Could he bring back the dead? But he stopped short of dripping wine onto the dead man's lips. Surely that was asking too much.

By the time he met up with Esme, the wine was nearly gone. How it had lasted this long was yet another mystery in a long line of unresolved mysteries Akolo had witnessed. She took a small sip, then dipped her fingers into the wine and pressed them against their son's sleeping lips.

"And then you," she said, holding the goblet out to Akolo.

He took the cup and lifted it, pretended to pour the last of the wine down his throat. But it was bone dry. He smiled anyway as he set the cup down.

"My father would have been proud of you," Esme said. She wiped away a tear and took his hands in hers.

"But all I did was ask," he began to object.

"And you waited for the answer," she said.

He had.

Still, those words haunted him.

There is always a price.

• • •

A mournful tune reached Akolo's ears, then faded away with the wind, drawing his thoughts to the latest news from afar. The king was dead. Killed in battle. "But the empire is strong," the courier had been quick to add. The king's son had already ascended to the throne and was gaining a reputation for being a strong leader. Stories of the king's fading influence were now old news.

The empire is strong.

Akolo had mixed feelings about the king. The charismatic leader had been generous to the people of Akolo's hometown after liberating them from the army that had nearly destroyed their fine city. But there was a cost to that liberation. Akolo knew that all too well. His entire family had been killed. And then he was carted away to serve the king and the high priest in a palace far from home.

Few who had lived through that event so many years earlier remained in the city, but Akolo remembered. The scent of smoke still sent him back to that moment when he was separated from his parents.

"What do you remember from the time I spent in the palace," asked Akolo.

Esme sat next to him on the small bench just outside their front door. He was still getting used to their new home. This one was closer to the temple, and nearly twice as big as where they had previously lived. But their growing family needed that extra space.

Esme tucked her pendant under her tunic and sat back, leaning on her hands, her face tilted up to the star-filled sky.

"I remember you were just a little boy," she answered, a smile in her voice.

"You were too!" he said, then added, "I mean, you were little too."

"I don't remember much more. My father kept a close watch on me back then. He wasn't eager to let me spend time with a strange foreigner."

Akolo laughed. "Well, that plan worked out well," he said with a smirk on his face.

They sat in silence for a few moments.

Esme sighed. "I miss him."

"I know. So do I." Akolo closed his eyes, trying to recall the first time he saw Esme. "All my memories of that time are hazy," he said. "No matter how hard I try to remember, I can only see glimpses of my time in the palace. It's like…" He paused. "It's almost like it didn't happen. Like it was a dream."

Esme reached over and gently stroked Akolo's beard.

"And what does that make me?" she asked.

"My dream wife?"

Esme laughed. There was no sound better than Esme's laugh. Except perhaps the giggles of their two sons.

"Perhaps we shouldn't be looking backward," Esme offered.

"Perhaps not."

"There is so much ahead of us, you know?" she added. There was a lilt in her voice, a familiar sense of wonder and hopefulness that buoyed Akolo when the challenges of his job threatened to diminish him.

But she was absolutely right. Since she began wearing the pendant fitted with his fire opal, Esme had essentially stopped aging. Their future was uncertain, to be sure, but it spread out ahead of them like an unending vista.

"Show me again," said Esme, tugging at the arm of his tunic.

He pulled back the sleeve to reveal the image that had been inked into his skin. The ouroboros—the snake eating its own tail. It was a way to honor the man who had trained him. His father-in-law. The high priest who wore an eye patch had a similar image on his skin.

A memory bubbled up of his first glimpse of the man.

"He never told me what happened to his eye," said Akolo.

"He never told me, either," said Esme.

"I guess that will remain a mystery, then."

"So much of life is a mystery, don't you think?"

Akolo nodded. "I just wish I had a few more answers."

"Sometimes you are too impatient, Akolo." She gently elbowed him in the side. "Answers will come in time, if they're going to come at all."

"I don't like waiting."

"Patience, my dream husband. We have all the time in the world."

All the time in the world.

CHAPTER TWELVE

ZACH WAS STARTING to zone out as his dad and Marshall droned on and on about some archaeological dig Marshall had been on years ago. It wasn't that Zach didn't find the conversation interesting—he was intrigued by the idea of digging up ancient artifacts—it's that his attention had been drawn elsewhere. Specifically, to a snow globe. He scooted his chair back, stood, then walked over to the bookshelf where the globe sat. A ray of afternoon sun streaking in through the window in Marshall's cabin lit the glass orb in such a way that it appeared to be glowing.

He lifted the globe and stared at the image inside. It was a simple scene of a singular, broad-trunked tree.

"It's an olive tree." Marshall's voice startled Zach and he nearly dropped the snow globe. He shook the globe and watched the artificial snow swirl, then settle inside.

"It looks old," said Zach. This wasn't a surprise. Most of the things on Marshall's shelves looked old. The only things that didn't look old were the carved animals that sat in various stages of completion on a narrow worktable that sat against the far wall of the small cabin.

"It is," said Marshall.

"Um...how old?"

"Maybe seventy years or more?" answered Marshall.

"That's kinda old," said Zach. But that was nothing compared to the books. According to his dad, some of them were a couple hundred years old. Still, all of that paled in comparison to the ancient world he himself had visited.

Or dreamed.

Zach carefully set the globe down on the shelf and turned his attention to a roughly made clay bowl that was partially hidden by an old wooden box that served as a bookend on one of the shelves. He pulled at the box, being careful not to tip the balance of the books it held in sway to get a better look.

"Hey, Marshall?" he asked.

"Yes?"

"Is that an oil lamp?" It looked a lot like the one his father had on his bookshelf. Like the ones Zach had encountered during his adventure.

Marshall scooted his chair back and walked over to join Zach. He gently pulled the wooden box out and reached behind it to collect the clay bowl. When his fingers touched it, Zach could swear time froze. Something shimmered in the air, and Marshall suddenly looked translucent, not unlike the holographic Obi-Wan Kenobi action figure his mother had found at a garage sale a couple of years back while visiting her sister. He had happily added the rare figure to his toy collection (he had learned it was a promotional item from a potato chip company) but didn't have it displayed in his room. He did a quick mental inventory of the boxes stacked in his closet and was pretty sure he knew which one held the toy. What else was in that box? He made a mental note to go through his storage boxes when he got back to his room.

All those thoughts happened in an instant. Zach returned to the present and looked at Marshall. He was just regular Marshall again. *Must have been a trick of the light*, thought Zach.

Marshall paused, turning the bowl over in his hand. "I'd almost forgotten I had this," he said. "Yes, it is an ancient oil lamp. From a Jericho dig, I believe."

"Were you there?" asked Zach. Marshall opened his mouth to answer, then hesitated. Zach quickly clarified, "I mean, were you at the dig."

Marshall's open mouth morphed into a smile. "Yes," he answered. "This was quite a few years ago, so I don't recall the details, but I was invited to join the team studying the city's architecture. They gifted me this lamp at the end of our time together. It probably seems like quite a generous gift, but it isn't quite as rare as one might guess."

"Yeah," said Zach. "My dad has one, too."

Ian nodded. "Still, that doesn't make it any less special." He set the book he'd been reading down on the dusty table. "Who knew that Marshall and I would have such similar interests. Strange coincidence, don't you think?"

"Yeah," said Zach. But what he really wanted to say was, "Do you really think it's a coincidence?" Because everything they'd experienced since moving to Littleton suggested otherwise—that something else, something much greater than any of them was orchestrating this series of inexplicable events. Zach smiled at this, pleased with the way he'd organized his thoughts into such a smart-sounding sentence.

"What are you smiling about?" asked Ian.

"Me? Just…I don't know. Just enjoying thinking about old things, I guess."

"Speaking of old things," began Marshall. "The city model you built is really quite something. So many clever details."

"Thanks. But I'm not sure I got it right. I mean, I guess there is no right or wrong. It's all from my imagination, right? But the more I look at it, the more I think it's missing something. Or lots of somethings."

"It's too bad you don't need a project for your history class," said his dad. "You'd get an A for sure."

The smile on his father's face was one of Zach's favorite things, and he was grateful he'd been seeing it a lot more recently. Their family had been a lot less stressed since Zach's return. Except for

Ariel. Of course she was gone a lot, hanging out with a boyfriend that she insisted wasn't her boyfriend. But when she was home, she seemed upset much of the time. Maybe that was just what it meant to be a teenage girl.

Zach shrugged and took one final survey of Marshall's shelves. There was a lot to look at, but he was tired of the cramped room and the ever-present dust motes.

"I think I'll head back home," he said, then walked to the door.

"Tell your mom I'll be a few more minutes."

"Didn't she go out shopping?" asked Zach.

"Oh, right. She went to get groceries for supper. Well, I'll see you back at the house soon, then, okay?"

Zach nodded, then exited the cabin and began following a path that had been worn into the dirt by all their recent visits to and from Marshall's humble home. He paused once he reached the open space and looked across the green lawn at the house. He had never really studied what the house looked like from the backyard. A flash of light caught his eye from one of the windows. His sister's room. But she wasn't home either, was she?

"Just another trick of the light," he said to himself.

He took a moment to inhale the welcome, redolent scent of the woods and the nearby gurgling creek, then continued on his way.

As he walked, a singular thought bumped all the others swirling in his head to the back of the queue: Light is just as fickle as time.

An image of a flickering oil lamp filled his head all the way back to the house.

• • •

Lyana preferred to shop at the small downtown market rather than the giant brand-name grocery store whenever she could. Today was one of those days since all she really needed was ground beef, flour tortillas and a couple other items. She had parked near the diner and was walking back to the car when a woman walking toward her stopped directly in front of Lyana and crossed her arms. Lyana didn't know her from Adam, but the woman's expression wasn't one of recognition. It was a sneer of judgment.

"You aren't fit to be a parent!" the woman said. She uncrossed her arms and pointed her finger at Lyana in some cartoon-like gesture of accusation.

"I'm sorry, I don't…" began Lyana.

"You need to go back to where you came from!" the woman continued, her voice shrill. The stranger paused for a second before briskly continuing on, bumping into Lyana as she passed and causing her to drop the bag of groceries.

"Hey…" Lyana began. But then she thought twice about engaging with the stranger. Lyana went to pick up the paper bag, but it tore as she lifted it. Her purchases fell onto the sidewalk. As she bent down to collect them, a shadow appeared on the sidewalk in front of her. She tensed, ready to deflect whatever accusation this new stranger was about to offer, only to realize it was Lloyd. He bent down to help her collect the groceries.

"That was…odd," said Lyana.

"Rude is what it was," said Lloyd. He gestured toward the diner. "I can get you a new bag. And maybe a coffee?"

Lyana exhaled. "Yes, a coffee would be good. But I can't stay long. I need to pick up Ariel from…a park somewhere. I have the address on my phone. I know this is a small town, but apparently there are still places I don't know about yet."

Lloyd carried the groceries into the diner and went around behind the counter to get a bag. Once filled and placed on the counter, he walked over to the coffee machine to fill a cup for Lyana.

The diner was known for pretty good coffee and espresso drinks and even better company. Lyana sat on one of the tall stools that lined the old-school service counter just off to the side of the register. The squish and squeak of the round vinyl cushion sent her back to a childhood memory. This was before her parents' divorce. She must have been six or seven. Her mother had taken Lyana out to eat at a diner not so dissimilar from this one. Her father must have stayed home with Eliza. Lyana had insisted on sitting at the counter—she knew the chairs could spin and she really wanted to spin. Her mother relented, and sure enough, Lyana started spinning as soon as she was lifted onto the chair. When she spun a little too fast, she nearly fell, but her mother caught her and steadied her, offering a gentle warning not to spin too fast, lest she turn into a tornado. This had made Lyana laugh. She smiled recalling the rare, sweet memory.

Lyana tested the chair. This one didn't spin at all. She was only mildly disappointed.

"Thank you," said Lyana as Lloyd set the mug on the counter.

"Of course."

Lyana lifted the mug to her lips and paused. "Not just for this," she said. "But for…everything. You've been…" The words caught in Lyana's throat.

"I really like your family," he said, gently breaking the awkward silence.

"How do you keep doing this? After all you've been through?" asked Lyana.

Lloyd pursed his lips and took in a breath. "Lyana, I'm not quite the saint you think I am."

Lyana set her coffee cup down and opened her mouth to speak, but Lloyd lifted his hand up to stop her.

"It's true that my wife and daughter died in a car accident, but… the story is more complicated than that," he said.

"What do you mean?" Lyana blanched. "Wait, you aren't going to tell me you were the driver, are you?" Lyana's imagination took off in all kinds of awful directions.

"No, no, not that." He took a deep breath. "There were actually two car accidents. The first happened a couple years before they were killed. I haven't talked about this with anyone for a long time, but I feel I owe you an explanation."

Lyana shook her head. "You don't owe us anything. You've been nothing but kind to our family." She took a sip of coffee.

"Please, let me share this. I think maybe I just need to say it out loud for myself."

"Of course. I can be a good listener."

"Yes, you can." Lloyd held up a finger to ask Lyana to wait, then walked back to pour himself a cup of coffee. When he returned to the counter, he took a long sip before beginning. "The first accident happened not far from here." He pointed toward the front door. "My wife and daughter were just leaving the diner when…a car ran a red light. It was a direct hit on the passenger's side."

Lloyd was struggling with his words. His vulnerability unnerved her.

"My wife escaped with just a few bruises, but my daughter, Mackenzi—I always called her Kenzi—ended up paralyzed."

"Oh Lloyd, that's awful!"

"It was the worst day I'd known…up 'til then anyway. Everything changed in an instant. But we were a good team. We buckled down and worked hard to care for Kenzi and keep our family strong. Months of appointments and physical therapy followed. It was a challenging time, to be sure." Lloyd stopped and gently shook his head. "I lost my way, Lyana. I became bitter, angry…at the drunk driver, sure. Maybe at God, too. I stopped going with them to appointments. I was a stranger to my own family. I didn't even recognize myself."

It was difficult for Lyana to imagine Lloyd being anything but kind and compassionate and giving.

"After a while, I was impossible to live with, so we separated. Not officially—neither of us could accept the idea of ending our marriage, but they needed to be in a healthier environment, and I needed time and space to fix whatever was wrong with me. At least that's what I told myself. Could we have done it differently? I can't tell you how many times I've asked that question. Therapy might have saved us. But...my stubbornness sealed their destiny."

Lloyd tilted his head back as if searching for a reserve of strength to continue.

"They moved in with her mother, about two hours from here. Just a week after they'd moved, they were out driving to a doctor's appointment and..."

Lloyd couldn't finish the sentence. He didn't need to.

"Lloyd," began Lyana. "It's not your fault."

Lloyd shook his head. "No, I know that. I wasn't driving either of those cars. But...well, I carry my fair share of guilt here."

"Maybe it's time to let that go?" said Lyana.

"I have come to accept my role in this and the parts of the story that were out of my control. And that's been healing for me..."

"But?"

"I can't fully put it behind me because the story isn't over. Not for my son, anyway."

Lyana looked up from her coffee at Lloyd. "Did I know you had a son?"

"Perhaps not."

"Where is he?"

"He's in New York City. Doing well, as far as I can tell."

"As far as you can tell?"

"You've probably already guessed this, but we had a falling out. I don't think he ever forgave me for the way I damaged our family. We haven't talked in years."

Lyana set her coffee cup down. "Lloyd, I'm so sorry for all you've been through. I truly am. You should have said something sooner."

Lloyd let out an awkward laugh. "I'm sorry, I don't mean to make light of anything, but you have had plenty of trauma of your own to work through. I didn't want to add to that."

"No, of course I understand. But you haven't added a thing, except maybe someone who's now in your corner," said Lyana. "Is it okay for me to share this with Ian?"

"Of course."

Lyana glanced at her watch. "Oh, I need to get Ariel. I'm sorry I have to run…"

"No apologies needed, Lyana. Family first, right?" His smile was as sincere as the tear that he was wiping from his cheek.

Lyana felt the weight of those words in her gut. So much loss. So much pain. And how awful it must be to have a son who won't talk to you, especially after all they'd been through together.

When she got to the door, she paused and turned back to Lloyd. "There's still time," she said.

"Time for what?"

"For repairing the relationship with your son."

The words had come unbidden, but the minute she spoke them she knew they were exactly the right words.

• • •

Marshall turned the oil lamp over in his hands, willing the vision he had experienced earlier when Zach and Ian were there to return.

He had lived thousands of years, but often could only see his past in snapshots, like someone watching the posters blur while riding the subway. With effort, he could focus in on a particular event, a specific time in his long life, but even then, those memories were incomplete.

He set the lamp on the shelf and walked over to his craft table. He picked up a piece of wood that he had whittled down to a vaguely bird-shaped object and ran his fingers across the rough surface.

"What do you want to be?" he asked the wood.

An image came to him, clear as day. It was a falcon.

But why? thought Marshall. *Why a falcon?*

CHAPTER THIRTEEN

AKOLO HAD ONCE again reached the apex of his unusual aging cycle. Over the years, he had learned his temporary aging followed a predictable pattern. He would age appropriately, if gracefully, for a period of fifty years, then, upon the occasion of his next interaction with the deity who had granted him the gift of immortality, would revert to his much younger self, only to repeat the cycle in another fifty years.

Immortality had more downsides than up. He and Esme had watched their children grow up and have children of their own, only to lose them to war or disease. The last of them, a grandson, had only just died a month ago. The sting of rejection from his unanswered pleas for the boy's healing followed him like a curse.

Perhaps his God was teaching Akolo a lesson. Or perhaps this was a consequence of Akolo's choice to extend Esme's life. Either way, it seemed his family was bearing those consequences. Every new loss confirmed those words whispered so many years ago. *There is always a price.*

Esme would be younger again when he returned home. His youth would soon follow, and once again they would cautiously embrace hope and the possibility that they could have another child and perhaps build a legacy that lasts.

Such a life seemed unreal. The ache in his bones was real enough, though. He felt every one of his seventy-five years as he reached the top of a hill and paused to rest. The morning fog was lifting and as it did, the city began to reveal itself. Of course, Akolo had heard plenty of stories about Alexander's great city. While he was alive, the military commander never shied away from touting his own accomplishments. After his death, the stories took on a life of their own, making a hero out of a man who had turned to rubble far more than he had ever built. But it wasn't the city that drew Akolo's interest; it was the rumor of a grand library. Akolo was desperate for knowledge.

For answers.

He didn't miss the irony of seeking information from a library in a city founded by the man who had destroyed Esme's people, the people who were like family to Akolo. But the world was changing and he intended to keep up. He had a secondary mission, too. One that had nearly driven him to madness. Akolo subconsciously pulled the satchel he'd been carrying tighter against his body.

The air here was different. Not dry as dust, but full of moisture, thanks to the lake to one side of him and the sea to the other. A light breeze brought the taste of salt to his lips. His bones still ached, but he felt strangely refreshed. He studied the city, a vast maze of buildings and arenas and walking paths and tried to identify the building he had traveled so far to find. But something on the horizon caught his eye and wouldn't let go. Just across a stretch of the sea stood a tower of immense size. A vague image of a much smaller tower flashed in his memory and just as quickly disappeared.

He began his descent. He would find the library soon enough, but first he had to visit that tower.

"It's a lighthouse."

Akolo turned to see a young boy standing in the shadow of the tower.

"Alexander's lighthouse," the boy added. "It shines a light to warn the ships. It's the tallest structure in the whole wide world!"

Akolo marveled at the construction. But was it really the tallest structure, or just another way to elevate Alexander's accomplishments? Akolo let out a bitter laugh, startling the boy. Someone would build something taller, something bigger, something more impressive someday. And he would likely be there to see it.

As Akolo looked up at the pinnacle of the structure, he saw a bird circling in the evening sky. A falcon pursuing a meal. Akolo inhaled, reveling in the scent of the ocean. He smelled something else, too. Ash.

He turned to ask the boy a question, but he was gone. Had he been there at all?

Akolo had told Esme this trip was important. He hadn't heard from his God in years. If the rumors of Alexander's library were true, perhaps he would find answers there. She knew of his secondary mission, too. She didn't argue, but he saw sadness in her eyes the morning he left. It wasn't that she feared for his life; she just felt the weight of everything that led up to this moment.

Akolo felt it too.

He wished this was one of the memories that blurred into obscurity, as so many others had. But no. He saw every detail in perfect clarity.

• • •

Alexander commandeered the temple room soon after his arrival. It was just one of many spaces the man took without asking. Akolo didn't care; he much preferred to spend his time at home with his wife and their grandson, whom they were raising as their own after the death of the boy's parents.

So much death, Esme often lamented. Sadly, grief had become a familiar friend.

"Alexander the Great," he clarified with a sneer when Akolo first greeted the powerful military commander as "King Alexander."

"Welcome to our humble village, King Alexander the Great," Akolo corrected himself. He half expected a reprimand, but the man merely raised an eyebrow and nodded.

The young man before Akolo looked nothing like the king who had taken Akolo into captivity so many years before. This king was a mere child by comparison. Alexander had already shown his mettle in battle, but his military success wasn't what caught Akolo's attention. Alexander was smart, clever, and well-spoken. He was obviously a learned man, having studied under Aristotle, a scholar whose influence had started to seep into Akolo's culture.

Akolo was in the thirtieth year of his latest renewal, so he appeared to be a man in his forties. Alexander paid him the respect due a man old enough to be his father, but the charismatic king spoke with the confidence of one who believed it was his destiny to rule. According to the news that preceded his arrival, one of his first acts after assuming the throne was to execute the men responsible for his father's death. Soon after, he had already won multiple battles to gain power and influence. Now Akolo was standing in his presence.

"I am surprised that you know my language," Alexander said as he sipped wine from the best goblet Akolo's assistants could find. His face turned sour at the sip and Akolo feared he'd throw the goblet across the room in disgust, but instead, he just set it back down on the table. "Where did you study?"

Akolo couldn't answer honestly because he didn't fully understand it himself. His God had granted him the ability to speak and understand a dozen languages. Esme, too, had been granted that gift.

"I am a student of many cultures," said Akolo, hoping that would suffice.

Alexander swung his feet up and onto the table and folded his arms in front of him.

"Word has it that your god is a powerful deity," he said.

So that's why he's here, thought Akolo. "He is a mysterious God indeed."

"Mysterious?"

"Much like your own gods, I presume," offered Akolo. It was a risky thing to say, especially since Akolo knew little of the man's religion. Akolo steeled himself for an outburst. Instead, Alexander laughed.

"Oh, yes!" He turned to one of the guards that stood on either side of him. "I like this one!" He turned back to Akolo. "I can see why you are revered as a leader in this 'humble village.' You have fire in you!"

Was he revered? Perhaps. He was certainly respected as the de facto religious leader for his people. But his story was far more complex than that. The locals believed him to be descended from the man who originally had his name. It was a clever ruse that he and Esme had orchestrated over many decades, but Akolo's God also played some mystical role in making it possible. Still, Akolo often worried that the truth of his unending life might someday be revealed. And what then? How would the people react? How would someone like Alexander respond to such news? And what would become of Esme?

"What brings you this far east?" Akolo ventured.

"I am embarking on a…let's call it a mission," he said. "And I'm looking for people who will join me."

Akolo furrowed his brow. "I am no soldier," he said. "I am far too old to be of use in battle…" And against whom?

Alexander laughed again. "I am not asking you to carry a spear. What I seek is an audience with your god."

Akolo gently shook his head. "My God is not only mysterious, but he is also a jealous God. Not just anyone can enter his presence."

Alexander raised his eyebrows. "I am not just anyone," he said. His voice remained calm, but entitlement and anger bubbled behind a forced smile. He took a deep breath, then let the smile relax. "I am told you can enter his presence."

Akolo nodded.

"I will give you something of mine to offer your god. Something of great value." He signaled to the guard on his right. The man handed Alexander a box Akolo hadn't noticed he was holding. Alexander took it in his hands and placed it gingerly on the table. It was a silver box with a strange symbol on its cover. Alexander opened it to reveal a book.

"This is my most prized possession," said Alexander. He lifted the book from the box and turned it toward Akolo, opening it to a random page. "Do you know it?"

Akolo did not.

"It is Homer's greatest work. The Iliad."

Akolo was entranced by the tome. Books were a luxury to his people, and none were as beautifully made and lettered as the one before him.

"Can you read it?" asked Alexander.

Akolo looked closely at the page before him. Yes! He could read it. He silently thanked his God for yet another unexpected gift.

"This is quite something," said Akolo. The book practically called out to him. He ached to hold it and spend time with it, soak up every word. "What story does it tell?"

"It tells many stories," said Alexander. "It is a book about the gods, but also about the ways of man. I treasure it." He placed the book back into the silver box, then slid it across the table toward Akolo. "Present it to your god. If he blesses it, he will be blessing me."

Akolo's hands shook as he gathered up the heavy box. He needed some time with this book. "God shows up when he wishes," he began, choosing his words carefully. "It may be some time before he appears to consider your offering." It was true. His God's presence was a fickle thing. The only time he could be sure of God's appearance was during a blood moon. The next one was at least a couple of weeks away.

Alexander shrugged. "Then I will leave it with you until such time." He stood. "I will return, but should anything happen to this book while I'm gone…" He stopped, then offered another smile. This one chilled Akolo to the bone. He signaled to his guards.

With that, Alexander the Great was gone, promising to return in due time to collect his prized possession, as well as his presumed blessing. Akolo didn't ask where he was going next, but he had a pretty good idea. Rumor had it that armies were amassing in the hills in anticipation of Alexander's arrival.

Perhaps someday wars will be no more, thought Akolo. He only hoped he would live to see that day.

• • •

Akolo set the book, still in its silver box, on top of the chest. The darkness around him seemed blacker than ever as he listened to the sound of his own breathing. He had spent weeks with the book, reading the epic poem over and over, sometimes aloud. Esme found it both beautiful and terrifying. Their grandson was mesmerized by the stories of great battles, acting them out with friends when they thought no one was looking. Akolo was. He didn't mention what he saw to Esme, fearing she would reprimand the boy for glorifying war. Perhaps she would be right to do so, but Akolo was just happy their grandson had found some friends and the freedom to express himself. He'd been isolated and almost mute since his parents died. Watching him at play brought Akolo a moment's joy, despite the nature of that play.

A fog slowly entered the room, and the silver box began to pulse with an eerie glow. Akolo watched as it brightened, first to a cool blue, then to a blinding white. The room stirred with a strong wind picking up the dust making it look like snow in the air as it reflected the light. Just before the glow subsided, it turned blood red and the wind instantly ceased. Silence. Usually, the deity's presence and power brought peace, but this time Akolo felt paralyzing fear. The fog grew thick and dark, and suffocated the room of light and oxygen. Akolo couldn't breathe. He started to feel faint. He fell to the hard, cold ground. Unaware of how much time had passed, he returned to his senses to find the room black as night. His elbow throbbed in pain.

"What does this mean?" he asked aloud, his voice dry like gravel.

He waited for an answer that never came.

Akolo collected the silver box and left the chamber. He placed the box on the table where Alexander had first sat and left it there. He would not read the book again.

Something had changed.

• • •

"How long will he spare the people of our city?" asked Esme.

Akolo shook his head. Alexander had not only returned to collect his book a month later, he claimed the city as his own, infiltrating their community with guards and soldiers who spoke a different language but expected to be treated as equals, as family even. The locals were rightly uneasy with the strangers as word of Alexander's battles made their way to them. He could not lose, they said. "His gods must be powerful," they opined as they wrestled with the reality of Alexander's mission: to rule the world.

Akolo's adopted people were being slaughtered, and the man responsible for this slaughter was living it up in the city of Akolo's birth. They had been spared, mostly, so far. Perhaps to honor Akolo's contribution to Alexander's great success.

My contribution, thought Akolo. He felt sick.

"I don't know," he said. Akolo had seen this kind of conqueror before—the very man who had killed his family and taken him captive as a child had similar world-domination aspirations. But now, that king's empire was in ruins, its people dead by the thousands.

It pained Akolo that he had ever respected Alexander, but he continued to play his part as he and Esme made secret plans to leave their beloved city.

"We would be leaving everything and everyone we love behind," said Esme. She wiped another tear away.

"Not everyone," said Akolo. He nodded toward the back room where their grandson slept. At least Akolo hoped he was asleep. This was not the kind of talk that would ease the boy's anxious spirit.

"What would happen with the temple artifacts?" asked Esme.

Akolo had struggled with this question. No one else could enter the holy room, so he didn't worry about the artifacts themselves. But what would that mean about his relationship with his God? He did not want to lose that connection, however complicated it had become. He secretly hoped that somehow, he could undo what had been done that night when he brought Alexander's book into his God's presence.

Surely it was why Alexander had become so "great," he thought.

Esme, once again, had been reading his thoughts. "It's not your fault, Akolo. You did the only thing you could do. It wasn't you who imbued the book."

Akolo knew this, but still he struggled. "I chose to bring it into God's presence during a blood moon," he said. "Any other day, and maybe none of this would have happened."

Esme placed her hand on her husband's shoulder. "You don't really believe that, do you?"

"I'm not sure what I believe." He pulled Esme into a hug. "But I do know that if anything ever happened to you, I would be lost."

"Then we will plan our escape carefully," she replied.

• • •

The news of Alexander's passing found its way to Akolo mere days after he and Esme learned of the death of their last surviving descendent, their grandson. Against their wishes, he had gone off to fight, only to die in a battle that did nothing to shift the balance of power. Right up until the moment of his death, Alexander's armies were unstoppable.

Akolo and Esme had chosen not to leave their hometown after all, fearing Alexander's response should they ever be found. They simply couldn't abide the thought of putting their grandson in harm's way. Akolo shook his head and a tear dripped down his ash-marked face.

He had pleaded with his God for his grandson's protection.

It didn't matter in the end. *What does, anymore?* he thought.

• • •

Akolo set his satchel down on the floor of the small room. Before him, red coals waited for fuel. Akolo had convinced the man guarding the lighthouse that he was on a holy mission. It wasn't exactly a lie, but it was enough. The man had not only granted him access to the tower, but he had also given Akolo the responsibility of adding fuel to the fire; to keep the light burning. Sunlight was fading fast, but Akolo had taken his time climbing the steps. He did not relish the thought of falling.

Akolo pulled the broken pieces of Alexander's silver box from the satchel and set them before him. He felt the sharp edge of a sword press into his back and turned quickly to see who was in the room with him. But the room was empty. Akolo shook his head, and with it, tried to erase the memory of what it cost to recover the silver box. He did not wish to relive that adventure. He had succeeded, at least in part, and now he had a job to do. His secondary mission had found new purpose upon the discovery of the tower. How appropriate to throw them into the sea from Alexander's lighthouse. They would be lost forever, their power no longer a threat. He gathered up the pieces and took a step toward the window.

No.

The long-silent voice of his God echoed in the small space. Akolo waited for more words. None came.

"Then what must I do?" Akolo yelled and raised his hands in frustration with the pain of the role he played in the destruction of Esme's people rising to the surface.

As his arms were lifted, the largest piece of the shattered box glinted in the light causing Akolo to notice the faded symbol on it. Though he originally believed it to be some kind of family crest, he later learned it was just a conflation of two Greek letters, alpha and omega. *The beginning and the end.*

Akolo looked into the polished mirror that was as tall as he. He studied his wrinkled face in the light of the glowing coals and saw hints of the young man he once was, the man he would be again someday.

A lighthouse was supposed to warn sailors of danger. This one served as a testament to one of the most dangerous men ever to live.

He knew what to do.

Without fear of burning himself, he buried the silver shards under the orange coals, then covered them with the fresh wood he'd carried up from the storage room far below.

The flame burst to life, flickering against the polished mirror. He took a step back, willing the flame to serve as a warning, not only to sailors, but to those who would be quick to champion a conqueror.

"Alexander the Great," he said aloud, his voice dripping with bitterness. He shook his head, then corrected himself. "No! Alexander the Horrible."

His secondary mission complete, he began his descent down the tower steps, vowing never to return to this place.

CHAPTER FOURTEEN

IAN LIFTED THE top of the lantern from the lamp-post, careful not to drop the decorative finial that held it in place, then backed down the ladder. He set the two items on the ground and climbed back up with the new light bulb in hand. As he unscrewed the burned-out bulb, he paused to study the inside of the lantern. He had never really looked this closely at the lamp-post before. It had saved them once, though that was Marshall's doing. Like the tall metal post, the exterior of the lantern was painted black, but the inside, apart from the glass panels, was silver. The dented and worn silver formed a mirror of sorts, patched together in various shapes and sizes with no clear design – other than what appeared to be a faded cut-off omega symbol. He looked closer at the bulb receptacle and guessed that it was a relatively recent modernization of what was likely an oil-fueled lamp in its original state. After replacing the burned-out bulb with a new one, he reseated the top of the lantern and twisted the iron finial onto its bolt.

"Don't fall too fast dear." Lyana's voice startled Ian.

"Wasn't planning on falling at all until you suggested it," he said, climbing down the ladder. He folded the ladder, then carefully pocketed the old bulb. They walked together into the garage.

"I think we need to have a sit-down with Ariel," began Lyana.

Ian leaned the ladder up against the garage wall, then dropped the dead bulb into a trashcan. "I thought the plan was to let her come to us."

"I know. But I'm worried about her."

"This isn't about that boy she's been seeing, is it?"

Lyana shrugged. "Maybe?"

Ian followed her into the kitchen and went over to the sink to wash his hands.

"Exactly what are you worried about? Do I need to have a man-to-man talk with him, too?"

"What? No. It's not that. I mean, she has been seeing a lot of him lately, but…"

"But what?" Ian opened the refrigerator door and stared at its contents for a moment, then closed it without removing anything.

"I think he's a good guy. I mean, he's a little odd, but I don't think he would ever do anything to hurt Ariel."

"He'd better not."

Lyana sat at the kitchen table. Ian wandered back to the counter and poured himself a cup of coffee. He held up an empty cup to Lyana.

"Sure. Yeah, I'll have a fresh cup."

They sat together at the family table, sipping coffee and not saying anything for a few minutes. It was Lyana who broke the silence.

"Doesn't this feel strange to you?"

"Is this still about Ariel?"

"No. Or yes. I don't know. It's just that here we are, sitting at a table sipping coffee, being normal people in a normal kitchen like everything is just…normal…"

Ian nodded. "And yet nothing about our story is 'normal.'"

"Exactly."

"'First the water, then the wind,'" said Ian.

"Yes! I was just thinking about that, too. Do you have any further thoughts?"

Ian shook his head. "I'm trying not to overthink it, but it's exactly the sort of thing that demands overthinking."

"Maybe that's what I'm doing with Ariel," said Lyana. "Overthinking things."

"She has been so strong in all of this," began Ian. "Maybe she's just run out of energy to keep that up. Maybe that's what's making her so…how would you describe it, angry? Surly? Confrontational?"

"Human," said Lyana.

"Human." Ian sipped his coffee. "That's what we are after all, isn't it? Merely human."

"Dad!"

Ian was startled again, this time by the urgency in Zach's voice.

"Come up here!"

Ian scooted his chair back and darted toward the stairs, Lyana close behind. Halfway up the stairs he began to imagine the worst, recalling the time when bees attacked Zach. When he turned the corner into Zach's room, he was confused. Zach was standing behind his palace model, pointing to the paper tower that dominated one side of the creation.

"What is it?" asked Ian.

"Just look!" Zach pointed again at the tower.

Ian didn't notice anything at first, but the more he stared, the more he began to see what had startled Zach. The top of the tower was slowly gyrating, as if guided by an invisible hand.

"Are you doing that?" asked Lyana.

"No!" said Zach.

Ian walked over to the model and moved his hands around all sides of the tower, expecting to encounter a stream of air that might be causing the tower to sway and swirl.

"Maybe it's just coming unglued?"

"No, Mom. It's not glued. It's taped," said Zach. His expression kept flipping between excitement and uncertainty.

"Untaped, then."

"Mom…just look at it, okay? And I already checked for airflow, Dad. It's doing this all by itself."

"That's not…" began Lyana.

"Normal?" Ian finished her sentence. "Wait…" He started to peel back the roof of the tower.

"What are you doing?" Zach was incredulous.

"You used a paperclip to help shape this," said Ian. He pointed at the paperclip that had been bent into a circle that lined the inside of the tower.

"It's gotta be magnets!" said Zach.

"Could be," said Ian. He looked on and around the table but found no magnets. He had no explanation for the strange event. A moment later, the tower stopped moving.

Zach's excitement faded. He sighed. "Guess it's just another mystery to add to our collection." He shrugged. "Maybe it's time to destroy it!"

"But you worked so hard on this," said Lyana. She, too, was looking all around the table, waving her hands in the air as if searching for invisible wires.

"I know. But…" Zach's smile returned. "Destroying it could be fun, too."

"Are you thinking what I'm thinking?" asked Ian. A day earlier he and Zach had found a small cache of firecrackers while cleaning out a bin in the garage.

"We can blow it up!"

Lyana lifted her hands and began to back out of the room. "You two are on your own with this one. Just don't do it anywhere near the house. And please don't lose a finger or an eye."

"You really want to, Zach?" asked Ian.

"I do, but…"

"But?"

"I'll let you light 'em."

Ian nodded. "I can do that."

"Can we do it now?" said Zach.

"We can."

Ian and Zach lifted the cardboard base of the model and maneuvered it out of Zach's room, down the stairs past Lyana, who was standing with arms folded and a half grin on her face, then outside onto the driveway. Just as they set it down, Ian heard a car coming up the driveway. As it emerged from the thick tree line, he recognized it as Sheriff Blackstone's vehicle. Ian's stomach dropped.

He jogged over to the car, meeting the sheriff as he exited.

Lyana ran up beside him, bending down to look in the back window. "Ariel? Is she okay?" The panic in her voice sent a similar panic into Ian's.

"What is this about, Sheriff?" he asked, his voice breaking.

The sheriff waved his hands out in front of him. "Everything's fine. Ariel is just fine..."

The back door of the car opened and Ariel climbed out. She looked unharmed but wouldn't meet Ian's gaze. She walked briskly past her parents without a word and disappeared into the house.

"What's going on here?" asked Lyana. "What did she do?"

"It's nothing," said the sheriff.

"I need to know right now why my daughter is being brought home in a sheriff's car."

"Look, it's not a big deal. Someone called in a report of a suspicious person breaking into..."

"She broke into a building?"

"...breaking into a cordoned-off construction site not far from the school."

"Why would she do that?"

Sheriff Blackstone shrugged. "I don't know. She wouldn't tell me anything. Nobody was hurt, and she cooperated when I called out to her. I think the citizen who called us was more worried about her safety than anything else. That house is falling apart. It's been scheduled for demolition for months. I guess the kids talk about it as being haunted or something. Maybe she was there on a dare..."

"She wouldn't do that," said Ian. Would she?

"She won't do it again," said Lyana.

"I suspect she won't," said the sheriff.

Ian hesitated. "Was she alone?"

"Alone? Yes. At least as far as I could tell."

"Is she being charged with anything?" asked Lyana.

"No, not at all. Of course, if she breaks into that site again, well..."

"Thank you, Sheriff," said Lyana. "We'll have a talk with her, but I'm sure she regrets her decision."

Ian wasn't so sure about that either.

"I guess that means we won't be blowing up the palace," said Zach.

Ian had nearly forgotten Zach was nearby. He turned to see him standing next to his cardboard-and-paper model, a look of disappointment on his face.

"We can do that later," said Ian.

"No, go ahead and do it now," said Lyana. "I'll go talk to Ariel."

Ian gave Lyana a long look before finally nodding.

"Okay," he said. "Let me know if you need backup," he added.

Zach laughed, then quickly turned his expression serious. "Sorry," he said. "That just sounded funny to me."

Ian turned to the sheriff. "Thank you for bringing her back. And please tell whoever called to report her 'thank you' as well."

Sheriff Blackstone nodded, then returned to his car and drove away. Ian waited until the car had disappeared into the trees before he turned his attention to Zach.

"Is Ariel gonna be grounded?" asked Zach.

"Your mom and I will talk with her. I'm sure she's going to be just fine." Ian ruffled his son's hair and began to arrange the string of firecrackers around the paper tower.

• • •

The machine-gun snap of firecrackers cracked the wall of silence. Ariel was curled up on her bed, her head on a pillow facing away from the door. Lyana sat on Ariel's desk chair, facing her.

"Why is he doing that?" Ariel finally spoke.

"Doing what?"

"Blowing up his model. I thought he liked it…"

Lyana shrugged. "I guess he was just done with it."

"Well, I think it's a shame."

Lyana didn't know where to begin. The tension between them had been high for too long. She didn't want to step on a landmine, but she had to say something. She decided to open with a general question. Surely that wouldn't be taken the wrong way.

"Everything okay at school?" she asked.

Ariel huffed. "Seriously, Mom? That's what you want to know? Why not just ask the question that you really want to ask? Hmm?"

"And what question would that be?"

"I'll save you the time. The answer is no. I am not crossing any lines with Garrett."

Lyana was taken aback. "I…I wasn't going to ask that question." She wasn't worried about that before, but now she wondered if she should be. "Why do you think I would ask that?"

Ariel turned and faced Lyana. There were tears in her eyes. "Because you don't trust me."

"What? Of course we trust you…"

"No, you don't. You say you do. You always say that. But that's a lie. You and Dad are liars!"

Lyana was stunned. This outburst appeared to come out of nowhere. Or maybe it had been brewing for a while. "Ariel, I don't know what you're talking about. Please, talk to me…"

Ian stepped into the room and looked over at Lyana, then Ariel.

"Why do you say we're liars?" he asked. Lyana was thankful his tone was calm.

"Grrr! You don't understand!" She turned abruptly and buried her face in her pillow again.

"Please, talk to us..." began Ian.

Lyana lifted her hand to gently shush him. "We'll give you some space. When you're ready to talk, please know that we want to listen. We do want to understand. We want to help. Okay?"

There was no response.

"Okay, honey?" Lyana repeated.

Ariel grunted and Lyana took that as acknowledgment. She ushered Ian out of the room, and they went downstairs to the kitchen.

"What is that all about?" asked Ian.

"I honestly don't know. But one thing I do know—when emotions start bubbling up to the surface quickly, and they feel out of control, they are nearly ready to be dealt with. We're not going to get anything out of her right now. She needs just a little more time. She's almost ready to talk."

"I hope you're right," said Ian. He poured a cup of coffee, then started down the hall toward his office.

Lyana stood in the kitchen, listening. Wondering. Waiting. Expectant, even. But no whispers came.

• • •

"I wondered what that sound was."

Marshall walked up to Zach, who was stuffing charred cardboard into a large trash bag.

"It was kind of disappointing," said Zach.

Marshall bent down to help him collect the last of the trash. "Really?"

"Yeah. It was a little...what's the word? Underwhelming."

Marshall laughed. "You wanted a big kaboom."

Zach's face lit up. "Yes! And all I got was a bunch of little pops. I mean, some of the paper caught on fire, but Dad put it out kinda fast with the hose."

Marshall lifted the half-filled bag and carried it to the trash can that sat just outside the Keanes' garage. Zach lifted the lid and Marshall dropped the bag in.

"You up for one of our walks?" asked Marshall.

Zach's disappointment disappeared in an instant, replaced by the expression Marshall secretly referred to as his "yes, please!" face. They had shared numerous nature walks together in recent weeks, and every time, Zach found something new to wonder over. Sometimes it was a leaf pattern. Other times the bend of a branch. As often as not, it was a rock along the creek bed. Marshall wished he could know that kind of wide-eyed joy again. When was the last time he felt so curious? So free of the weight of the world?

"I'm worried about Ariel," Zach said as they walked along their preferred path by the creek.

"Why?"

"She's really angry at Mom and Dad," he said. "But she won't tell me why."

"Have you talked to her about this?" Marshall paused as Zach bent down to pick up a stone, turn it over in his hand, then toss it into the creek.

"Not really. It's just something I know. I can feel it."

Marshall nodded. "You know lots of things, Zach. You are quite perceptive." One of Zach's abilities was being able to feel the atmosphere around him. Even if he couldn't always discern why, he could pick up on unspoken tension, chaos, or peace quicker than most people.

"Thanks."

They walked along in silence for a while. Marshall looked forward to his visits with the young boy. His memories had started to come into clearer focus, and every time he looked at Zach, he saw a vision of himself as a young boy.

"It was probably magnets," said Zach. This was his pattern: to be silent for a long period, then just state something out of the blue as if they'd been talking all along.

"What was magnets?"

Zach explained what he had witnessed with his palace model, then went silent again, awaiting Marshall's thoughts.

"Could have been something to do with magnetism. That house is full of surprises," he said.

They walked a little further, then Zach abruptly stopped. He didn't bend down to pick up a rock or leaf. He just stuffed his hands into his pockets and turned his face to the sky.

"Do you think the sky has changed much?" he asked.

"Changed? What do you mean?"

"I mean, do you think the sky is different today than it was thousands of years ago?"

"I suppose it is different in some ways," said Marshall.

Zach dropped his gaze and looked directly at Marshall. He rarely made eye contact with anyone, so this caught Marshall off guard.

"Was it you?" he asked.

Marshall had expected this conversation. Thus far, Zach had said little about his time-travel adventure, apart from sharing details he could remember about the palace itself.

"What do you mean?"

"I mean, in my adventure. Or my dream. Whatever it was. Was that you?"

Marshall didn't respond, hoping Zach would continue on his own. He did.

"You were little. Like, younger than me."

"What specifically do you remember?"

"Specifically? Not much." He paused, then started walking along the creek again. After a couple of steps, he bent down to pick up a small wildflower. He lifted it and stared at it intensely. "There was a garden!"

Zach's exclamation rolled like a wave over Marshall. Yes, a garden!

"It was gigantic. Shaped kind of like a pyramid or something, but every level was full of trees and plants and vegetables and flowers."

They were quiet for a few more minutes, then Zach turned around and started heading back the way they'd come. This was also like Zach, to suddenly decide their walk was done, without so much as an announcement. Marshall caught up to him, his gait lightened by the door Zach's recollection opened to his own memory. He was a little boy again, walking beside his new friend as they discovered together one of the wonders of the world.

Oh, to be that young boy again, thought Marshall. How marvelous it would be to discover the beauty of the world for the very first time.

To fall in love again with a green-eyed girl.

Marshall's eyes misted over at the memory of meeting Esme. Of the genesis of their life together.

They reached the clearing at the end of the woods. Marshall wiped away a tear just before Zach stopped and spun toward him.

"Thank you," he said.

"For what?" asked Marshall. He was reeling from the whiplash of being thrust back into the now.

"For helping me with the bees."

Marshall nodded. "Of course."

Zach raced off toward the house, leaving Marshall to wonder if he was referring to the time he helped with the beehive they'd found in the walls of Zach's room, or the bee that stung Zach millennia ago.

He sighed. Time was relentless.

Esme, my love. I would give anything to go back and spend a moment with you again.

Before heading back to his cabin, Marshall followed a hunch and wandered to the east side of the house. Lyana had questioned him extensively about the strange yellow plant that had sprouted up almost overnight just before Zach returned. He had confirmed what she found through research. It was indeed Silphium. An ancient flowering plant that should not have existed in this timeline.

It was gone. The plant had withered and died.

This felt like an omen.

But what kind of omen?

• • •

Dear Diary,

I did something stupid today. I was supposed to hang out with Cassie. But she had to leave early because her little brother was home alone or something. I didn't even get to tell her about Garrett. I should have just texted Dad to come get me, but I didn't.

Instead, I went to the Dead House. It's an abandoned house not too far from the park where I was with Cassie. Everyone at school says it's haunted. I know a few things about a haunted house so, yeah. I had to see if it was true. I wasn't scared or anything. Just curious.

Apparently some nosy neighbor saw me heading that way and followed me, because the sheriff showed up before I'd even gotten in the front door. He drove me back home. Talk about embarrassing.

But that's not the stupid thing I did. The stupid thing was that I called Mom and Dad liars. It's out there in the open now and they're going to want to talk about it.

I'd rather spend the night in a haunted house than vomit my real feelings to my parents.

I mean a different haunted house, not the one I live in.

Ha. I just made myself laugh.

You know who else makes me laugh? Garrett.

Sigh.

CHAPTER FIFTEEN

AKOLO HAD LONG ago lost count of the number of times he and Esme had been renewed to younger versions of themselves. They continued to be creative in how they handled the dramatic change in public so that few would have any reason to think anything was amiss. But Akolo knew the real magic of their transformations was in how his God would cloud the memories of any who might wonder what had happened to the old man and his wife.

He and Esme were in their fifties when news arrived of an uprising developing in a nearby town. This wasn't like the many wars Akolo had endured; this was something different. Something organic and small. But growing. As it was told to him, a group of rebels were championing a man they claimed was God in the flesh.

It was a ridiculous claim, to be sure. But the movement wasn't going away. It had even spread to Akolo's city. Word spread about healings. About miracles. This troubled Akolo more than he would have liked. Could this be the work of the very God he himself had been serving for centuries? Could God really talk to men and work miracles outside of a temple? Without a blood moon? The same gifts he and Esme enjoyed?

Enjoyed.

Now there was a loaded word. Yes, thought Akolo, he had indeed enjoyed a long and meaningful life. A life made infinitely better because Esme was by his side. But the heartache of being unable to get pregnant after the ages-ago deaths of their earlier children and their families remained. Long ago, Akolo had stopped pleading with God to give him and Esme the gift of one more child. It was not to be.

He glanced over at Esme, who was asleep on their bed. Sunlight filtered through the window, highlighting the grey streaks in her hair. It would turn white someday, and then she would be young again and that hair would be black as night. Akolo marveled at every shade, every curve of her body, every line that graced her perfect face. There was no season in Esme's life that he didn't find compelling. She was a wonder at every age and in every way.

Perhaps he could let go of his heartache after all. Esme was more than enough.

Her eyes opened and he smiled at her.

Yes, perhaps he could.

"What is occupying your thoughts, my love?" Esme's voice was smooth like glass when she was young, and rich like velvet the more she aged. This was her velvet voice.

"You, as always," he said.

She laughed her honey laugh and sat up. "I mean besides that," she said.

"This rebel uprising," he said. "It has been growing for a few years now. I'm just wondering what it will lead to."

"Maybe it will just die out. Like so many others. Our overlords are not so easy to defeat."

Akolo nodded. The latest conquest had been as comprehensive as ever, but there was a layer of civility to the newest champions of the land. Akolo picked up a coin that was sitting on the table in front of him and turned it over in his hand.

"They put his face on a coin," he said, mostly to himself.

"He can have it back, then," said Esme.

Akolo set the coin down. He and Esme had lived through so many wars and conquests. He was once again thankful that so many of his memories had blurred to insignificance. Still, the weight of war weighed heavily on his heart. Most notably, the loss of his only descendants. If someday he and Esme should die, there would be no one left to carry on their legacy. But what really was their legacy? He sighed. "Do you think peace will ever truly come to our world?"

Esme thought for a moment, then stood and walked over to Akolo. She wrapped him in a hug. "I pray it will."

Akolo hugged back and nodded. But inside he wondered: How does a seemingly unknowable God decide which prayers to answer and which to ignore? *If only I could know this deity more*, thought Akolo.

• • •

Akolo stood in the temple building, staring at the curtain that hung in front of the door to the holy place where the chest and its artifacts lay. The temple had endured for centuries, but this was the fourth or fifth curtain that had hidden the entrance to the one room in the city that only Akolo could enter. God lived behind that curtain. And maybe behind other curtains like it, he thought as he pondered the stories that continued to find their way to his city from nearby towns. The latest was truly perplexing. Rumors of a temple being cleared of merchants. Akolo's temple had certainly faced its challenges over the years, but every issue had been deftly dealt with, due in great part to Esme's wisdom in dealing with people who were driven more by greed than compassion. Sometimes he wondered if that's why he himself hadn't fallen prey to the temptations of wealth and status.

Today Akolo would ask his God about the rumors. Was there any truth to them? And if so, what did this mean for Akolo and his city? For his people?

But unexpectantly, at midday, things suddenly changed. The sky went dark as night, covering the sun for almost three hours. Akolo ran up to the temple to see what was happening. He took one step toward the curtain, and the ground began to shake.

Akolo had experienced the ground shaking a few times before and still had no answer to why the earth would rattle. But this time, the shaking was especially violent and accompanied by the ominous sky. He grabbed the edge of a table nearby and held on to keep his balance. Shouts filtered up the steps from the courtyard below.

"What is happening?"

Akolo knew the people would look to him for an answer. They always turned to him for answers. But what answer could he give?

Just then, there was a rumble like thunder, then a snap, then the sound of tearing.

The stone frame to the holy place began to crack, blasting dust into the air. And then the unthinkable happened: The heavy curtain was torn right down the middle. Akolo steadied himself against the aftershocks, then stared at the temple room before him.

Silence.

Destruction was everywhere, with billows of dirt and dust floating in the air. What was once a secret and mysterious place seen by only one man had now been fully exposed to the world. The roof had cracked and tumbled, allowing the evening light to spill into the space, illuminating the chest that held the holy artifacts. The very room where his God had imbued weapons and goblets—and, once, an old book—was lit up for everyone to see.

After the earth had stopped shaking, the people started to appear. A few brave souls at first. Then many more began to climb the temple steps. They would find Akolo standing before the broken room, the torn curtain, his hands raised to the sky in prayer.

But he wasn't praying. He was pleading.

"What does this mean?" he asked. His entire world had shifted in an instant. "What do you want from me?"

The crowd grew and the hushed murmurs grew with it. Then, a strange silence. Akolo turned toward the people, prepared to humble himself before them. He had no assurances to give. No hope to offer. This was an event without explanation.

But when he turned, he saw the crowd had turned their attention to someone walking up the stairs. They parted, and from among them emerged Esme. Even in the dim light of the setting sun and the flickering lamps, he could see something was wrong. She continued up the steps until she was standing before him. She didn't look like the same woman he had held earlier that very day. She looked tired. Sickly. And older than she ought.

"Akolo..." she said, then she fell into his arms. He caught her and held her tight. "Something is very wrong," she whispered. And then, "And something else is very right."

Akolo called for the physician to come, but he was there before Akolo got all the words out. The man helped Akolo carry Esme down the temple steps. As they descended, Akolo caught a glimmer of light off Esme's necklace. He paused, nearly causing the physician to stumble.

"What is it?" Esme asked.

The stone in her necklace had cracked. The stone that had granted his wife immortality was split in two, mirroring the rent curtain.

"It's nothing," he lied.

It wasn't nothing.

It was everything.

• • •

The "something very wrong" was exactly what Akolo had feared. The stone was no longer protecting her. He could see it in her eyes. He could feel it on her skin. He could even taste it in her kiss.

There was no good news in that.

And yet...

"I'm pregnant," she had said when the physician left their bedroom to get his supplies.

Akolo didn't need to ask how she knew.

"And I'm going to grow old," she said. She smiled at that, but the sadness in her eyes was too much for Akolo to take.

"I can fix it," he said. "I'll take the stone into the temple and…"

"The temple is broken," she said.

"No, no. The building is broken. It can be repaired. And when it is, we will repair your stone. We will have a healthy baby, and you will be fine and everything will be good and, and…"

Akolo felt a rising panic. How would he ever live if his Esme died? He couldn't fathom it. No, he wouldn't let that happen. Whatever it took, whatever the cost, he would find a way.

With shaky hands, Esme reached up to her neck and removed her necklace. She gently placed it into Akolo's hand, then closed hers around his. Her hands were cold. She looked as if she might speak, then closed her eyes.

"She needs rest." It was the physician, back with his supplies.

Akolo didn't want to let go. But at the physician's urging, he finally did. He started to pace, but this time the physician wasn't so gentle with his urging.

"Go outside!" he said. Then, more politely, "Your wife needs a calm, peaceful place to rest. Get some air. She will be fine."

Akolo acquiesced. He stood outside their door for a few minutes, then decided on a plan. Slipping the necklace in his pocket, he began a determined walk back to the temple. The damaged temple.

Surely the God who resides there isn't damaged, he thought.

Akolo stepped through the torn curtain into the holy room and stood beside the chest. It was intact. A stray breeze caught his attention, and he glanced up to see a hole in the roof of the small space. Moonlight peered through the crack.

Pink moonlight.

It was a blood moon. How could he have missed that?

Gently, hopefully, he took Esme's necklace out of his pocket and laid it on the chest. And then he waited.

He stood there until his knees buckled. Once on his knees, he bowed his head in supplication. What plea would his God understand?

"Please," he began. And just as soon as he began to speak, he lost his voice. There were no words.

Tears began to stream down his face.

After a timeless moment, the air stirred again. He looked at the necklace. The stone remained cracked, but it was glowing. Not blue or white like the first time, but red.

Was this because of the moonlight? he wondered. No. Something about this moment was different. It didn't feel like any other time when he'd seen his God work in the temple. Yes, there was still power here. He felt that. But it was not the same. Not like the turn of the air before a storm, but more like the storm itself.

Still, if it helped to keep Esme alive…

A crack of thunder interrupted Akolo's thoughts. Rain began to fall, pouring through the hole in the ceiling. He looked up and his tears disappeared in the rain.

If only his fears disappeared so easily.

• • •

"Akolo, come!"

It was the physician's assistant. She had found Akolo standing near the pen where the horses once were kept. Now, the fence was nothing but ruins, but he could still see the gentle beasts in his memory. He could smell their earthy scent, hear their gentle snorts. But mostly he saw the love in his wife's wide green eyes. How they came whenever Esme called out to them. She was wise and strong and full of opinions, but her love was beyond compare. She loved all of God's creatures, including men and women who were driven by a lust for power or wealth. People Akolo himself struggled to tolerate, let alone love.

Esme was everything good about the world.

Akolo ran to his house, nearly knocking the physician over when he awkwardly fell to his knees by his wife's side. She was propped up in bed with a pillow and holding a tiny bundle.

"It's a miracle!" said the physician's assistant, a pure sense of wonder in her voice.

The physician gently shushed the young woman. "Let us give them some privacy," he said as he led her out of the house.

"We have a son," said Esme.

The joy of those words was nearly stolen by the sound of her voice. It was neither smooth like glass nor rich like velvet.

It was brittle. The rattle of death.

"No," said Akolo. He bent forward and wrapped his wife and the infant in a hug. "No, you're going to be fine," he whispered. "Everything is going to be fine."

The baby offered a small cry.

"What shall we name him?" Esme asked in her still, small voice.

Akolo swiped at his wife's silent tears, brushed her hair from her face. Her hair had gone white during the pregnancy. She looked far too old to bear children, and yet here they were with a newborn son.

A miracle indeed. But at what cost?

"Ask for help," whispered Esme.

Akolo didn't understand. "What do you mean?"

"Help raising our son," she added.

Akolo shook his head. "No, Esme. We will raise our son. You and I."

Esme gave a small laugh that turned into a lingering cough. Akolo offered her a sip of water from a nearby goblet. Some of it dribbled down the side of her mouth. He wiped at it with the sleeve of his tunic, then returned to wiping her tears.

"You can be so stubborn, my husband," Esme said, a renewed energy in her voice. "Please, promise you will ask for help in raising our son."

Akolo could not speak the word, so he nodded.

"I love you," she said. "Always and forever."

"Always and forever," he repeated.

Time stood still.

It started up again with the sound of a baby crying. His son. They would leave a legacy after all. What should they call him indeed? Akolo gently extracted the tiny bundle from his wife's arms and held the baby close. He began to hum a song Esme had sung to their other children so many years ago, but somewhere along the way, he forgot how it went. He looked to her, hoping she might join in like they used to do.

Her eyes were closed. Her face was drawn. Her skin was sallow. The stone had not saved her.

The love of his life was dead. Were it not for the child cooing in his arms, he would have happily joined her.

But not yet.

Not yet.

Akolo wept.

CHAPTER SIXTEEN

"IS ARIEL OKAY?"

Lyana looked up from pulling weeds and saw real concern on Zach's face.

"What do you mean?"

"I mean, she's obviously upset about something, and she won't tell me what, and I'm worried about her."

Lyana wanted to dismiss Ariel's recent behavior as the result of "simply being a teenager," but that would be incomplete at best and a lie at worst. She knew full well it was more than that. But what the "more" was continued to elude her.

"Your dad and I are worried, too," she said. Was that too honest? she wondered. She thought back to when the kids were young and how she and Ian would reassure them that they would always be safe, despite a world in which safety was anything but guaranteed. But they weren't young children anymore, and with all they'd been through, such a promise was impossible. Speaking the truth was her best option, even when the truth was hard. Zach had proven he could handle difficult things. She continued, "She seems angry at us, but I can't get her to tell me why. I know your dad and I make mistakes—of course we do—but it's hard to fix things if we don't know what's wrong."

"Yeah, I know what you mean." Zach pointed to a clump of plants that was growing next to the house. "Are those things wrong?" He smiled. "I mean, are those weeds?"

Lyana laughed. It felt good to laugh, even if it was short-lived. "Yes. You can pull them."

After weeding the garden, Lyana had suggested they do a perimeter walk of the house and clean that up of weeds as well. They were on the final leg of that project, and she had enjoyed every sweaty moment of spending time with her son. Ian was expected to return soon with burger buns, and her plan of a family picnic out back was moving along nicely.

"I'm thinking of doing another model," said Zach. He was holding a clump of dried plants in his gloved hand, staring at them.

"Oh? What kind of model?"

"You know about the Hanging Gardens of Babylon?" he asked.

"I've heard of it." Ian had pointed it out when they were discussing what Zach had shared about his incredible adventure. The details were few, but he talked at length about a fantastical garden. The description matched that of the Hanging Gardens—which have never been proven to have existed in history, as Ian was quick to point out. "It's one of the original seven wonders of the world, isn't it?"

"Well, I was thinking about my adventure, and then I did some research and thought it would make a pretty cool model. I mean, mostly it's just a bunch of terraces built around a pyramid, but I could draw the plants and things on the paper before I put it together." He dropped the weeds into the overflowing wheelbarrow. "I forgot how much I like drawing," he added.

"Your imagination knows no bounds, Zach. I love it." He often talked about his adventure so casually, like it was no big deal. But clearly it was the biggest deal. Time travel was far more unbelievable than the existence of the hanging gardens, and yet the only thing that could truly explain Zach's adventure was that he did indeed travel back in time. Lyana shook her head, clearing another impossible thought from the growing queue.

First the water. Then the wind.

Lyana was startled by the voice. It was more insistent than ever this time. She looked over at Zach. He hadn't flinched. Why was she the only one who heard voices?

• • •

Ian paused at the display and considered adding a bunch of flowers to his mostly empty cart. He almost never bought flowers—Lyana had always made a point to grow them in their own garden. But a family picnic in the backyard seemed like the perfect opportunity to show that he could still surprise his wife and his kids. He chose the most colorful bunch from the display and gently laid them in the seat of the grocery cart.

As he rolled the cart to the front of the store, a familiar song came on the store's sound system. Thankfully it was the original version, not some lame instrumental knock-off. Those always made Ian cringe. Ian parked his cart near the candy aisle so he could listen to the rest of the song. It was one of Lyana's favorites too. There are some songs you can't ignore. This was one of them.

Welcome to the planet
Welcome to existence
Everyone's here
Everyone's here
Everyone's watching you now
Everybody waits for you now

What happens next?
What happens next?

When the chorus came around, he couldn't help himself. The store was mostly empty, so he started singing along with more confidence and volume.

I dare you to move
I dare you to lift yourself up off the floor
I dare you to move
I dare you to move
Like today never happened
Today never happened before

Halfway through the chorus, a strange voice interrupted his moment of musical joy. Ian stopped singing and looked around for the source of the voice. The aisle was empty. He resumed his singing, only to be interrupted again. The words spoken were unintelligible, maybe foreign? He looked around again and only saw one customer—an older woman who was collecting grapefruit from a bin. Ian thought back to the words he himself had uttered at the storm cellar door weeks before. He and Marshall had later determined they were Akkadian, an ancient language no one spoke anymore. Why would he be hearing this in a grocery store? He resigned himself to the fact that little had made sense in their family's story over the past year and focused his attention on the remainder of the song. The voice didn't return. Perhaps it was just a glitch in the sound system.

• • •

"Ah, there you are," said Lyana. Ian was carrying a single grocery bag in one hand and a bunch of flowers in the other. "Flowers? You never buy flowers," she said. "What's the occasion?"

Ian walked up and kissed Lyana, then presented the floral arrangement to her in overly dramatic fashion, eliciting an exaggerated "ew" from nearby Zach. "Who needs an occasion? I just thought they looked pretty." He turned to Marshall, who was arranging place settings on the long folding table Lyana had set up on the lawn. The wind was picking up just a little, so he was dropping silverware on top of the paper napkins to keep them from drifting away. "Marshall, glad you could join us."

"Was tricky to clear my schedule," he said. Then he offered a sly smile and added, "No place I'd rather be." He pointed to the grill. "Grill's all ready for burgers. We were just waiting for you to return with the buns."

"You did remember the buns, didn't you?" asked Lyana. She took the flowers from Ian.

He produced the package from the bag and set it on the table. "Of course."

"I'm just going to get something to put these in," said Lyana. She headed off toward the back door.

"Let Ariel know we'll be eating soon."

Lyana waved her acknowledgment as she disappeared into the house.

Ian went to the grill and started arranging the burger patties in neat rows across the grate. Marshall walked up to observe Ian's work.

"That one is a little too far to the south," he said, pointing to one of the burgers.

Ian laughed, then gently nudged the patty a little bit north, aligning it with the rest.

"Meticulous in all things," said Marshall. "That's a handy trait to have."

Ian raised an eyebrow. "Most of the time, anyway. Sometimes I get a little lost in the details. Lyana could tell you a story or two."

Marshall turned a chair around and sat, his back to the neatly set table.

"I really do admire you," he said. His voice sounded tired, labored.

"Really? Why do you say that?"

"Because we're complicated and interesting," said Zach, who was standing next to the ice-filled cooler, fidgeting with the handle.

Marshall laughed. It was a rare sound from the caretaker. "Yes, because of that," he said. "But mostly because you are such a strong family. You have endured much, and yet here you are, celebrating a regular day together with a backyard picnic. I think that's a rare and wonderful thing."

Ian smiled. It was wonderful. And far too rare since their move to Littleton. He decided in that moment he would remedy that. They would have regular family picnics as long as the weather allowed. "Thank you," he said.

"Hey, you're kinda like family, too," said Zach. Zach glanced over at Marshall and offered what Ian thought was a knowing look, then returned to his fidgeting.

Ian closed the lid to the grill and turned to Marshall. He had so many questions for the man who had sold them this house. This amazing and wonderful and insane and inscrutable house. He chose one at random, hoping it wasn't too personal. "You haven't told us much about your family history," he began. "Since you're part of ours, now"—he winked over at Zach—"maybe you could shed a little light?"

Marshall didn't respond immediately. Ian started to regret his choice of question, but a moment later Marshall began. His tone was quiet, reserved, and a bit sad. "I was married once." He paused and looked up to the sky. Ian followed his gaze. Fluffy white clouds dotted the blue, looking all the world like the animated clouds featured in the opening credits to *The Simpsons*. "She was the most amazing woman.

Beautiful, strong, loving, and wise beyond her years." He laughed the small laugh of an inside joke. "And honestly, that was quite a feat."

"What was her name?" Ian asked.

"Esme," said Zach.

Ian turned toward his son, then back to Marshall. "Have you guys talked about this already on one of your walks? How am I always the last to know?"

"Know what?" Lyana carefully set a bucket of flowers on the table. "Sorry, couldn't find a big enough vase. You bought too many flowers, Ian."

"Not possible," said Ian. "Marshall was just talking about his wife. Did you know about her, too?"

Lyana finished adjusting the flowers to her liking and looked over at Marshall. "We haven't really talked much about her. I mean, I didn't even know her name."

"It's Esme, Mom," repeated Zach. He had stopped fidgeting with the cooler and was tossing a piece of ice from one hand to another. It was clear he was tired of waiting and eager to get to the eating part of the picnic.

"Yes, Esme," said Marshall. He had turned away from them and was staring off into the woods. Or maybe back in time. "I miss her," he said, his words nearly a whisper.

"Hey, Dad?" It was Zach. He was staring at the ice in his hand.

"What's up, Zach?"

"Look at this!" He held out his hand.

Ian watched as the ice cube began spinning in his hand.

"How are you doing that?" Lyana raced over to him and reached for his hand. She grabbed it, and the ice cube skittered off Zach's hand.

"I don't think it's me," said Zach. He was looking over Ian's shoulder. Ian turned.

"What in the world?"

"I've never seen a sky like that," said Ian. A dark green wall of clouds had risen above the tree line and was growing in intensity.

"That's...not normal," said Lyana. "We should take our picnic inside."

"But what does that have to do with the ice cube?" asked Ian. "Why was it doing that?"

"Something's coming," said Zach. "Something bad." He wiped his hand against his pants.

Marshall was already grabbing the plates and bowls of fruit to carry into the house. Zach started dragging the cooler while Ian removed the burgers from the grill and shut off the burners. Before he took a step toward the house, the wind suddenly picked up, blowing the plate from his hands. The half-cooked burgers fell to the ground, and the plate flew Frisbee-like toward the woods.

Ian abandoned the burgers and made it to the house as the rain began. The wind was howling now.

"Dad, you need to see this," said Zach. He was holding his phone out.

"What is it?" asked Lyana. She came over and looked at Zach's phone. "What am I looking at?"

"Sudden drop in air pressure," said Ian. "And temperature is dropping too."

"Something bad," said Marshall, repeating Zach's warning.

"It's the conditions for a tornado, Mom." He looked scared.

"We need to go to the shelter," said Lyana.

"Mom, no. I don't want..." began Zach, remembering what happened to him the last time he was in the shelter with bad weather.

"We will be with you," said Ian.

The wind howled, rattling the windows.

"We should hurry," said Lyana. She grabbed a water bottle off the kitchen counter and scooped up one of the bowls of fruit and began heading toward the door. When no one followed, she paused. "We don't have much time! Let's go!"

Ian nodded. "Right. I'll get Ariel. Zach, you lead the way. We'll be right behind you."

Marshall put his hand out to stop Ian. "I'll get Ariel," he said. "That storm cellar door is heavy. I can't lift it, but you can. Get Zach and Lyana to safety. We'll be right behind you."

Ian hesitated. The wind howled again. This time it sounded like a freight train.

"Okay, go!" Marshall started toward the stairs. Ian followed Lyana and Zach out the back door into the pelting rain. "Hold hands!" he shouted over the tempest. Lyana grabbed his hand and Zach took hers, leading them on a run toward the woods. Ian had been to the storm shelter many times, but fog continued to mess with his memory of how to get there. Zach knew. He always knew.

Ian turned his head as he ran, nearly tumbling into Lyana. He righted himself and looked back again, trying to see if Marshall and Ariel were following. But all he could see was a wall of rain.

CHAPTER SEVENTEEN

MAYBE YOU SHOULD talk to them.

Garrett's text message stared back at Ariel like judgment. He made it sound so easy. This was the opposite of easy. Ariel loved her parents. Of course she did. But she had reason to believe they had been lying to her for years. How do you reconcile those two things?

Maybe you should just talk to them.

She heard the words bouncing around in her head in Garrett's voice. His calming, caring voice. Garrett was one of the good guys. Not only was he smart and funny and handsome, he was totally *for* Ariel. He was her cheerleader. He was on her side. Then why did she feel attacked?

A rattling sound interrupted her thoughts. She pulled off one earbud and tried to locate the source of the noise. A moment later, the sound repeated. It was her window being buffeted by the wind.

She laughed and reached for her journal and a pen. She wrote quickly, her handwriting messier than usual.

Okay, just writing this down so I don't forget. Garrett wants me to talk to my parents. I know he's right, but GRRR! This is the worst thing. Also? The wind is really picking up outside. Probably another insane storm brewing. I mean, of course it is. My whole life is on the edge of a storm! This is so on the nose I actually laughed out loud.

Ariel dropped her journal and pen on the nightstand, closed the messaging app on her phone and turned up the volume on her headphones. She wasn't ready to talk to her parents. Not yet.

She lay back on her pillow and closed her eyes, willing herself to disappear into the music and forget about real life for a while.

Welcome to the fallout
Welcome to resistance
The tension is here
The tension is here
Between who you are and who you could be
Between how it and how it should be
I dare you to move
I dare you to move…

The sound of someone crying bleeds into her earbuds. But it's muffled, distant, like the person is in another room, or behind a door somewhere. Ariel shakes her head to clear her dizzying thoughts and finds herself standing in a colorless, empty hallway, leaning against cold metal. A locker. A school locker. But this isn't Littleton. She is in Boston. In the school she attended for years before they moved. The blurring resolves into focus, and she sees two of her friends standing in front of her, books cradled in arms, faces tilted toward Ariel as if awaiting her response to a question.

What was the question?

"Well?" says Amber. She shakes her head. "Anyway, I think he's weird."

"Me too," says Mandy. "It's like he lives in a totally different universe."

"It's freaky," says Amber.

Ariel's memory snaps into place and she remembers this interaction. Her best friends had stayed over at Ariel's house the night before. They were talking about her brother. About Zach.

"What's the deal with all the counting?" asks Amber.

Ariel remembers what she says next. "You're right. He's weird."

This is the moment she crosses the line. For the next year, she will treat Zach horribly whenever it serves her social status. Future Ariel is watching this play out but has no agency to change her younger self's words.

"He's totally annoying," Ariel adds. She hates the sound of her voice. There is no remorse in it. This version of Ariel will do anything to maintain her social status.

Her friends' conspiratorial laughter fades as the hallway scene dissolves into black. The sound of crying returns, only now it is no longer muted, distant. It is close. Louder.

It is coming from her own throat.

She opens her eyes wide, trying to glimpse anything, but she is in total darkness.

A vertical line of light appears in front of her, and she looks down at her arms wrapped around her knees. They are not her arms. They are not her knees. And the cries are not hers at all.

She is Zach and he is hiding in his closet, crying.

"You okay in there, bud?"

It is their father's voice. Ariel wants to call out, tell her father that it's all a big misunderstanding. That she didn't mean to be so cruel to Zach. She didn't mean to make him cry. Why didn't she see this back then? Why didn't she notice she was being so awful?

Because she was too focused on herself. She sees this now.

The cracked door opens further and Ariel, in Zach's body, looks into their father's kind eyes.

I'm sorry, she wants to say. To Zach. To her father.

But the words come out in Zach's voice. "I'm okay," he says.

He is not okay. She has hurt him.

The song she had been listening to bled into the memory.

Maybe redemption has stories to tell
Maybe forgiveness is right where you fell
Where can you run to escape from yourself?
Where you gonna go?
Where you gonna go?
Salvation is here

A loud banging snapped Ariel back to reality. She looked over to see her door had slammed shut. Her window was open. She didn't remember opening it. And her room was surprisingly dark for the middle of the afternoon. She pulled off her earbuds and sat up on the edge of her bed. The wind was whipping around like it was angry. She walked over to the window to close it. The sky was a strange shade of green.

Right then the house shook so much she nearly lost her balance. This was just like the day Zach returned from his time-travel adventure. Her parents hadn't believed her then. Surely, they would now.

She called out for them but only heard the howl of the wind in reply.

This was not good.

Not good at all.

A muffled voice reached her ears.

"Zach?" She raced over to the door. She turned the knob, but the door wouldn't budge. "Zach, is that you?"

"No, it's Marshall," came the reply. "We need to get to the shelter."

"What?"

"The storm shelter!"

The door rattled but did not open.

"It's stuck!" Ariel cried out. "It won't open!"

"Stand back. I'll try to break in."

Ariel backed up until she ran into her bed, then caught her balance before tumbling. There was a moment of eerie silence, then a loud thud, but the door still didn't open.

"I'm going to get a crowbar or something to pry it open," said Marshall.

"Wait, don't go!"

Ariel jumped off her bed and began wrestling with the doorknob. It spun, but the door remained firmly closed. She pressed her ear up to the door and listened.

"Are you still there?" she asked. The house shuddered in reply. She was well and truly stuck in her room with a terrible storm raging outside.

A loud snap was followed by the sound of something crashing into the house.

"Marshall?" Again, no reply. "Mom? Dad? Zach?"

Shattering glass behind her made Ariel scream. Instinctively she ducked. When she turned around, she saw shards of glass scattered across the floor and her bed. Her window had been blown inward. She called out for Marshall's help again, but the wind stole her voice. Ariel looked around the room in a panic. Her heart was racing. Rain was blowing into the room through the empty window frame.

The sky had turned nearly black. There was only one place to hide.

The closet.

She walked around the broken glass, shielding herself from the pelting rain, grabbed her journal and phone, then stepped over to her closet, bending down to squeeze herself in among the boxes and bins and hanging clothes. With some effort, she pulled the door closed.

Ariel sat down too hard, landing on a pair of boots she'd nearly forgotten she owned. She fumbled for her phone and tried to message

Garrett, then her parents. But the phone wasn't working. The screen had frozen and there was no resetting it.

She pulled up her knees and wrapped her arms around them, her face turned down as she'd been taught during the tornado drills they'd had when she lived in Boston.

Ariel began to cry.

"Please don't let me die," she whispered to the house.

The house shook in reply.

• • •

Marshall descended the stairs as quickly as he could, but the house shifted and threw him off-balance. He caught the railing just in time to keep from tumbling down onto the floor below. He steadied his breath and continued down the stairs, through the kitchen, and into the garage. He searched frantically for something to pry Ariel's door open, but Ian's tool collection was sorely lacking. He finally grabbed a hammer and a garden trowel and raced back into the house. Just as he arrived at the bottom of the staircase, a voice like velvet thunder froze him in his tracks.

Wait.

Marshall looked around, searching for the source of the sound, but he wouldn't find anyone there. He knew this voice. He had heard it so many times before. It was the voice of the God he had served for so many centuries. The voice that would speak to him in the holy temple. The voice that would abandon him for decades at a time.

Marshall stood still at the bottom of the stairs, the relentless storm buffeting the house with rain and wind, holding a hammer and a trowel and feeling like a fool. For a moment the fog in his mind lifted and he remembered. He remembered everything. *Everything.*

"What do you want from me?" he said aloud.

There was no reply.

He would not wait. Ariel's life was too great to risk. He had to get her to safety. He'd promised Ian and Lyana he would protect her.

That was now his only mission in life.

He tossed the useless trowel aside and began climbing the steps, numbering each one as he ascended.

• • •

Ian was using his body to hold the door open as the rain continued to soak him. He was squinting into the downpour, hoping to see Marshall and Ariel, willing them to appear so he could usher them down the steps into the safety of the shelter. The freight train roar of the wind increased. He turned toward the opening below.

"I'm going to go after them!" he shouted down to Lyana.

"Hurry, Ian!"

Ian pushed the heavy door up. The wind pushed back. He climbed a single step, but the stair was slick with rain and he slipped. He put his hands down to stop his fall, and the storm door fell above him with a slam. Thankfully it hadn't hit his head.

"Ian!"

"Dad!"

"I'm okay. I…just slipped." He climbed up another stair and put his shoulders against the closed door. "Just a bruise or two, that's all," he said. He reached up and pushed, expecting the door to rise. It didn't move.

"What's wrong?" asked Lyana.

He tried again, using his body as a lever. But the door wouldn't budge even an inch.

"It's stuck!" he said.

Zach had already climbed the stairs and was crouched beside him, mimicking his posture to press up against the door. "We got this, Dad," he said.

"Watch your feet. The stairs are slippery." He reached over and ruffled his son's drenched hair. A faint glow from Lyana's phone below painted shadows on his son's young face, making him appear ten years older.

"On three, okay, Dad?" said Zach.

"On three."

Together they counted. One. Two. Three. They pressed upward with their shoulders.

The door refused to comply.

After several failed attempts, Ian reached over and put his hand on Zach's arm.

"It's good and stuck," he said. "I think we'll just need to wait this out."

"But what about Ariel? And Marshall?" asked Zach. The fear was palpable in Zach's voice.

"Marshall is clever. So is Ariel. They'll figure something out. They'll be fine."

"You don't know that!" said Zach.

No. He didn't know that. But he had to believe. What else was there? "They will be fine."

"Still no luck with the phone," said Lyana. "It's frozen and none of the buttons work."

Ian helped Zach down the stairs into the deep darkness of the small shelter, lit only by Lyana's home screen. The three of them sat on the cold, wet floor. Ian chastised himself for not stocking the space with non-perishable foods and the heavy-duty flashlight they'd found there that worked just fine once they'd replaced the slightly corroded batteries. It's not like he thought they'd ever need to use it.

"Wait, do you hear that?" said Lyana.

Ian started to reply but she shushed him.

"I hear it," said Zach.

Ian focused in on the sounds around him. The thunderous roar of the wind had been supplanted by something else. Something almost human. It was a low humming sound. The hum was joined with another, harmonizing with the first. Ian knew the interval.

"Fifths," said Lyana. She knew it too.

"What do you mean?" asked Zach.

"The tones," said Ian. "They're a fifth apart. Like on a keyboard…"

"That's not the storm," said Lyana.

"I…I don't know what it is," said Ian. The sound was as beautiful as it was haunting.

And then Ian heard something else.

First the water. Then the wind. Then the end.

"Did you hear that?" asked Ian. "That voice?"

"Yes," said Lyana.

"Is…is that the voice you've been hearing?" he asked, but he already knew the answer.

Lyana nodded.

Zach scooted closer to his dad and reached for his hand. Ian took it, then reached for Lyana's with his other hand. "I heard it too," he said.

"What does this all mean?" asked Lyana.

"I don't know," said Ian. They had been through so much together, but this was something new. Something sinister. A chill raced through Ian's veins. He silently prayed Ariel and Marshall had found a safe place to ride out the storm.

A moment later Lyana's phone went completely dead, and they were buried in total blackness.

Zach swallowed loud enough for Ian to hear.

"I think I know what this means," said Zach, his voice brittle as parchment, his fear as palpable as the humidity in the shelter.

"What does it mean?" asked Ian.

"Didn't you notice?" said Zach. He squeezed his dad's hand.

"What?"

“The steps in this shelter are all wrong.”

“What do you mean?” asked Ian.

“There aren’t enough of them.”

Zach didn’t need to say another word. Ian had felt the shift, the sudden change in air pressure. The missing steps confirmed his suspicions. The door above them would open now, he was certain of it. But what would they find when they opened it?

CHAPTER EIGHTEEN

"I DON'T HEAR ANYTHING anymore," said Lyana.

"Me neither," added Zach.

The humming had ended and they were surrounded by a roaring silence. It was clear to Ian something significant had occurred above them while they waited in the damp darkness of the storm shelter.

"Do you think it's safe to try the door again?" asked Lyana.

"What if it's still stuck?" asked Zach.

"Only one way to find out," said Ian. He let go of his son's and wife's hands and carefully felt his way up the steps until his head bumped into the heavy door. Positioning himself just so, he pressed upward. The door didn't move at first. Then, after a popping sound that Ian felt in his neck and his ears, it rose upward. He pushed and the door lifted, then fell open onto the ground above. Ian was frozen by what he saw.

They were still in the woods, at least it appeared to be the same woods where they'd gone to escape the storm. But the sky above was blue. It was midday, by all accounts, and there were no signs that a storm had visited this place. He breathed in and relished the scent of fresh air after spending an uncertain amount of time in the stale, cramped shelter. Zach appeared at his side, then Lyana followed. They all stepped out of the shelter onto the soft forest ground.

"Wow," said Zach.

"How long were we in there?" asked Lyana. She was turning in a slow circle, taking in their surroundings.

"I don't know," said Ian. It hadn't seemed like long, but time had messed with them before, so it wasn't entirely surprising that things weren't adding up.

"Do you smell that?" asked Zach.

"The air…it's different," said Lyana.

"It's so…fresh," said Ian.

"Not that. I mean, yeah, it does smell fresh. But there's another smell."

Ian inhaled another breath through his nose.

"Something's burning," he said.

"Yes!" said Zach.

Ian took in his surroundings. He couldn't be sure, but it seemed like the trees were different too. Something had indeed changed while they were inside the shelter.

"There!" Zach was pointing in the direction of the clearing. At least that's where he believed the clearing should be. Ian continued to find it strange he was so bad at directions on his own property when he was so good at detail in every other aspect of life.

A thin plume of smoke was rising above the trees in the distance. He started to walk toward it.

"Ian, wait," said Lyana.

He stopped.

"We don't know what we're walking into," she added.

"That's the way to the house," said Zach. "Maybe it's on fire!"

"Ariel!" Lyana started running toward the plume.

Zach and Ian chased after her. After a moment, Ian overtook Lyana. He came to an abrupt stop at the edge of the woods. What he saw made no sense to his brain. Their house was unfinished. The framing had been done, and the walls were mostly complete, but this was a work in progress. A single figure stood behind a fire pit that was sending up the trail of smoke. His face was obscured by the smoke.

"This can't be…" began Lyana.

"What happened to our house?" asked Zach.

Ian shook his head. "I think I know the answer to how long we were in the shelter," he said. An unexpected sense of wonder wrestled with a gnawing, uncertain fear in his gut.

Zach exhaled a loud sigh. "Yeah," he said. "Me too."

"What? What are you both not saying?" asked Lyana.

"Um, Lyana…I think…I…know…we went back in time," said Ian. A smile came to his face, despite the utter impossibility of the situation. Or maybe because of it.

"But Ariel! And Marshall," began Lyana.

"I think they're…I don't know what to think," said Ian. Were Ariel and Marshall still in the middle of the storm somewhere in…the future? He prayed again for their safety, then just as quickly wondered how any God could orchestrate such a convoluted storyline for his family. What was the point of all of this?

The man tending the fire in the distance stepped out from behind the smoke and looked directly at them.

"I think he sees us," said Zach.

"So, this is real, then," said Lyana. "I was really hoping this was just a bad dream."

"A dream we're all having?" asked Zach, but then he nodded. "Yeah, that happens."

"I think that might be Marshall," said Ian. "Does he look younger to you?"

"I can't tell," said Lyana.

Ian took a step forward, then paused. As the man's face came into focus, there was no doubt: This was indeed Marshall. Or could this be Mr. Goodpasture, Marshall's uncle? Ian looked again at the unfinished house. He recalled the stereoscopic slide Ariel had found.

Most of those slides were from the late 1800s, but the one with their house under construction was clearly much more recent. *It could be from around this time,* he thought. Maybe a little earlier, since the house seemed more complete.

The man began to approach them. Ian stepped cautiously toward him, gesturing for Zach and Lyana to stay where they were. Unaspiringly, they didn't comply and instead joined him to meet the man in the space between.

The man wore overalls and an old-style beanie on his head that looked like something out of an old black-and-white gangster movie. He appeared to be in his late fifties, but the salt-and-pepper beard made it difficult to know for sure.

Ian stepped up to the man and held out his hand.

"Ian Keane," he said. He introduced Zach and Lyana as well.

The man studied the three Keanes, then he presented his hand.

"Goodpasture," he said.

"Are you sure?" asked Zach. Ian turned toward him and subtly furrowed his brow.

"Mr. Goodpasture, it's good to meet you. We seem to be...a bit lost," said Ian. He wasn't exactly sure how to broach the subject of their sudden appearance on his property. On *their* property. This was so confusing.

Mr. Goodpasture looked them up and down, and in that brief silence Ian wondered how out of place they must look. Did he recognize them somehow? But how could he?

"Well, you're not lost now," said Mr. Goodpasture. "I know right where you are," he said, then offered a small laugh. "You're just in time for tea," he added. Then he turned and started walking across the empty lawn toward the woods. He didn't break stride as he called back, "I promise my humble abode isn't made of gingerbread."

Ian laughed a nervous laugh and whispered to Zach, "Hansel and Gretel."

"Yeah. I got it," said Zach.

Lyana tugged on Ian's arm, and they held back before following Mr. Goodpasture at a distance. "Are you sure this is a good idea?" she asked in a low voice.

"I'm not sure we have many options," said Ian. They could try climbing back into the shelter in hopes it would send them back to their time. But that seemed like a longshot. Maybe they needed to be here. But for what?

"You should ask him what year it is," said Zach.

"Don't you think that might make him suspicious?" asked Lyana.

"Pretty sure he already is a bit suspicious," said Zach. "What if he remembers us?"

"Remembers us? How?" asked Lyana. "This is Marshall's uncle. Right?"

"I think it's really Marshall, but who really knows with all this timey-wimey stuff," said Zach. Ian could tell his son was intrigued by their current circumstance. His head was on a swivel, eyes wide, looking all around the property they called home.

"I'll think of something," Ian said.

They followed a worn footpath into the woods. Up ahead was a cabin. It appeared to be the same cabin Marshall lived in during their time but looked much newer. A line of sawdust painted the dirt between two sawhorses in the front yard. A small wooden table and bench sat just outside the front door. Ian noted that the window he could see didn't seem to have any glass in it. On the table sat a wooden tray and four mugs. It was almost as if he'd expected them.

"And no," Mr. Goodpasture began, "I did not know you were coming." He indicated the tray. "I was expecting a crew to arrive later today to work on the house. I like to be prepared." He indicated the mugs, then picked one up and turned it upside down, dumping out a wayward leaf. "Give me a few minutes and I'll have a pot of tea ready." He excused himself and went into the tiny cabin.

"This is totally weird," said Zach. He walked up and lifted one of the mugs, looking it over. "It's heavy," he said.

Lyana once again tugged on Ian's shirt and pulled him aside. "Do you think it's safe to be here?"

"I don't think this man is dangerous, whoever he really is."

"No, no. I don't mean that. I mean…" She waved her arms around, indicating their surroundings. "I mean the timeline. What if we screw something up? Remember that short story you had me read?"

"I'm going to need a little more here, Lyana."

"The one by Ray Bradbury…something about thunder?"

"'A Sound of Thunder'?" said Ian.

"Yes! That's the one. It's the butterfly effect. What if we step on a metaphorical butterfly and accidentally change the future? What if…" Tears began to form in her eyes. "What if we never see Ariel again?"

Ian wrapped Lyana in a hug. "We'll see Ariel again," he said. "I don't understand what's happening here, but it's all going to be okay."

"How can you be so sure?"

"Because I just am," he said. Was he?

A few minutes later, Mr. Goodpasture appeared carrying a teapot and a tin over to the table.

"Please, sit," he said, gesturing to the long bench. "You must be tired from your journey," he added.

"I didn't say we were on a journey," said Ian.

"Oh, no, you didn't," he said, shaking his head. He began to pour tea into the mugs. "But there's not much out this way, so you must have walked a long time to end up here."

Lyana nodded. "Thank you…Mr. Goodpasture. We are indeed tired," she said, carefully wiping the tear streaks from her cheek.

Mr. Goodpasture opened the tin to reveal a variety of small cookies and set it on the table. The tin looked old, but it could just be a keepsake from another time. Ian scanned his surroundings, hoping to find clues that could help him determine the year. The cabin was relatively new, but Marshall had never told him when it was built. There was so little to go on. He had no choice but to simply ask outright.

"Mr. Goodpasture, I have a rather strange question to ask you." He hesitated.

Zach couldn't abide the wait. "What year is it?" he nearly shouted.

Mr. Goodpasture's expression had been mostly unreadable to that point, but Zach's question clearly caught him off guard.

"What year?" the bearded man repeated.

Zach nodded.

"1974," Mr. Goodpasture said, a look of puzzlement on his face. He sipped his tea, all the while staring at Zach. It was almost creepy how intensely he stared. "You really aren't from around here," he finally said, turning to Ian.

Lyana set her teacup down and placed her hand on Ian's. He knew that signal: She was prepared to take over the conversation. He just needed to sit there and listen. And back her up, whatever path the conversation took.

"I absolutely love Zach's imagination," said Lyana. "He's a huge science fiction fan, aren't you, Zach?" Zach scrunched his face into a question, but Lyana didn't wait for him to respond. "What Ian wanted to ask was…" She paused and Ian squirmed, wondering what she was going to say next. "How long have you been building that house?" she said.

Ian breathed a sigh of relief, then tried to conceal the action by blowing on his tea.

"Hot," Ian said. Lyana squeezed his hand.

"I've been working on this house for about a year now," began Mr. Goodpasture. "I bought the property a while ago, but…" Marshall paused. "It's taken me some time to source all the materials." He smiled, but Ian sensed sadness in that smile. "I like doing things right," he added, bending the sad smile into a sincere one. "Would you like a tour?" Mr. Goodpasture asked.

Zach nodded vigorously.

"We'd love one," said Lyana.

"It's still a work in progress," said Mr. Goodpasture, "but the bones are good and it's mostly safe to walk around in." Zach grabbed a cookie from the tin and stood up. His tea sat on the table, untouched.

"Not a big fan of tea, are you?" said Mr. Goodpasture.

"Not really," he answered.

Ian helped Lyana stand and the three of them stood there waiting for Mr. Goodpasture to finish his tea. He took a long sip, gently placed the mug on the table, then stood and led them back along the dirt path toward the clearing. Ian glanced back at the cabin, half wondering if it would still be there when he looked.

It was.

• • •

Mr. Goodpasture felt unsettled as he led the three strangers through the clearing. Why did this family seem so familiar? And what was with the clothing they wore? *Maybe they're from California*, he thought. He shook the random thought away, but one big question remained: What were they doing here?

Mr. Goodpasture started the tour at the lamp-post out front. He tried to read Zach's face as the young boy took in the sight of the imposing post. Did the boy recognize it somehow?

"That lamp-post makes quite a statement," said Lyana.

He nodded. "I like that it's the first thing people see when they come down the driveway." There was so much more he could say about the lamp-post, but that was a story he'd have to keep to himself. Even if they'd heard about the Lighthouse of Alexandria, there was little chance they'd believe a piece of it had not only survived but was right there in front of them. He had learned long ago to choose his words carefully. He would continue to do so now.

"How is it powered?" asked Zach.

"What an astute question," Mr. Goodpasture said.

"And the answer is?" said Ian.

"Magic," was the reply.

Zach's face twisted into a question. "Really?"

"Why yes, of course," answered Mr. Goodpasture. "That is, if you consider electricity magic. I certainly do."

Zach's wonder morphed into an eyeroll, bringing a smile to Mr. Goodpasture's face.

He took them through the front door into the main section of the house. They stood in the entry foyer while he described all the ways the house was going to be finished, being careful not to say too much about the origin of the components he had gathered to turn the Tudor-style home into his masterpiece. Lyana marveled at the stained glass that would eventually be fitted to the front door. Ian was impressed by the stone wall that was mostly complete in the room down the hall. Zach was clearly disappointed that they couldn't tour the upper floor, but the makeshift steps were too risky to traverse at this stage of construction, and the framing there was also incomplete. Still, he tried to paint as complete a picture as possible about what the house would look like when finished.

"It's beautiful," said Lyana. Did he detect more tears in her eyes? He had seen her wipe some away back at the cabin, too. She didn't seem like the overly emotional type. She appeared strong and wise.

Like Esme.

Mr. Goodpasture sighed and embraced a moment of awkward silence. The sound of the nearby stream trickled in through the sheets of plastic that served as temporary windows. He felt calmed by that sound.

"What's that lead to? Is there a basement?" Zach asked. He was pointing to a hole in the floor at the far end of the living room. "I mean, I know there's no basement, but..." He stopped.

"No, there's no basement. That's just temporary," said Mr. Goodpasture. "I'm still doing some work on the plumbing and electrical."

"Can we look down there, too?" Zach asked.

"It's just a bunch of dirt and concrete," began Mr. Goodpasture.

"I don't think we need to go down there," said Lyana.

"Please?" pleaded Zach. Ian looked over at Mr. Goodpasture with raised eyebrows. It was obvious he, too, was interested in seeing the foundation.

"Why not," said Mr. Goodpasture. He walked toward the hole and began climbing down a makeshift ladder constructed of two-by-fours. "But be careful down the ladder and watch your head down below."

He climbed down, then reached over to a stud where he'd tacked up a simple switch that would turn on the trio of bare bulbs he'd strung below the floor joists he could work into the night on the fussy electrical system.

A moment later, Zach and Ian had joined him. There really wasn't much to see under the house, but Marshall understood the draw of the unknown to a young boy. He had once been that curious boy himself.

A long, long time ago.

"What do you think?" asked Mr. Goodpasture.

"It looks like the foundation of a house," said Ian. "A solid foundation, that's for sure."

"I think it looks totally awesome," said Zach. He started to follow the line of lights strung above.

"I don't think we should do much exploring here," said Ian.

"Why? Because of spiders?" said Zach. He started looking around. "I'm not afraid of spiders."

"Maybe more because of nails?" Ian said, pointing to one that Zach's hand had just missed while reaching for a foundation timber.

"Your dad is right. It's not particularly safe down here."

Ian was running his hand gently across one of the vertical beams. "What kind of wood is this? It looks…"

"Old?" said Mr. Goodpasture.

"Yes."

"I had it imported from overseas." That much was true anyway. They didn't need to know the rest of the details. "It's supposed to last forever."

"I can see why," said Ian. He seemed duly impressed.

"What's in there?" Zach had inched forward and was pointing to a metal door that stood half-open in the very center of the room, wedged into the concrete footing. Mr. Goodpasture's heart ached as he recalled the day he'd poured the concrete for that footing.

"That's…it's like a memento box," he said.

"Kind of like a time capsule?" asked Zach.

"Yes, like that."

"Can we look inside?"

"Zach, I think that's a private sort of thing," said Ian. He turned to Mr. Goodpasture, who nodded. Ian gestured for Zach to come back to the ladder, then ushered the boy up before following behind.

Mr. Goodpasture walked over to the small metal door and stood there for a moment before closing it. After climbing the ladder, he slid a sheet of plywood over the opening and led the others back outside. Zach immediately went over to the lamp-post and began studying it again.

"Do you have supper plans?" asked Mr. Goodpasture.

"I'm not sure exactly what our plans are," said Ian. He gave a curious look to his wife, then turned back to Mr. Goodpasture. "Is there a restaurant within walking distance? Or maybe we could call an Uber…" Lyana coughed and then Ian continued, "I mean we could call a cab? Our transportation options are a little limited."

"You can say that again," said Zach. Mr. Goodpasture noted that Lyana was quick to shush the young boy. What were they hiding?

"There's a new diner in town, but I can't vouch for the food. Never eaten there."

"Never hasn't happened yet," said Zach.

Mr. Goodpasture smiled. "Now there's a true statement if I've ever heard one."

"The diner sounds great," said Lyana. "Do you have a phone we could use to call for a cab?"

"A phone? 'Fraid not. Haven't gotten that wired up yet. But I could take you if you don't mind squeezing into a small truck."

"Oh, I didn't see a vehicle out front," said Ian.

"It's behind the cabin. There's another road back there, though it's a bit of a stretch to call it a road. Still, it can get us places."

"Then let's go," said Zach. "I'm starving!"

Mr. Goodpasture ruffled the boy's hair, then immediately wondered why he'd done that. This was so unlike him.

"Sorry," he said. "You just remind me of someone," he said, hopeful that his vague excuse would be enough.

"It's fine," said Zach. "I'm getting used to it."

Zach looked over at his father, and the intimacy between them was almost too much for Mr. Goodpasture to bear.

The ache of longing returned with a vengeance.

CHAPTER NINETEEN

"ARIEL!"

Ariel heard Marshall's voice above the commotion of the raging storm that had forced its way into her bedroom. She reached for the closet door and cautiously pushed it open with some effort. Papers swirled in her room, her own private tornado. She was momentarily mesmerized by the sight, but frantic pounding at her door quickly brought her back to reality.

Pound. Pound. Pound.

The doorknob rattled, then twisted, then fell to the floor. A second later, the door burst open. Marshall stood there holding a hammer in mid-strike. He called out to Ariel, and she pushed the closet door fully open. In the strange greenish light of the storm, Marshall's wrinkled face looked like that of a crazed lunatic. An image from a movie she wished she'd never seen flashed in her memory. *The Shining.*

Ariel hesitated. What if he wasn't really there to help her?

"Ariel!" Marshall shouted. "We need to get to safety. Now!"

The wind howled another warning, blowing the closet door closed. She tried opening it again, but it wouldn't budge. Something had fallen in front of it.

"I...I can't open it," she called out. Again, the house shook. Ariel had never experienced an earthquake, but this was exactly how she imagined it would feel. She tried the power on her cell phone again. Nothing.

"I hate this house!" she shouted through her tears of fear, as if somehow her anger could convince the storm to subside. Instead, boxes fell from the shelf above her as the wind rattled the house once again. She pushed them away and resumed the tornado position, praying to a god she didn't believe in that she would be spared. Or that her death would be quick.

The tornado was coming for this house.

For her.

"Ariel."

Ariel looked up to see Marshall standing outside the closet, fighting with the wind to keep the door open. Her dresser was lying on its back just to the side of the door. Marshall reached his free hand to her.

"Ariel," he said again, his voice unnaturally calm amidst the turmoil. "We need to go."

Ariel felt the wind on her face as she took Marshall's hand and fought her way out of the tumble and disarray of her closet into a mess that barely resembled her bedroom. Marshall's grip was strong, his hand marked with calluses that suggested a lifetime of physical labor. She contrasted this with a memory of visiting his cabin, of the delicately carved fauna that decorated a shelf there. Marshall was more than just a strange old man. He was a true enigma. Seconds after he pulled her from the closet, the unrelenting wind ripped the closet door from its hinges and threw it to the floor with a vengeance. If she had remained in the closet...She shuddered and pushed the awful thought away.

Down the stairs they went, holding tight to the railing as the house continued to rumble. Ariel couldn't shake the image of Dorothy's house spinning away in a twister as they reached the bottom of the stairs. Marshall didn't let go as he led them to the front door. When he twisted the knob, the door flew open, smacking Marshall's head before slamming against the wall. He reached up and his hand came back red with blood.

"Marshall!" Ariel let go of his hand and ran into the kitchen. She grabbed a kitchen towel and returned, handing it to him. He held it up to his head.

"I'm okay," he said. "Just a superficial wound." He reached for Ariel's hand again.

She hesitated, seeing that it was covered with blood. He looked down, wiped his hand against his shirt, then reached out again. A gust blew through the open front door and knocked over a table lamp.

"We're out of time," Marshall said. He didn't wait for Ariel to take his hand but grabbed it and started pulling.

Stepping outside was like stepping into another world. The sky was emerald green and black, the trees were being whipped into a blur like an impressionist painting. Branches and boards and who knows what flew by in front of them, caught up in the twist of a massive tornado, as if they were somehow standing in the very middle of it.

"It's too late," said Marshall. He nearly dragged her back inside the house, then struggled to close the front door. "We'll have to ride it out and hope for the best."

First the water. Then the wind. Then the end.

Ariel froze. "Did you hear that?"

Marshall's face fell and Ariel's confidence in him fell with it. The sudden change in his demeanor scared Ariel almost more than the terrifying storm. He just stood there in the foyer, his face ashen.

Then, suddenly, he came to life again. "The closet under the stairs!" he shouted, then once again grabbed her hand. He led her to the door, opened it and ushered her inside. He didn't follow.

"I'll be right behind you. I just need to get something first," he said.

Ariel started to object, but the door closed and she was alone. Outside, the wind howled, the house groaned, and everything rattled as she once again assumed the position of a child hiding from the tornado that was tearing her world apart.

• • •

First the water. Then the wind. Then the end.

Marshall sorted through the words for their meaning as he raced up the stairs and down the hall to Ian and Lyana's bedroom.

It was a long shot, but the unrelenting storm left him with no other option.

He bolted through the bedroom door and ran to the dresser where he had seen the pendant once before.

"Please be here," he said to himself.

He opened the jewelry box and scanned the contents for the familiar stone, shuffling through rings and bracelets and necklaces. But it wasn't there. The fire opal was missing.

Marshall tried to recall what Lyana looked like when he'd left them earlier. Could she be wearing the opal pendant? He closed his eyes, and a snapshot of Lyana's frightened face came into focus. And there, hanging on a chain around her neck, was the fire opal.

His heart fell.

This was his last resort. There was nothing more he could do.

A loud snap followed by a sound like rolling thunder turned Marshall's attention to the bedroom window. But before he could race out of the room, a huge tree trunk came crashing down onto the house, breaking through the roof and pinning Marshall to the floor.

He cried out in pain, feeling every bit of the heavy trunk pressing down on him.

He began to laugh at the insanity of the moment but stopped when he felt a sharp pain in his chest. He had cheated death for millennia. Or maybe death had cheated him. Surely this was not how it was destined to end.

Marshall looked at the bedroom door. The tree that had pinned him to the ground was also pressed up against the closed door. The only thing he could do now was pray for Ariel's safety. For all the Keanes' safety.

But before he could put together the words, he heard pounding on the door.

"Marshall!"

The door budged just a little, and the wind whipped through the broken wall in response.

"Ariel, don't worry about me. Get yourself to safety!"

"I won't leave you," she said. The door budged again, then fell closed as the branch pressing up against it slipped down further. "I…I can't move it."

"Esme…"

As he called out the wrong name, the storm suddenly stilled. It was as if someone had pressed "pause." Even the curtains that were hanging askew from the broken curtain rod stopped flapping.

The pounding on the door stopped.

"Marshall?" Ariel's voice was small, scared. "What…what is happening?"

"I…I don't know," he said. But he had his suspicions. Like so many of the strange events that had happened in the last few months, this was surely the work of a supernatural power. Perhaps an intervention from the very God he had served for so long.

The door pushed open a few inches. "Maybe I can move it now that the storm has stopped."

"Ariel, I don't think the storm is over. Not yet. I think this is merely a pause."

"A pause for what?"

Marshall looked at the crack in the door and saw Ariel's eyes staring back at him. He saw fear, but he also saw something else. Anger. He sighed and felt the sharp pain in his chest once again.

"I know you've been upset about all that's been happening to your family."

"Ya think?"

"I do."

Ariel pushed against the blocked door again, and it budged another inch or so.

"There's a lot that even I don't understand," he continued. "But some things…there are some things I think you should know."

• • •

In frustration, with tears running down her smudged face, Ariel stopped pushing against the door and leaned against it, then slid to a sitting position. She trained her ear on Marshall's voice. His voice was strong but labored, and he sounded sad.

"It's all my parents' fault!" she shouted.

"What?"

"This," she said, waving her arms around the house that was falling apart in front of her. "All of it. We should never have moved here in the first place."

"Ariel, this house…"

"This house! This house has tried to kill us! And even after all of that, what do my parents do? They say, 'This is where we're meant to be.' That's insane! Don't you see how insane that is?" She shook her head. "Why am I even telling you this? You've been lying to us from day one. And don't even get me started on my parents. They're worse! They've been lying for years!" Ariel swiped tears along with the rain-soaked hair from her face.

"You're right," said Marshall. "I haven't been entirely truthful with you. And I'm sorry for that. I've been careful with my words because..."

"Because you don't think we can handle the truth?" Ariel said with disdain.

"Well, in a way, yes. But it's more complicated than that."

"Why is telling the truth so hard for adults?"

"Things aren't always what they seem," said Marshall. "But there is a way for you to see the truth. The whole truth."

"What do you mean?"

"Downstairs, in the pantry, is a mirror."

"Yeah, I know. So what?" Ariel's patience with Marshall was growing thin.

"Do you trust me?"

"What? No. I don't trust anyone right now." Did that also apply to Garrett? The thought made her stomach ache.

"Go to the mirror. Look in it. You will find the truth there."

Ariel shook her head. "That's a big fat nope." There was no way she was going to stare into a cracked mirror in a house that was intent on destroying her family. Not alone, anyway. She stood, braced herself against the door, and pushed with all her might. The door budged a little more. She did it again, and again. Finally, the door burst open, snapping a branch before slamming against the wall. Ariel stood in the doorway, looking across the room to the man who was pinned to the ground by a large tree trunk. She shook her head again, disbelieving the scene before her. It was as if the tornado had lifted a tree and flung it with purpose into the room where Marshall now lay. Like it was targeting him. His eyes were bright, but he looked small and broken.

"I know how crazy it sounds..." began Marshall with a heavy breath.

"Do you really?"

"...but you really need to trust me on this."

"I'm not looking in that mirror all by myself," she said. She stepped around a shattered chair and walked up to the tree trunk. "You're coming with me." She tried lifting the branch, but it was too heavy.

"We don't have much time," said Marshall. "The storm could be back any second. Just go!"

"No! I will not go alone!" She scanned the room for something to wedge under the tree trunk but found nothing. "Hang on," she said, then raced out of the room. She bypassed her room and went straight to Zach's. After digging around in his closet, she found an old aluminum baseball bat. Zach had tried to play baseball once but struggled to find his place in that team environment. Ariel could still recall the day he came home from practice and slammed the bat onto the floor of their foyer, chipping the tile. She was sure her parents would be angry at him for the outburst, but instead they had been calm and patient. They gave him the space to express himself before sitting down to talk with him. She had marveled then at how her parents handled the situation. Oh, how she longed for those simpler times.

Ariel carried the bat to her parents' room. The eerie pause in the storm continued, but the air smelled oddly familiar. She shuddered when she recalled the pungent scent of melting plastic and cat urine from back when the wiring in the house tried to kill her mother. Wordlessly, Ariel went to work, wedging the bat under the tree trunk in the only place she could, then began pulling, pushing, prying it upward. At first there was no movement, but then the tree trunk shifted. Marshall dragged himself out from under the massive obstacle. Ariel let go, and the heavy trunk slammed back onto the carpeted floor, sending a cloud of dust into the stilled air.

"Can you walk?" asked Ariel.

Marshall stood slowly, then cautiously took a single step. "I can," he said, then immediately stumbled.

Ariel caught him, hooked her arm around him and ushered him out the door, then carefully down the stairs. They shuffled toward the pantry. The mirror had slipped to the floor in all the chaos of the storm and was lying there face up, its cracked surface looking for all the world like a doll's skating rink. Marshall leaned on the door frame and carefully lowered himself to the floor. He sat to catch his breath.

"What do I do?" asked Ariel.

"Look into it," he replied.

Ariel had seen enough scary movies to know that this was a terrible idea. But the winds suddenly whipped up and the storm was raging in earnest again. It was as if the tornado was a living thing and it was just hovering outside their house, waiting for the right moment to strike again. Maybe she should just hide in the closet under the stairs after all.

Something in her gut told her to stay put. She stepped up to the edge of the mirror and looked down into it. At first, all she saw was her dirt-crusted face and unkempt hair. She brushed a wayward strand from her bruised cheek. She was just about to tell Marshall how stupid this idea was when the cracks in the mirror began to brighten, like there was a light shining from behind. And then, a sudden flash…

Lyana is on a couch. Ariel knows this couch. It's the one they had back in their Boston home. The one that sagged just a bit in the middle. Ariel had loved that couch and the way the curve of the cushions drew her and her mother closer when they sat on it together.

Her mother looks different. Ariel can't remember when her mother looked like this. She is so young here. She is curled up in the fetal position and crying. Ariel wants to call out to her mother to comfort her, but she is a ghost without a voice, observing this scene playing out in front of her with no opportunity to intervene.

The scene blurs and now Ariel's father is standing in front of Lyana, his briefcase on the floor next to him. He is wearing a tan blazer that Ariel doesn't recognize. It is so soaked from an apparent rainstorm it's almost brown. Water drips from his hair. A muted roll of thunder interrupts the silence.

"I'm so sorry," says Ian.

Sorry for what? Ariel wants to ask.

Her mother doesn't reply.

"I should have been here," Ian says. He walks up to her, hesitant, then kneels in front of the couch and takes her hands. She uncurls from the fetal position and sits forward while Ian wraps her in a hug. The intimacy is almost too much for Ariel to bear, but she can't look away.

"We lost her," says Lyana. "We lost our little girl."

Wait. What? Ariel is confused. She wants to shout, "You didn't lose me! I'm right here!" but still she has no voice.

Rain continues to drip from her father's hair. No, not just rain. Tears. Her father is crying. She can't remember the last time she saw her father cry.

And then she hears a small voice in the distance.

"Mama…" says the voice. It repeats the word over and over.

"I'll get her," says Ian. He gently removes himself from their embrace and leaves the room. The edges of Ariel's vision are blurry, so she can't see where he's gone.

The scene shifts again and he's back, sitting next to Lyana, holding a little girl in pink pajamas who is rubbing her eyes.

"Mama," says the toddler again.

"Your mama is sad," says Ian. "I'm sad, too."

The little girl reaches out toward her mother. Ariel knows now that she is that little girl.

"Mama," she says again. It is her only word.

Lyana swipes at the tears on her face and takes the little girl into her arms. "I'm sorry, sweetie…" And then her words fail.

"We so wanted you to meet your new sister," says Ian.

No, thinks Ariel. That's not the way it happened. This is a lie. You only told me you lost the baby because you wanted to hide the truth! This can't be the truth.

"Someday we'll tell you about her," says Ian.

Ariel wants to shout at them. Call them liars. They didn't lose the baby. They got rid of it. They killed her sister in the womb because they were young and stupid and selfish. So selfish. She overheard them shouting at each other about it. They even separated for a while over it. There were so many clues along the way. Things hinted at. Things unsaid. It took Ariel a while to piece those clues together, but she is certain she got it right. Ariel isn't wrong about this. She got it right.

Things aren't always what they seem.

Marshall's words. But what does he know? He's not a part of her family. He's just a weird old man who lies. How can she trust anyone at all…

Ariel is in a hospital room, standing next to a bed where her mother lies. She is in pain. Doctors and nurses are attending to her in ordered panic. Monitors are beeping their warnings. And then a doctor is beside her, holding her hand.

"I'm so sorry," he is saying. "I'm so very sorry."

The nurse standing beside him is wiping away a tear.

The truth washes over Ariel like a tidal wave.

Ariel feels it in her bones and knows it in her heart.

Ariel was wrong. So wrong. How could she get this so very wrong?

When Ariel opened her eyes, a tear fell onto the mirror. It landed on a crack, and then something impossible happened. Where the tear fell, it followed the path of the crack and congealed into gold. Beautiful, glimmering gold. She watched in wonder as the gold traveled along all the fault lines, turning each one gold, healing the mirror. It was the most beautiful thing Ariel had ever seen.

"Oh my."

It was Marshall's voice. He was standing now, holding his aching chest with eyes wide in wonder, leaning against the doorframe and watching as the mirror healed itself.

Ariel turned to Marshall and did something she never thought she'd do. She rushed over to him and hugged him. Tight.

"Thank you," she said through the fountain of tears.

Marshall winced in pain but hugged Ariel back. In a quiet voice, he responded, "I know what I need to do."

CHAPTER TWENTY

LYANA PICKED UP the menu and glanced at the offerings. "Can you believe these prices?" she whispered to Ian. "Everything is so cheap."

"I hope no one is hungry," he whispered back. "I don't think the bank where I got my debit card even exists yet, and I only have five dollars in cash."

"I didn't think to bring my purse to the storm shelter," said Lyana, shrugging.

She turned to Zach.

"Don't look at me," he said. "All I have is a rock." He reached into his pocket and pulled out the fire opal he'd discovered after returning from his adventure. Lyana knew he rarely went anywhere without it. He turned the stone over in his hands.

"We can just get drinks," said Lyana.

"Maybe fries, too?" said Zach.

"Maybe fries, too," said Ian.

Mr. Goodpasture finished talking with the worker at the counter and walked back to join them at the table in the back of the small café.

"This is their third week of business," he said, pulling out a chair and sitting down. "Family-owned business. See that young man over there?" He pointed to a young man sitting next to a woman about the same age. They were both seated on the same side of the booth.

Lyana nodded.

"He's the owner's son. He wants nothing to do with the café. He's planning on moving to Spain once he graduates."

"He's totally into that girl," said Zach.

Lyana was surprised by Zach's comment. Did he really just say that?

"Oh, yes, he's definitely into that girl," said Mr. Goodpasture. "That's why his dad isn't too concerned about losing him to some pipe dream of living abroad."

Lyana shook her head. "You learned all that just from talking to that man?"

"That man is the owner. And yes, you can learn a lot from a single conversation in a small town," said Mr. Goodpasture. "I really should make an effort to get out more," he added, presumably to himself. "Please order whatever you like. My treat."

Lyana looked over at Ian, but before either of them could talk, Zach practically shouted, "Fries! With cheese."

Mr. Goodpasture laughed. "Of course," he said.

"That's very generous of you, Mr. Goodpasture," said Ian. "But you don't have to…"

"I insist. It's not often I get a visit from three strangers. Since none of you are ghosts and it's nowhere near Christmas, I'm just happy this isn't some kind of intervention."

"Huh?" said Zach.

"He's talking about *A Christmas Carol*. You know, Scrooge and the three ghosts?" said Ian.

"Oh, right. Yeah. Pretty sure we're not ghosts," said Zach. The way he measured his words told Lyana he was actually considering that possibility.

"Well, thank you," said Lyana.

The owner came over and took their orders. When he walked away, Mr. Goodpasture was staring at Zach's hands.

"What's that you have there?" he asked.

Zach held up the stone, and Lyana could swear Mr. Goodpasture stopped breathing.

"Where…" he paused. "May I?" He reached out, and Zach paused before dropping the opal into Mr. Goodpasture's hand.

"This is beautiful," he said, studying the stone. "I had one like this…" And then he stopped. The air around them seemed to shift again. Lyana looked over at the window, expecting to see thunder-clouds. But it remained a perfect, blue-sky day.

"Oh, Lloyd, it's beautiful!" A squeal from the young woman at the booth grabbed Lyana's attention as the girl lifted a sparkling necklace from a velvet box. The young man was beaming almost as brightly as the shimmering stone that hung from the silver chain.

Mr. Goodpasture looked over at the booth. "He's smitten."

Lyana tugged at Ian's sleeve and whispered, "*His name is Lloyd.*"

Ian was already staring at the couple.

"It can't be…" he began.

"I did the math. It *could* be," said Lyana.

They were a little too far away for Lyana to get a good look at the young man's eyes, but the smile on his face was too familiar to ignore. In a few decades, that young man would become one of their greatest allies and friends.

"Do you think the girl…?" began Ian. He didn't need to say any more. Surely this was the young woman Lloyd would one day marry. The rest of the story fell into place, and Lyana felt the weight of Lloyd's eventual heartbreak. Here he was, a young man, so in love. So full of hope. Clueless about what the future would bring.

If only she could warn him…

Ian reached over and took Lyana's hand. The message was clear. He was feeling the same way, but there was nothing they could do.

That's when the weight of their own story landed with a thud in Lyana's thoughts. They needed to get back home. They had to get back. *Ariel!*

What if they couldn't?

Tell your story.

Lyana looked at Ian, but he was still watching the young couple. Was the voice just inside her head this time? There was no going back once she broached the subject, but she had little choice.

"Mr. Goodpasture," she began. He was still turning over Zach's stone in his hand, studying it as if looking for a distinguishing mark.

"Hmm?" He looked at her.

"What I'm about to say is going to sound totally unbelievable." Ian opened his mouth to object, but she squeezed his hand. He nodded for her to continue.

"Try me," said Mr. Goodpasture. He set Zach's stone on the table.

"When we said we're not from around here, that was both true and a lie."

Mr. Goodpasture didn't flinch.

Lyana paused to look around the restaurant. "Maybe we should have this conversation elsewhere?" She turned to Ian.

"We're actually from around here," said Zach. "Just not yet."

This time Mr. Goodpasture raised an eyebrow. "Not yet?"

"What Zach means is..." Lyana lowered her voice. "We're pretty sure we traveled back in time."

"Oh?" Mr. Goodpasture leaned back, a smile on his weathered face. Then the smile faded. "Oh," he said again, but this time it was a statement. "Please, say more."

Lyana turned to Ian.

"Let Zach tell it," he said.

Zach picked up his stone and eyed it as if trying to see what Mr. Goodpasture had been looking for. He took a deep breath, then began talking, his voice animated. "Okay, so we're from like forty years in the future or something like that. And we live in that house you're building. My room is the second one down the hall upstairs. It's totally awesome, by the way. The house, I mean. Apart from the bees...Anyway, there was a huge storm and a tornado, and we raced to the storm shelter in the woods to be safe, but my sister and Marshall were still in the house, and my dad was going to go back to get them, but the storm door wouldn't open, so we got stuck there. Then some strange stuff happened with the air, and we could finally get out but when we climbed out it wasn't then anymore, it was now. And..." He took a deep breath. "And we need to get back."

Mr. Goodpasture didn't respond for a moment. Then he nodded toward the booth across the restaurant. "You know them," he says. "In your time."

Lyana looked over at the couple. "Only the young man," she said, "I think."

Mr. Goodpasture nodded. "I know a few things about time," he said after another long pause.

Lyana leaned forward, and her pendant slipped out from under her shirt. She began to stuff it back under her collar when Mr. Goodpasture held up his hand.

"Wait," he said. "That pendant." He pointed.

Lyana held it out in front of her. "This? It's a family heirloom. I don't think it's worth much to a jeweler, but it means the world to me. It's been in my family for..."

"Decades," said Mr. Goodpasture.

"What?"

"Okay," he said with a sigh. "Now it's my turn. What *I'm* about to say is going to sound totally unbelievable," began Mr. Goodpasture. "I know that stone. And I think..." He pointed to Zach's stone. "I know that one as well."

Zach scrunched his face into a question. Then, slowly, his face morphed into something like recognition.

"I'm remembering a word," Zach began, his face wide with wonder. "I don't know where it comes from, but it's there in my head as bright as a neon sign." He closed his eyes, his mouth moving but not saying anything. Then, just one word, "Akolo."

Mr. Goodpasture's expression changed in an instant. He looked intently at Zach.

"I've seen that word somewhere before, too," said Ian.

"Not a word," said Mr. Goodpasture. "A name."

"Yes!" shouted Zach.

Mr. Goodpasture took in a deep breath, then let it out. His countenance changed with the exhale. "*My* name," he said at last. The words lingered with the weight of his revelation.

"Akolo," Zach repeated cautiously. A smile slowly formed on his face as his eyes opened wide. "Akolo!"

"I don't understand," said Ian, looking puzzled.

Mr. Goodpasture reached across the table and placed his hand on Zach's. Lyana thought for sure Zach would pull his hand back. He was so sensitive about touch, especially the touch of strangers, but Zach didn't move his hand.

"What do you remember?" asked Mr. Goodpasture.

"Just bits and pieces," said Zach. "It's mostly blurry. Like how the trees look when you're driving on the highway."

A tear had formed in Mr. Goodpasture's eye. "Most of my memories are filed away in a box hidden among a multitude of boxes..."

"Like in *Indiana Jones*!" said Zach.

Mr. Goodpasture tilted his head. "I'm not familiar..."

"Zach, that doesn't come out for another six or seven years," said Ian.

"Oh, right. Sorry. It's a movie. A good one. Should have started with 'spoiler alert,' then." Zach shrugged. "Anyway, there's a scene after Indy finds an ancient chest where they box it up and put it in a giant warehouse that's filled with similar-looking boxes..."

"A gold chest?" asked Mr. Goodpasture.

"Yes," said Ian. "It was a religious artifact..."

Mr. Goodpasture nodded. "I'm also familiar with religious artifacts."

Just then, their food arrived.

"I think we should eat. We can continue this conversation back at the house," said Mr. Goodpasture. Zach nodded eagerly and started stuffing his face with cheesy fries.

Lyana was hungry, but she could only nibble on the club sandwich in front of her. A different kind of hunger was vying for her attention. A hunger for information. For resolution.

For the truth.

Lyana fingered the stone in her pendant, and a memory flashed before her.

She is sitting on a park bench on a cold December day, holding a sandwich wrapped in butcher paper. A distinguished older man comes up to her, engages her in conversation. He notices her pendant, calls it lovely. And then he offers advice that alters the course of her life. "Sometimes a change of scenery is exactly what a person needs."

Lyana returns to the moment. "You," she begins. "I met you while I was sitting on a park bench in Boston."

Ian had lifted his burger to his mouth, then stopped. He slowly lowered the burger. "I was lecturing at the Seeon Abbey in Bavaria, Germany. I sensed a presence, and saw a figure watching me in the wings…"

Mr. Goodpasture smiled and offered half a shrug. "These things have not happened yet. Perhaps they yet will."

"Argh," said Zach with a mouthful of fries. "This time-travel stuff is so confusing."

Mr. Goodpasture laughed. It was the best sound Lyana had heard all day. She continued to pick at her sandwich while everyone else finished their meal. As they left the café, Lyana made a slight detour to walk by the booth where the young couple still sat.

"Sorry to interrupt," she said. "But I just had to say…you two make such a cute couple." Lloyd didn't take his eyes off his girlfriend but managed to offer a polite "thank you." The sound of his voice brought a lump to Lyana's throat. She quickly excused herself and turned to join the others before the tears began to fall.

CHAPTER TWENTY-ONE

"WHY ARE WE doing this again?" asked Ariel. She shivered in the wind-whipped rain as Marshall unlocked the door that led to the crawlspace below the house.

"This is the safest place to be right now," said Marshall.

Ariel didn't think that could remotely be true, but she didn't want to be alone in the house as it shook in the unrelenting storm. She glanced back and saw what looked like a battalion of black clouds encroaching upon their backyard. The word *menacing* only scratched the surface of what they looked like.

"There," said Marshall. He held the small metal door open, fighting the wind, and gestured for Ariel to climb through it into the crawlspace.

"I don't know if I can do this..."

"I know you can," said Marshall.

Slowly, she bent down, then crawled through the opening into the darkness below. "We should have brought a flashlight," she said as Marshall followed her down, the door swinging closed behind him.

"As long as the power still works..." he said. Marshall brushed past Ariel, sending shivers down her spine. A moment later, there was a soft *click*, and a single bare bulb lit up somewhere in the middle of the surprisingly vast, mud-lined space.

She had never been under the house before. Not because she was claustrophobic. She was fine with small spaces. What she wasn't fine with was spiders. She gave the crawlspace a once-over, noting the juxtaposition of beams and joists and all the shadowy places where spiders could be lurking. She shivered again.

"You said, 'I know what to do now,'" said Ariel. "What did you mean by that? And…you saw the cracks in the mirror turn gold, didn't you? Please tell me you saw that."

"I did. It reminds me of Kintsugi," he said. He was making his way toward one of the foundation beams. In the flickering light of the swaying bulb, his shadow appeared to be stalking him.

"Kin-what-y?"

"Kintsugi. The Japanese art of repairing broken pottery by mending the cracks with gold. It highlights the damage rather than hiding it, creating a more valuable and resilient object. It's a way to honor or celebrate the piece's history. Its imperfect journey, making it unique. A one-of-a-kind. I've never seen it done to a mirror, though. That was…unexpected."

"It's a metaphor, isn't it," she said. "The K-word thingy is about healing, isn't it." Ariel sighed. "Why does everything in this house have to be a metaphor? It's exhausting trying to keep up." She followed him over to a thick, vertical wooden beam. As she got closer, she saw something that looked like a metal door fitted into the concrete footing under the beam.

Marshall laughed. "God works in mysterious ways," he said.

"I didn't know you believed in God," said Ariel.

He had stopped at the small door and crouched down to inspect it. She shuffled over next to him and sat on a wooden log that was just lying there in the mud, hoping it wasn't some critical structural element that had fallen because of all the shaking and rattling caused by the storm. She looked up. A shimmering web blinked back at her in the uncertain light. She quickly looked back down, focusing on the small door.

"What is that?" she said.

"A kind of time capsule," he answered. He brushed his fingers across the metal, caressing it. That seemed odd to Ariel, but then again, wasn't everything these days?

"Are you going to open it?"

"Yes. Yes, I am." He turned toward her, his face more shadow than not. "But first I need to tell you a story."

"Storytime? Really? In the middle of a tornado?" At that, the roaring of the wind outside intensified.

"Ariel, how do you feel?"

"What...what do you mean? I feel scared to death."

"No, I mean, how do you feel about your parents?"

"I..." She took in a deep breath. "I feel like I owe them an apology. I was wrong. I believed something about them that wasn't true. I'm still not quite sure why I did that." She turned to look at Marshall. "Why did I do that?"

"I'm not really sure, Ariel," said Marshall. "Perhaps it was because you were so young your little mind couldn't fully understand what was happening. Fear can cause us to fill that void with negative thoughts. But you're free of that now. You know the truth."

"Yes! That's how I feel," she said. And, despite the desperate circumstances she found herself in, she did feel free. "I need to talk to them! I need to explain and ask forgiveness." She started to stand. "Maybe the storm will let up soon. We can go to them. We can get to the shelter..."

Marshall gently grabbed Ariel's arm and guided her to sit again.

The house rumbled, and the bare bulb shook so much the shadows danced like they were possessed. When the shaking subsided, Marshall continued.

"I think you've known for a long time that I'm not exactly who I appear to be," he began. She started to pull away. "It's not what you think."

"You don't know what I'm thinking," she said. She looked up at the spiderweb again, then back at the small metal door.

"You're afraid," he said.

"No. Yes. Of course I'm afraid."

"What are you afraid of?"

"I'm afraid…" Her words caught in her throat. "I'm afraid of losing my family. Of losing everything I love." Scenes from her life replayed in her mind. Even an image of Garrett's goofy smile joined the memory parade. Was this what it was like to have your life flash before your eyes?

Marshall blew out a long breath and leaned forward, folding his hands in front of him.

"I know a little something about losing everything," he began.

He told Ariel a story that couldn't possibly be true. A story that spanned millennia. A story about a man named Akolo who once consorted with kings and conquerors. A story about brutal wars and ancient cities and magical artifacts. And a story about family. When Marshall talked about Esme, his eyes filled with tears. Even in the dim light, she could see how much he loved her. How much he missed her.

When he had finished his story, Ariel had no words.

"You are a very insightful young woman," said Marshall. "I know you're struggling to make sense of what I just told you. Believe me, some days I have a hard time believing it. But it's true. All of it…"

"I…I think I saw you," she said. "In a dream." The dream she had shared with Zach bubbled to the surface. "I saw a young boy, and a…a tent? A temple? There were soldiers and a high priest. Zach saw it too…"

The truth hit her like a wrecking ball. Zach *had* traveled back in time. There was no doubt in her mind now. His adventure wasn't merely a dream or a hallucination. Everything he had told her was the absolute truth. And everything Marshall just said, too.

"But what does it mean? And what does any of this have to do with my family?"

"Ariel," said Marshall. A loud rhythmic clanking sound made her jump. She turned around, looking for the source of the sound. "It's just the wind, blowing the crawlspace door," said Marshall. He was far too calm.

"Do…do you still have special…abilities?" she asked. "I mean, can you see things that others can't?" Marshall opened his mouth to speak, but Ariel grabbed his arm and continued, "Can you see them now? My family? Are they safe?"

Marshall shook his head. "I'm sorry. It doesn't work like that."

"You didn't answer my question. What does this have to do with my family?"

"I am your family," he said.

Ariel shook her head. "No, that can't be. I'd know about you."

"Do you know that pendant your mother wears? The one with the fire opal?"

"Yes…"

"That was once mine. It has been passed down through generations. Too many generations to count. And when I open that door"—he pointed to the metal door in the footing—"you're going to see exactly what I mean."

"That's…that's why you were up in my parents' room. You were looking for her pendant."

"Yes."

"But it wasn't there."

"No."

"Because she's wearing it."

Marshall nodded.

"All the more reason to go to the shelter. We can get it from her! I'm sure…"

Marshall gently pried Ariel's fingers from his arm. She looked down and caught a glimpse of the ouroboros tattoo. Small droplets of blood surrounded it where her fingernails had dug in.

"Oh, I'm so sorry," she said. "I didn't know I was holding on so tightly."

"It's okay," he said. In the dim light, the droplets of blood looked black.

Marshall crouched and shuffled over to the small door. The storm sounds intensified. The sound was so loud, Ariel had to cover her ears with her hands. Then the light bulb burst, and they were left in complete darkness.

Except…no. It wasn't completely dark. Marshall had opened the small door. A soft white glow emanated from inside.

Marshall grabbed something from the box.

"Oh," he said.

And then he fell backward onto the muddy ground.

"Marshall!"

CHAPTER TWENTY-TWO

MR. GOODPASTURE SAT in the living room of the unfinished house and gestured for the others to join him. It was an odd scene, the four of them seated in a circle on the subfloor of the house they would someday own. The sun had begun to set, and the only light in the house was coming from a series of work lamps situated in various places on the main floor. All they needed were a few candles and matching cloaks to complete the picture.

Ian shook the image away. If there was one thing they didn't need right now, it was a portal to darker dimensions.

"I am Akolo," Mr. Goodpasture repeated. He let the words settle before continuing. "I have lived a long, long time." As he spoke, he looked from person to person. When his gaze landed on Ian, he had to turn away. The intensity in his eyes was too much to bear. "Many years ago, a boy appeared out of nowhere in a palace where I'd been taken after the siege of my hometown and the death of my family." He paused again, settled his gaze on Zach. "That boy became my friend. I can only see bits and pieces of that chapter in my life, but what I do recall is how much I needed a friend during that season.

This young boy helped me to see hope where previously I had only known heartache." Mr. Goodpasture paused again. "As I've said, my memories are incomplete, but the *feelings* from every chapter in my life are as clear as day."

Ian had so many questions, but he held his tongue and let Mr. Goodpasture continue. As the sun continued to set, a breeze appeared, causing the plastic sheeting covering the unfinished windows to flap. The gentle slapping sound reminded Ian of lapping ocean waves.

Mr. Goodpasture talked at length about the role he, as Akolo, played in the temple at the palace, then back in the city where he had been born. When he spoke of the God he served and the ways that God would use Akolo to imbue power in artifacts, Ian began sorting through his vast knowledge of ancient history. Mr. Goodpasture didn't offer much detail—perhaps those memories were hazy, too—but that didn't stop Ian from imagining Akolo's potential role in artifacts he had learned about in his studies. The prospect was mind-blowing. Ian was sitting in a circle with a man who actually shaped the course of history.

After a particularly long pause in Mr. Goodpasture's story, Zach, who had been uncharacteristically quiet, spoke up.

"We visited a garden," he said. "It was really big and I got stung by a bee."

This was a new detail from Zach. He'd mentioned the garden before, but not the bee sting.

"I have to know," began Ian. "Was this the Hanging Gardens of Babylon?"

Mr. Goodpasture nodded slowly. "It wasn't called that back then, of course. But...yes."

Ian turned to Zach and ruffled his hair. "Hey, kiddo, you got to see one of the seven wonders of the world!"

Zach smiled. "Wish I could remember it better," he said.

“This is such a fantastical story,” said Lyana. “I mean, no one in their right mind should believe a word of it.”

“Good thing we’re not in our right minds, then,” said Zach.

Mr. Goodpasture smiled. “You are a clever boy,” he said. His face turned serious. “I want to thank you, Zach. For being such a good friend so very long ago.”

Zach shrugged. “Feels like yesterday to me,” he said with a smirk, showing his usually hidden dimple on the corner of his mouth.

This brought a laugh from all four of them. The sun had just about disappeared when Mr. Goodpasture began speaking again. This time, his voice was more subdued. The sadness in his tone was palpable.

“I’m sure you’ve all heard the phrase ‘Time heals all wounds,’” he began. Everyone nodded. “Well, I’m here to tell you that’s a bunch of baloney.”

Ian snickered at this, then just as quickly apologized. “Sorry. I know that’s not funny.”

“It’s okay, Ian,” said Mr. Goodpasture. “Sometimes laughter is the only way through the difficult times.”

The wind picked up, and the flapping plastic sheets sounded less like the ocean and more like an advancing army. “A storm’s coming,” he said.

Mr. Goodpasture nodded. “Yes. I feel it too. I think I need to move this story along a little faster.” He stood, then started pacing back and forth as he talked. “I lost my Esme so very long ago. But…” He looked over at Zach. “It feels like yesterday. Some might say my long life is a gift, and in many ways, that is true. But ever since I lost my love, it’s been more of a curse. I have tried everything within my power to bring her back…or…to go to her. But all my attempts have been thwarted.” He stopped pacing and spread his arms out in front of him. “But this? This is going to work. It has to work.”

“What do you mean ‘this’?” asked Lyana.

"You told me that you buy this house in the future. Why? What led you here?" asked Mr. Goodpasture.

Ian spoke first. "We wanted to move out of the big city. Lyana found this listing…"

"No," she said, interrupting Ian. "It found me."

"Yes!" said Mr. Goodpasture. "It found you because you are the answer to the puzzle."

"I don't understand," said Zach. "What puzzle?"

"When Esme first got sick, I petitioned God to heal her and he offered a solution. I gave her a pendant, not so different from your own, Mrs. Keane," he said, gesturing to Lyana. "Except the stone in that pendant was imbued with a supernatural power. It didn't just keep her alive, it gave her a full life. We enjoyed many centuries together because of that stone. But then one day, something happened and the stone cracked, then broke in half. I tried everything in my power to repair it. But Esme's fate was sealed. She began aging that very day."

"What caused the stone to break?" asked Ian.

"There was an event," said Mr. Goodpasture. "An event that some say is myth and many claim is a historical fact. I…I'll let you decide for yourselves what to believe. It happened right around the time where our modern day calendars change from BC to AD. This event and the breaking of the stone occurred at the very same time."

Ian swallowed hard. It didn't take a history degree to remember exactly what happened around that time.

"What does one have to do with the other?" asked Ian.

"I…I don't know. Some mysteries are too big even for me to understand."

"That must have been devastating," said Lyana.

"She was everything to me. I couldn't lose my Esme. But there was some good news. Esme was finally able to become pregnant, after centuries of barrenness. Sadly, she died giving birth," he said.

He turned to Lyana. “The baby survived. And because of that, here you are,” he said.

“I…what?” Lyana’s face was a mixture of shock and confusion.

“You are my descendent,” said Mr. Goodpasture.

“I knew it!” said Zach.

“How is that even possible?” asked Ian.

“Surely I don’t have to explain how babies are made, now, do I?” Mr. Goodpasture offered a sly smile.

“Marshall!” shouted Zach.

Mr. Goodpasture seemed confused by Zach’s outburst. But Ian knew immediately what he was saying. He had come to the same conclusion not long after meeting Mr. Goodpasture.

“You’re Marshall!” Zach said. He stood and walked to Mr. Goodpasture. “You’re Akolo and Mr. Goodpasture and Marshall!” He offered Mr. Goodpasture a brief but energetic hug.

“I…” began Mr. Goodpasture. “I don’t yet know that name,” he said. Zach stepped back and studied Mr. Goodpasture, squinting, looking for Marshall in the man’s face. “But I like it.”

“So, what now?” asked Ian. “We’re back to the big question: How do we get home?”

“Every seven generations, hope is renewed,” said Mr. Goodpasture, seeming to ignore the question. “And I believe that you, Lyana, are a seventh generation. Fate has brought us to this moment. Fate, or is it faith?”

Ian watched as Lyana unclasped the pendant around her neck and handed it to Mr. Goodpasture. He held it in his hand like the most precious of stones.

“But that one is broken,” said Zach. He reached into his pocket and presented his stone. “You can have this one.”

Ian felt a lump in his throat. Everything they had endured in the past year had led up to this moment.

"Thank you, Zach," said Mr. Goodpasture. "But this will do just fine." He held the pendant up, and it glowed in the dimming light. "We need to reunite it with its other half," he added. He started toward the opening in the floor that led to the crawlspace. "I don't quite know what happens next, only that I must obey what my instincts are telling me."

"Your instincts? Or the voice?" said Lyana.

Mr. Goodpasture gave Lyana a genuine smile.

All three of them followed him down the ladder into the crawlspace. Mr. Goodpasture flipped the light switch, and the three bulbs lit up. Ian took up the rear, his mind cluttered with history and mystery and calendars and timelines and a jumble of possibilities that made his head spin.

When they got to the box in the footer, Mr. Goodpasture gently suggested the three of them stay back a bit. "I don't know what will happen," he said. "Maybe something big. Maybe nothing at all."

He opened the small door and pulled out a stone that was the perfect match for the one in Lyana's pendant.

"Is it okay if I..." began Mr. Goodpasture, indicating Lyana's pendant.

"Please, do whatever you want with it. It's yours now," she said.

"Here, use this," said Ian. He handed a small pocketknife to Mr. Goodpasture.

"I didn't know you had a pocketknife?" said Lyana.

Ian shrugged. "I didn't either," he said. He found the knife in his pocket after they became locked in the storm shelter. He didn't say anything then because he didn't know how it got there. He concluded that he must have absently collected it from Marshall's worktable when they were in his cabin. That possibility made his convoluted thoughts spin even faster.

Mr. Goodpasture pried the stone from the setting and held both halves in one hand.

Nothing happened. Ian was more than a little disappointed by this.

"Maybe you need to say something?" said Zach. "Like an incantation or magic words?"

"Or maybe you're missing an ingredient," suggested Lyana.

"Like eye of newt?" offered Zach. He quickly apologized. "Sorry."

"Not eye of newt," said Mr. Goodpasture. He nodded solemnly, then placed both stones into the small box and closed the metal door. "Time," he said. "The missing ingredient is time."

"Of course," said Ian. "It's not time yet. Some of us haven't even been born yet."

Mr. Goodpasture gestured for everyone to head back to the ladder. "All we can do now is wait," he said.

"For forty years?" said Zach. They all climbed out from the crawlspace. Mr. Goodpasture led them into the unfinished kitchen. "We can't wait here for forty years…we need to get home."

"Yes, home," said Lyana. She reached back and grasped Ian's hand. "Ariel."

"You mentioned she was with someone," said Mr. Goodpasture.

"Yes…" began Zach. "With Marshall. She's with you!"

"Then I hope I'm as clever as you in the future."

"So, what do we do now?" asked Lyana.

Ian saw Marshall in the way Mr. Goodpasture touched his chin as he considered his response. "We need to get you back to the shelter."

Mr. Goodpasture found a flashlight in a toolbox Ian hadn't noticed before and clicked it on, then led them out of the house into the coolness of the evening. They really didn't even need the flashlight. The moon was full.

"It's a pink moon," said Lyana, as if she heard Ian's thoughts.

"No," said Zach. He had stopped walking and was looking up into the night sky. "A blood moon."

"Yes," said Mr. Goodpasture. He urged them on. "A blood moon."

The storm shelter door was open, lying on the ground the way they'd left it hours earlier.

"So...what, we just go in there and wait?" said Zach.

"Not quite," said Mr. Goodpasture. The air stilled around them. The air suddenly smelled of electricity. "You go in there and hope."

Hope, thought Ian. That was certainly the operative word.

"Mr. Goodpasture," began Lyana. "Thank you."

"Please, call me Marshall," he said. Lyana gave him a hug, then started down the shelter steps.

Zach started to follow but paused after counting four steps. "You might want to make this a little deeper," he said. "Add a few more steps."

"Really?" said Mr. Goodpasture. "That would be a lot of work."

"I know," said Zach. "But it'll be worth it. Trust me." He counted two more steps, then paused again. "See you in a few decades," he said before continuing downward.

Ian shook Mr. Goodpasture's hand. "I hope you're right about this," he said.

"Hope is a funny thing, don't you think?" Mr. Goodpasture replied.

"It is," said Ian. He pulled the door up off the ground and climbed down into the shelter, carefully lowering the door behind him. After a loud *thunk*, they were once again in total darkness.

Ian shuffled over to his wife and son and wrapped them in a hug.

"Do you hear that?" Lyana asked.

"The humming sound," said Zach. "It's back."

Hope.

CHAPTER TWENTY-THREE

"MARSHALL!"

Ariel was crouched over him, shaking him. He stirred, then sat up. He opened his closed hand to reveal not one but two stones.

No. Two halves of the same stone. Not only were they glowing, but they also appeared to be moving of their own accord, like magnets that were the same pole, pushing away from one another.

"I am here," Marshall said with a low tone, but he wasn't speaking to Ariel. His head was tilted up, with his eyes eerily reflecting the stones' glow. They continued their strange dance in his open hand.

"Marshall, can you hear me?" He appeared to be in some kind of trance. Ariel tried shaking him again, but he didn't even register her touch. She sat down on the muddy ground and wrapped her arms around her legs for the third time since the storm began.

"Why is this happening?" she cried.

Marshall looks down at his hands. The stones spin and blur and morph into the image of the ouroboros, the very image that is tattooed on his arm. Then the shapes and lines and shadows around him bend into a snakelike liquid, reforming into something new. He is in a temple. Before him is the ancient chest he spent so many hours with over the millennia. He has not seen this chest in over two thousand years. It is old and battered and decorated with spidering cracks.

The voice speaks to him without sound. He doesn't so much hear it as feel it in his head, his heart, his bones.

Welcome, servant.

"Who am I to be called your servant?" he says.

You have served me well.

"But I have made so many mistakes."

Yes.

"I chased influence and power."

And what did that cost you?

"My people. My family. My Esme."

What do you seek now?

"I want the curse over my family to be broken, and I want this family to be healed, to be whole, to be safe."

They are not here.

"What must I do to bring them home?"

Give me the one thing you have yet to share.

"I have worked tirelessly to repair my mistakes. To fix what I have broken. For centuries I did whatever you asked. What is left to give?"

I don't want your works.

"Then what do you want?"

I want you.

Marshall holds out his hands, and they begin to glow with an intense light. The light flows from them toward the chest, creating streams of liquid gold in the air. It pours into all the ancient cracks, filling each one and making the chest new again, healing it. The scene around him quickly dissipates, and he is back in the dark, damp crawlspace with Ariel.

After a few minutes of silence, Marshall opened his eyes and turned toward Ariel.

"Your family is stuck," he said.

"What do you mean, stuck?"

"They are not here."

Ariel wanted to scream. "What do you mean they're not here?"

"They are trapped in the past."

"Trapped?" said Ariel.

"Like Zach was," said Marshall. He winced. "But unlike Zach, they do not have a way home."

"There has to be a way!"

Marshall's gaze turned back to the stones in his hand. They continued to dance around each other. Marshall let out a small cry, as if he'd been bitten by a spider.

Ariel brushed away imaginary spiderwebs, her voice rising in panic. "How do we bring them back? Can you bring them back? Please tell me you can bring them back!" She grabbed Marshall by the shoulder to shake him but felt a sharp electric shock that made her stumble backward.

"I know what I must do. But I will need a knife," Marshall said, struggling with the words. "A sharp knife."

"Where..."

Marshall winced in pain but did not answer. "Please, hurry," he said.

"What's going on?"

Marshall didn't respond. Was he in his trance again? Ariel didn't know what to do, but she couldn't just do nothing. She felt her way through the darkness across the muddy floor to the crawlspace door, squirming every time her hands touched something other than mud. Outside, the storm raged. She pushed at the door, and it flew open in the swirling wind. Lightning flashed, painting ominous shadows across the yard where she'd enjoyed so many cookouts. The crawlspace door flew back toward her, and she moved her hand away just in time as it slammed closed.

This was too much. She didn't want to be in the crawlspace. She didn't want to face the storm. She didn't want to be anywhere. "I can't do this!" she shouted.

Marshall's voice reached her ears just as the thunder roared.

"You can do this," he said.

"Marshall, please. I can't..."

"I believe in you," came his voice again. She looked across the dark crawlspace to see his face glowing in the light from the stones. He had not moved.

Ariel steadied her fraying nerves and pushed on the crawlspace door, then crawled out onto the rain-soaked ground. She got to her feet and raced around to the back door. Black clouds continued to swirl around the house. At any moment she feared the menacing storm would swallow the house up, and her with it.

Once inside, she ran to the kitchen. She grabbed a steak knife from the woodblock on the counter and headed back outside. Two steps out the door, she paused and looked across the lawn to the woods. She could make a run for it. Go to the storm shelter. What if Marshall was wrong? Maybe they were still in the shelter. What if a tree had fallen across the door? She turned to look up toward the second floor of the house. In the next flash of lightning, she saw the large tree that had crashed into her room. Roots dangled at the base of the unearthed tree like serpents reaching for the ground below.

Ariel started toward the woods.

They are not here.

This time, it was not Marshall's voice.

She stopped, turned and ran back to the crawlspace door. Her face was wet with rain and mud and probably blood, too. She wanted to laugh at the absurdity of the moment. But this was no laughing matter. She squeezed through the opening and dropped to the ground below. Marshall remained frozen.

Ariel shuffled up to him and held out the knife.

"Marshall," she said. "I'm here."

Marshall's gaze remained fixed. "Draw the knife across my palm," he said, his voice strained. "The stones...need my blood."

"What? No way. I can't do that!" The stones in his hand increased their frantic dance.

"Fear is a luxury, action is required," he said, his voice strangely calm.

"Please, Marshall…that is asking too much."

"It's time to make things right."

"I…can't…"

Marshall turned toward her. "It's time to heal your family," he said.

"Okay, okay," she said. Ariel held the knife out, her hand shaking. Marshall gently grabbed it with his left hand and steadied it.

"Do not be afraid," he said. He guided her hand so the knife's edge rested on the hand where he still held the two stone halves.

"Give me strength," said Ariel, speaking to whatever god was listening.

Slowly, she dragged the knife across Marshall's palm. A stream of bright red blood appeared. Marshall closed his bleeding hand on the stones and began to cry out in obvious pain. When he opened his fingers, the two halves had become one. Their glow brightened, slowly at first, then more rapidly, until Ariel had to shield her eyes.

"It's going to work," said Marshall.

And then, a blazing flash of light. When Ariel's eyes adjusted to the darkness that followed, she was alone.

"Marshall?"

She listened intently for a response. But it was quiet. Even the storm outside was silent.

Marshall was gone.

CHAPTER TWENTY-FOUR

THE HUMMING STOPPED.

"Do you think we're back?" asked Zach.

Lyana squeezed Ian's hand. "I don't hear a storm," she said. "But honestly, I don't know if that's good news or bad."

"I can try the door," he said. "Or should we wait?"

"Try the door," said Zach. "I'll help."

The two of them brushed past Lyana and climbed the steps. Zach was counting aloud as he went, pausing when he reached the door. Ian grunted as he pressed upward. As the door bent upward, he pushed it over and onto the ground. Zach continued his count as the two of them stepped out of the shelter, Lyana following close behind.

It was twilight. The golden hour. The air was rich with humidity, but there was no sign of a storm.

"It's the right number of steps now," said Zach. He was beaming. "We're back!"

Lyana hoped he was right.

"This way," said Zach. He made a beeline through the woods, Lyana and Ian following close behind. When they got to the clearing that marked the edge of their backyard, Lyana's heart nearly stopped. A tree had been thrust into their house. *It must have been uprooted by the tornado...*

"Ariel!" She started running. Ian and Zach raced past her, then all three of them stopped short as they watched someone climbing out from the crawlspace window. At first, Lyana thought it might be Marshall, but then the figure stumbled into the golden light.

"Ariel!" she shouted. Her daughter was caked with mud and blood, her hair wet and wild. She looked like she'd been through a war. "Are you okay? You're bleeding..."

Ariel hugged her mom tight. "Not my blood," she said.

"Then whose?" said Ian. He was brushing the wet hair from her forehead.

"Marshall!" shouted Zach. He ran over to the crawlspace door, then fell to his knees and called into the opening. "Marshall!" he shouted again.

There was no response.

Zach looked up from his knees at Ariel.

She shook her head. "Marshall is gone," she said.

"No!" Zach started to crawl through the opening, but Ian grabbed his legs and stopped him.

"I'll go," he said.

Lyana helped Zach to his feet.

Three long minutes later, Ian returned. He climbed through the door, then walked up to Ariel.

"I don't understand. What happened?" he asked.

"Strange things were happening, and then a bright flash of light and then...he wasn't there anymore," she said.

"But he's coming back, right?" said Zach.

Ian turned to his son. "What does your gut tell you?"

Zach shook his head in disbelief. "My gut tells me that he needs to come back," Zach said with tears streaming down his cheeks. The two had become close not once but twice. First when Zach went back in time to befriend a young Akolo, then once again after his return to the present. Losing Marshall would be a heavy blow to Zach.

Lyana wrapped him in a hug.

"I didn't get to say goodbye," said Zach. The heartache in his voice brought tears to Lyana's eyes.

Ariel was crying too. "Mom, Dad, I'm so sorry," she said. "I've been awful to you. I've been so angry. I believed a lie about you for so long. But now I know the truth and…" Lyana pulled Ariel into the hug.

"It's okay, honey," she said. "It's okay."

Ariel continued, "And, Zach, I owe you an apology too. A big one. I treated you poorly for too long. I was selfish, and I'm so, so sorry…"

Ian stepped over to complete the family hug.

They remained there, holding each other tight, until the sun disappeared behind the trees.

Ian finally broke the reverent silence. "Everything is going to be okay," he said.

Lyana looked over at the heavily damaged house, brushed Ariel's matted hair away from her face, squeezed Zach tighter and looked into her husband's eyes. She saw love there. And grace. And most of all, hope.

"Yes," she echoed. "Everything is going to be okay."

For the first time in months, she actually believed that.

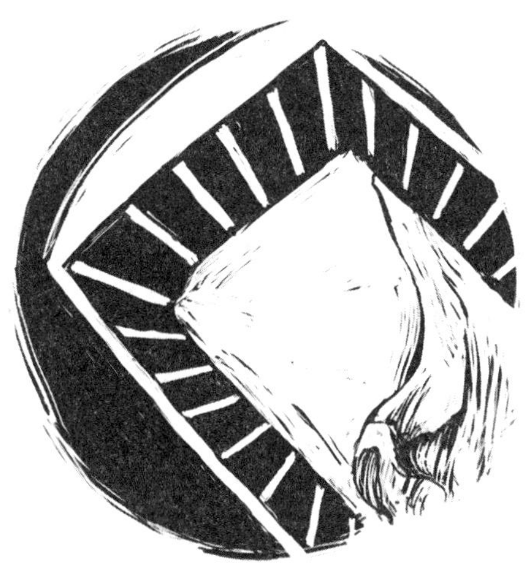

CHAPTER TWENTY-FIVE

"I'M SORRY TO interrupt. But I saw you sitting over here and had to say hi."

Ian looked up from a menu he knew by heart to see Kelly, the real estate agent that sold them the house more than a year earlier.

"Kelly! We haven't seen you in ages," said Lyana.

"I took a new job in Worcester, Mass. I love it here in Littleton, but I have family there and it's a great opportunity. I had just come back to visit my friend Angela when I heard about the storm. Was it really a tornado?"

"That's what they tell us," said Ian.

"A highly localized tornado," added Lyana. "Seems like it just had it out for Farr Hill."

"That's crazy!" said Kelly. She shook her head. "Well, I'm just glad you're all fine." She started to walk away, then paused and turned around. "Is it true that the caretaker went missing?"

Ian looked over at Zach. He seemed lost in his own little world. The thought that his progress in social situations had stalled, perhaps even reversed, was of great concern to him and Lyana. Maybe he just needed more time.

Lyana answered, "We honestly don't know what happened to Marshall. Perhaps he disappeared like his uncle all those years ago."

"Hmm…perhaps so. I only met him a couple of times. He was odd, but I really liked him," said Kelly.

"We did too," said Ariel. Ian watched out of the corner of his eye as she reached over to place her hand on Zach's. He pulled his away when he felt her touch.

"Well, I don't want to keep you from lunch. I'm sure it'll be delicious. I really miss this place. Good to see you all."

They said their goodbyes. Lloyd stopped Kelly to offer a quick "hello" and "goodbye" before walking up to the Keanes' table. He removed his apron and sat in the empty chair.

"That was a nice surprise," Lloyd said, indicating Kelly, who was exiting the diner.

"That's the best kind of surprise to have," said Lyana.

Lloyd laughed. "You've certainly had your share of the other kind." He leaned forward, lowered his voice. "Still no word from Marshall?"

"None," said Ian.

"They didn't find a body," said Zach. "That means he's still alive. Somewhere."

Or some-when, thought Ian.

They'd had this conversation numerous times since the storm. Zach insisted that Marshall was alive and that he'd be back someday. Ian and Lyana tried to gently suggest that he could be gone for good, and that Zach might need to accept that. He resisted. It was only after Ariel talked with him that he began to soften his anger at a world that somehow wouldn't include Marshall.

"He sacrificed himself for us," Ariel had told him. When Ian later confronted her about this claim, Ariel admitted that she didn't know for certain that's what happened. But she sensed it was true. All the clues pointed to sacrifice. And it had worked, just as he said.

Ian thought back to the first time Marshall had saved them. The incident with the house wiring. The creative solution with the lamp-post. He had said the same thing then.

It's going to work.

"It's all arranged," said Lloyd, pulling Ian back to the present. "I'll have a crew out at your place tomorrow to start clearing all the debris."

"We haven't heard back from our insurance yet," began Lyana.

Lloyd smiled. "We've already secured donations of materials and time from two local contractors. If the insurance eventually comes through? Well, you can offer to pay them, though I doubt they'll accept any money. We are a community here, and you are part of that community. You are family."

Ian was shaking his head. "This is…too much," he said. "But thank you, Lloyd. You don't know how much this means to us. We…" The words caught in his throat, but Ariel must have heard his thoughts.

"…we love that house. And we love Littleton," she said. The smile on her face said it all. She was truly home.

They all were.

"Oh, I have some news, too," said Lloyd.

"News?" said Lyana.

"I reached out to my son in New York," he said.

"And?" prompted Lyana.

He shrugged. "And…he responded."

"Are you going to see him?" asked Ariel.

"It's much too soon for that. He's still quite angry, and I don't blame him. But…it's a start."

"There's still time," said Lyana.

Lloyd nodded. "Yes. There's still time."

Ian looked over at his wife. She glanced back, and in that look Ian saw the most beautiful part of his wife. Her relentless hope.

Hope is what got them through this.

He looked at Zach, ruffled his hair. Zach only resisted a little.

And hope is what would get them through whatever was yet to come.

• • •

"The bad news is that a couple of the foundation beams will need to be replaced," said Ian. "But the good news is we found out before the house fell apart. After the flooding earlier, and the tornado, we had an engineer inspect the place."

"Hadn't you done that before you bought it?" asked Jeb, Eliza's husband.

Ian looked over at Lyana. "We did. And they didn't find anything then. The inspector thinks the high winds from the tornado helped to reveal the extent of the damage. We might not have noticed it for years if not for that storm."

Lyana took a sip of her lemonade and reached across the picnic table. "I'm so glad you two could come," she said.

Eliza squeezed her sister's hand. "Well, it was about time we saw this amazing house of yours." She gestured to the scaffolding and the tarps covering the mostly repaired hole in the house. "Although I must say, I didn't expect it to have quite so much…charm."

Lyana laughed. "I know we've been a bit isolated since moving here. We had a lot to deal with…"

"Which is exactly why you should have called me so I could come to your rescue," said Eliza. "Isn't that right, Jeb?"

"I'm sure they had good reasons," he replied.

Eliza huffed and shook her head. "I wanted to be here for you."

"And here you are!" said Lyana.

Eliza squeezed Lyana's hand again, and a curious look came to her face. She stood up abruptly from the picnic table. "Come with me to the kitchen," she said.

"What…"

"Just come. We need to refill the lemonade." At that, Eliza yanked the half-full pitcher off the table and began walking toward the back door. The upper floors of the house were still being repaired, but the main floor was already back to full functionality. Lyana excused herself from the table and started after Eliza. She paused to look across the yard, where Ariel and Garrett were walking hand in hand where the chicken coop used to be.

"Don't stray too far," she called out. She got a rolled-eye glare and a drawn-out "Mom," from Ariel, just as she expected.

Lyana met up with Eliza at the kitchen sink. Eliza held out her hands, and Lyana, perplexed, took them.

"What is this about?" she asked.

"You…you're pregnant, aren't you?" said Eliza.

"What? No…I can't be. That's…" began Lyana. Her hands went instinctively to her stomach. And with a big smile she said, "I want to show you something."

Lyana grabbed Eliza's hand and led her through the door into the garage. She weaved around the furniture that had been removed from the upstairs rooms until she reached something covered in a heavy tarp.

"Ian has been working on this in secret for a few weeks. Ever since the storm," she said. She pulled the tarp back to reveal a mostly completed crib.

"Oh, Lyana! It's beautiful. Ian made this? With his hands? How did he know…?"

"Remember when I told you there was something special with this house?"

"Yes…" Eliza said with a confused look.

"Well..." she hesitated. "After the storm, Ian and I walked through the rooms to survey the damage. It was quite overwhelming. We knew it would be a huge undertaking to rebuild, especially after everything our family had been through. We stood in the middle of the rubble, cried and held each other. Then we both heard it."

"Heard what?"

"A single word, *architect*," said Lyana. "I don't know how to explain it, but we both instantly knew what it meant. As I looked into Ian's eyes, something changed. He looked up, and in a whisper back, he said, 'Okay, God, if we rebuild this house, would you rebuild our family?' It was in that very moment that we knew we were supposed to add a nursery to the house." Lyana paused again, giving Eliza a moment to digest her words. "I know this all sounds crazy, but Marshall assured us we could trust the voice."

Eliza was stunned to silence.

"So, I didn't know for sure. But I hoped. *We* hoped. And..." A tear formed in Lyana's eye. "As of this morning, I know it's true. We're going to have another baby!"

Eliza pulled Lyana into a bear hug with tears in her eyes. They had lamented and hoped together for years about Lyana's desire for another child. Eliza understood Lyana's longing for this miracle. At that moment Zach walked into the garage.

"Mom, I'm going to visit the cabin," he said. He looked at the half-revealed crib. "What is that? What are you..."

"You're going to be a big brother," said Lyana.

"What? Are you serious?" he said. A big smile came to his face. "Does Ariel know? Does Dad know?"

Lyana laughed. "Yes, your dad knows. But I haven't talked with Ariel yet. We just found out for certain today."

"Good luck getting a minute alone with Ariel. She's pretty much attached to Garrett these days." He shrugged. "He's a good guy, so that's okay. I could just do without all that mushy stuff," he added.

"Mushy stuff?"

"You know, hand holding and kissing…"

"You saw them kissing?" Lyana's mom-radar spiked.

"Ew, no. I am not prepared to see that."

Neither am I, thought Lyana. *Neither am I.*

"I think it's a girl," said Eliza, still processing the big news.

"You think so?" said Lyana. A brief wave of sadness washed over her as she relived the heartache of losing Avril, but that was quickly followed by a bigger wave of gratefulness. Boy or girl, the child was a miraculous gift. They would treasure her. Or him. All of them would.

"I hope it's a boy, like me," said Zach.

"Another Zach?" said Eliza. "Do you think the world could handle two of you?" She smiled and ruffled his hair.

"I don't know," he said. "I just like the idea of a little brother, ya know?"

Lyana knew.

"Anyway, I'll be at the cabin for a bit," said Zach.

He turned and walked out through the open garage. Lyana watched him leave, even took a step to follow him, but Eliza gently took her arm.

"He'll be all right," said Eliza. "He's a clever young man."

"Yes. Yes, he is," she answered.

• • •

Zach knocked on the cabin door, then waited. He knew the cabin was empty but held on to a thread of hope that his parents were wrong, that Marshall wasn't gone forever. When there was no response, he opened the door. It was a full-circle moment for Zach. He and Ariel had explored the cabin briefly soon after they'd moved into the Farr Hill house. Back then they were essentially breaking and entering. But now? The cabin officially belonged to their family. Or at least would eventually, once all the official paperwork was complete. That's what his dad told him anyway.

Still, it felt wrong to walk right in unannounced. Zach called into the empty space, "Hey, it's just me, Zach," then walked inside, absently brushing his fingertips across the ouroboros symbol on the door. He flicked the switch by the door, and the overhead light came on. The cabin was exactly as it had been the last day he'd visited. Before the tornado.

Tornado.

A new memory unlocked in Zach's brain.

He was sitting on what passed for a bed in the tower room, feeling desperately homesick. A young Akolo was there with him. A strong breeze blew through the open window and stirred up dust. Zach called it a "dust tornado." Akolo wasn't familiar with the word.

Akolo.

Zach walked over to the worktable and sorted through a wooden box that contained some of Marshall's carvings. He picked up and studied each one, marveling at the meticulous detail. The falcon was Zach's favorite. He had intended to ask Marshall if he might carve one for him, but then…

Zach sighed.

"Why did you have to go away?" he said aloud. He didn't expect an answer but continued as if having a conversation with his old friend. "We had more exploring to do." Zach thought back to the last time he and Marshall had wandered in the woods. He had felt particularly proud that day because he'd studied up on plants after their previous walk and could name just about every one that they saw.

Another latent memory surfaced in Zach's brain. This had been happening regularly since the Tornado Incident, as the local news had called it. Randomly, recalled images and sometimes even full-on scenes would appear in Zach's head in vivid detail.

He had just been stung by a bee. The clarity of the memory made Zach wince. He looked down at his arm and watched a ghostlike Akolo pull out the stinger, then coat the angry welt with powder from a nearby yellow plant.

"I still don't understand how you knew to do that?" Zach said aloud. "I mean, what if I was allergic to that plant or something?" He laughed, and the sound fell flat in the small room. "I don't like that you're gone," he said.

He continued to explore the cabin, looking for any tiny clue that Marshall was still out there somewhere. He ran his fingers across the spines of the old books, pausing when he reached one that looked newer than the rest. He pulled the book out and set it on the kitchen table. It was one of the books Zach's dad had worked on. He flipped to the title page. There it was, his dad's name, listed as "contributing editor." Did his dad know Marshall had this book? Or maybe his dad had given it to him? He reshelved the book and walked up to Marshall's bed. It was a single bed, with a hand-carved wooden frame. Nearly everything in the cabin was handmade. Zach sat on the bed and traced the intricate pattern on the headboard, following the curves with his fingertips while imagining Marshall working on this so many years earlier. Or was he Mr. Goodpasture then?

Zach sat down on the edge of the bed.

"I'm remembering more lately," he said. "Thing is, I don't know if that's a good thing or a bad thing. You know what I mean?"

Zach sighed, then looked once more around the small space Marshall had called home for, what, decades?

"If you're out there somewhere, send me a sign, okay?" said Zach. "Just nothing too creepy," he added, then laughed again. He stood and started for the door, then turned around and went back to the worktable. He lifted the carved falcon again.

"Is it okay if I take this?" he asked. Unsurprisingly, there was no verbal reply, though Zach wondered if the shimmer of dust motes stirred by a sudden breeze might be Marshall's doing. "How about a trade, then?"

He reached into his pocket and removed the fire opal that never left his side. He held it up in the light streaming through the window, then set the stone in the wooden box. "That ought to cover it," he said.

He ran his fingers across the fine, smooth lines of the carved bird and slipped it into his pocket.

Halfway through the door, he paused and turned back, giving Marshall just one more chance to not be dead. But the room remained empty and silent. Zach pulled the door closed and turned to walk away, but his foot caught on something, and he went sprawling to the ground. He looked back to see what had tripped him and saw a vine running across the walkway he hadn't noticed on the way in. He stood, brushed off sticks and stones, then followed the vine around to the side of the cabin, where it spidered in a dozen different directions across the east wall. Most of the vines looked old and dried up, but one branch demanded closer inspection. He stepped up to the wall and reached out his hand to caress the fresh green shoots.

"Huh," he said.

EPILOGUE

THE BRIGHT WHITE light remained as the air around him swirled. Memories of familiar scenes flashed in his mind.

Marshall sensed their presence before he heard their voices. They were calling out his name.

"Akolo!"

He knew these voices. His sisters. His father. His mother.

"Ima!" he cried. He spun around, looking for the source of the sounds, but all he could see was the white light. The voice that spoke next came from nowhere and everywhere.

All is put right. You are now here, with me.

He knew that voice.

A deep sense of peace washed over Marshall. Over Akolo.

"The Keanes..." he began, but he already knew the answer. They were safe now.

Well done, servant.

Silhouettes began to appear all around him. There to his left, his sisters. And to his right, his mother and father. He wanted to run to them, but his feet were fixed in place.

More familiar voices joined the chorus. His children. His grandchildren. All those who had been lost to war and sickness and time. A multitude surrounded him, their faces coming into focus as the white light dimmed. The crowd of witnesses parted, and a woman appeared among them. She walked toward him with a slow, purposeful stride, her smile beaming, her green eyes sparkling.

Tears poured down Akolo's face, each one a gift.

Esme stepped in front of him and gently caressed his cheek with her hand.

"What took you so long?" she asked, a sweet smile on her perfect face.

Akolo laughed. The laughter spread through the crowd like good gossip. He wrapped Esme in an embrace that he'd been aching to share for centuries. When they parted a few minutes or a hundred years later, he couldn't believe his good fortune. All the people he ever loved, all the people who loved him, were here, in this place.

This was joy personified. This was grace and love and beauty and hope.

This was family.

This was everything.

"I got a little lost along the way," he said with a shrug.

Akolo took Esme in his arms and the two of them walked into the crowd of smiling faces. They all began walking together. To where, Akolo did not know. But he did know one thing for certain. He spoke that truth aloud.

"I think we're finally home."

ACKNOWLEDGEMENTS AND THANKS

Completing the final book in our trilogy was not possible without the beautiful community of people who surrounded us with compassion, love, grace, wisdom and understanding for what it has taken us to accomplish this huge feat.

Aaron and Jennifer Sanders, for being great examples of legacy and family which gives us hope. Stephen Parolini, for helping us chisel through this rock to find the gold. May it continue to bring you inspiration and creativity that changes your life, like it has for us. Jill Pickering, for carrying our story even when we couldn't. May it remind you that sacrifice is always honored. Karen Hampton, Melanie Waltz and Kelly Cline, for holding space for our shattered hearts, and making room for healing with such love and grace. Hope UC, it's been almost 30 years since we have experienced healing and peace for our souls to this level in a building, and you all have cultivated and stewarded it well.

Our biggest thanks to Anani, the One who covers and leads through the dessert, the One who imparts wisdom and reveals truth in the pain, the One who calms the storm of chaos, and the One who refreshes the weary soul. Our stories become your testimony. We are forever humbled.

ARCHITECT
Writing Consultant | Stephen Parolini (noveldoctor.com)
Cover Art and Illustrations | Charlie Swerdlow (HistoryDepicted.com)
Interior Layout | Alice Briggs (Kingdomcovers.com)
Copy Editing | Lisa Gilliam
Lyric Permission Acquisition and Additional Photography | Emily Coey (1885Atelier.com)

One More Night
Words and Music by Phil Collins
Copyright © 1985 Phil Collins Ltd.
All Rights Administered by
Concord Sounds c/o Concord Music Publishing
All Rights Reserved Used by Permission
Reprinted by Permission of Hal Leonard LLC

Dare You To Move
Words and Music by Jonathan Foreman
© 2000 Meadowgreen Music and Sugar Pete Songs (ASCAP)
Meadowgreen Adminstered by CapitolCMGPublishing
All Rights for Sugar Pete Songs Administered by
Penny Farthing Music (ASCAP) c/o The Bicycle Music Company
All Rights Reserved Used by Permission
Reprinted by Permission of Hal Leonard LLC

Viva La Vida
Words and Music by Chris Martin, Guy Berryman,
Jon Buckland and Will Champion
Copyright © 2008 by Universal Music Publishing MGB Ltd.
All Rights in the United States and Canada Administered by
Universal Music - MGB Songs
International Copyright Secured All Rights Reserved
Reprinted by Permission of Hal Leonard LLC

COMING SOON...

The Adventures of Akolo

The next exciting chapters of The Goodpasture Chronicles

Across the world, throughout history.
One quest to break the curse.

GoodpastureChronicles.com

ABOUT THE AUTHOR

R.J. Halbert is a sixteen-time award-winning, and best-selling husband and wife team who have collaborated as authors of The Goodpasture Chronicles, a supernatural fantasy trilogy that blends mystery, suspense, endurance, and triumph into an epic adventure. Book one in the series, *CARETAKER*, received the 2025 Bill Fischer Silver Award, and book two, *SERVANT*, received the coveted Blue Star from Kirkus Reviews.

Jason Halbert, one-half of R.J. Halbert, is an Emmy and Grammy Award winning producer and songwriter. His songs have reached millions of listeners worldwide through multiple #1 and Platinum selling albums. In addition to his 23+ year career as Music Director and Producer for Kelly Clarkson, he has left his creative mark on numerous works in film and television, and as well as a copious amount of recording artists over the years. When not creating music, he loves bee-keeping, Sci-Fi, and is known to be quite a storyteller.

After homeschooling their two children around the world on a tour bus, Rhonda Halbert, the second half of R.J. Halbert, has spent the past 15 years as a successful music and television manager, guiding her clients' relationships with labels, networks, and producers. She is also a published photographer, music supervisor, passionate cook, garden enthusiast, and spiritual practitioner.

Together, Jason and Rhonda have woven their 33+ years of life together into a riveting story, based somewhat on truth and experience, but even more so, brimming with imagination.

Learn more at rjhalbert.com